ZANE PR

A NOVEL

NO
BOUNDARIES

Dear Reader:

Allison Hobbs is talented and there is no denying that. And I do mean all-around talented when it comes to being a prolific writer. From the word imagery to the thorough storylines to the incredible erotic scenes to an always climactic ending. In *No Boundaries*, she does it again since she is a writer that has never believed in boundaries.

Sometimes in life, we meet one person who literally changes our entire life. Such is the case with the main characters in this book, Fonia and Jaguar. Fonia was raised in a strict, dysfunctional household with a mother willing to do whatever it took to keep a man. She has no sense of normalcy when it comes to healthy relationships. Jaguar has had more casual sex than any one man can appreciate and decides that he wants to refrain from the random acts of blowing out backs until he can find emotional attachment. Two strangers leading completely different lives end up finding the missing pieces to happiness within each other. Both will have to make a certain degree of sacrifice to make it work, but it is all well worth it in the end.

As always, thanks for supporting myself and the Strebor Books family. We strive to bring you cutting-edge literature that cannot be found anyplace else. For more information on our titles, please visit Zanestore.com. My personal web site is Eroticanoir.com and my Facebook page is Facebook.com/AuthorZane.

Blessings,

Zane

Publisher
Strebor Books International
www.simonandschuster.com/streborbooks

ZANE PRESENTS

ALLISON HOBBS

A NOVEL

NO BOUNDARIES

SBI
STREBOR BOOKS
NEW YORK LONDON TORONTO SYDNEY

Strebor Books
P.O. Box 6505
Largo, MD 20792
http://www.streborbooks.com

ISBN 978-1-59309-415-7
ISBN 978-1-4516-5688-6 (e-book)
LCCN 2013933637

First Strebor Books trade paperback edition July 2013

Cover design: www.mariondesigns.com
Cover photograph: © Keith Saunders/Keith Saunders Photos

10 9 8 7 6 5 4 3 2

Manufactured in the United States of America

For information regarding special discounts for bulk purchases,
please contact Simon & Schuster Special Sales at 1-866-506-1949
or business@simonandschuster.com

The Simon & Schuster Speakers Bureau can bring authors to your
live event. For more information or to book an event, contact the
Simon & Schuster Speakers Bureau at 1-866-248-3049 or visit our
website at www.simonspeakers.com.

To Aletha Dempsey

JAGUAR

B utt-ass naked and covered with water beads, I came out of the bathroom and froze. The woman in my room covered her mouth and released a sound of shock. Neither of us had expected this encounter. She took a step backward, and I reflexively concealed my privates with both hands.

The cleaning woman gawked at me, and then lowered her eyes. "I knocked. You didn't put out the *Do Not Disturb* sign; I thought you had gone for the day!"

"No, I'm still here," I said dumbly. Momentarily stunned from the surprise of finding an unfamiliar woman in my room, I stood unmoving as I shielded a dick that had become overly active, thumping against my hand as if it wanted to come out and say, "hello."

"I'll come back later." She backed up a little more, yet her eyes remained glued to my face, and then scanned the length of my naked body.

She was basic-looking. Late twenties, medium height, with wide hips and average-sized breasts. A Latino chick with red-tinted hair that was pulled back in a small bun.

On a scale of one to ten, she was a five. Despite her plain face and unremarkable figure, my dick jerked spastically beneath my hands. I think it was the uniform that had me going; the maid's uniform was a turn-on.

Noticing the movement below, her eyes shot down to my crotch.

"I'm so sorry," she repeated with a Spanish accent. The accent was sexy, and had a hypnotic quality, influencing my dick the way a snake charmer's melody draws a serpent out of hiding. I felt the head of my serpent pressing against my palm and then peeking through the space between my fingers.

"Oh," she murmured. And my dick took that single utterance as permission to stand fully erect, shoving so forcefully, it pushed my hands aside. At that point, my mind grew hazy, and the primitive part of my nature took over. I was instantly motivated by my animalistic side. Like a dog in heat, I was aware of nothing except my sexual urges. The business appointment that had been lined up for me no longer seemed important. All that mattered was pacifying my throbbing phallus—appeasing its desire to plunge inside something warm and wet.

But despite being mentally incapacitated, I wasn't so far gone that I'd overpower the maid...or any other woman for that matter. I'd never forcibly take what I wanted; I'm not a rapist. I understand a firm "no," and hearing that word would immediately bring me back to my senses.

And so, wondering if the maid and I were in mutual agreement, my questioning eyes locked on to hers. She didn't say a word, and I took the excited glimmer in her eyes as consent.

Propelled by lust, I took steps toward her. I glanced at my image in the mirror and saw what the maid saw: a tall, milk chocolate brother with a body that was well-toned from years of playing basketball. I didn't own any workout equipment, and during law school, my demanding schedule prevented me from working out at the gym, but I'd always made time for recreational basketball. Even if it was only two or three times a month, I found time to get my hands on a basketball. I'd been shooting hoops for as long as I could remember. Where I come from, dudes start practicing their dunk shots as soon as they can hold a basketball.

The maid began to undo the first few buttons of her uniform. It was on the tip of my tongue to say, *"Leave the uniform on,"* but her fingers were working so quickly, I couldn't stop her. Maybe I'm a little twisted, but to me, there's something extremely erotic about a woman wearing a uniform—any kind of uniform. A policewoman, waitress, postal worker, flight attendant, even an aggravating meter maid could make my dick get hard.

The grayish-blue housekeeping uniform dropped to the floor, and I noticed the nametag pinned to the front. *Rayna.* Stripped down to bra and panties, I was pleasantly surprised when Rayna unsnapped her bra, exposing pert breasts with dark, rose-colored nipples. Rayna's nipples were distended, jutting out like tiny corkscrews, and seemed to scream, "*Suck me!*"

I advanced toward Rayna with my lips parted. She pulled down her panties and kicked them off, showing off a forest of curly, pubic hair. Female genitalia could be waxed clean or hairy as a jungle; it didn't matter to me. All that mattered was the way it felt inside. With no time for foreplay, I practically dove on top of her, lifting up her right leg as I fitted the head of my dick into her moist opening.

"Oh, papi," she whimpered, gyrating and taking in several inches of dick-length. Her pussy was good and gushy, and I moaned with pleasure as I sank into a swamp of warm honey. I slow stroked for a few moments, and then kicked it into high gear. I was ready to start plunging in and out like a ferocious madman, but forced myself to slow down and savor the experience.

My lips sought out those erect, suckable nipples, and I made all kinds of heathen-like grunting sounds as I sucked her titties and fucked her pussy at the same time. Rayna may have only been a five in the looks department, but her pussy was off the scale. It was sloppy wet like it was crying, and her inner walls clutched and grabbed possessively; it felt like her pussy was throwing a tantrum. Her walls were like a velvet vise around my dick—a vise that kept getting tighter and tighter.

"Damn, baby. This shit is…" I couldn't even finish the

sentence. Could only breathe like a dragon and groan like a tortured beast.

"Go deeper, papi," Rayna moaned, throwing up her other leg. I knew what she wanted. When a chick says go deeper, she doesn't necessarily want you to knock her uterus out of place, she wants you to find that elusive patch of pleasure known as the G-spot. She wants you to go deeper so she can bust a prolonged and powerful nut. Finding that hidden pleasure place can be a daunting task, especially when you don't know the woman's body, or when you're pressed for time. From my experiences, I'd discovered that if I turn a chick over on her stomach, and take her from behind, I stand a good chance of locating the pleasure zone.

So I repositioned Rayna, and slipped my dick between her voluptuous thighs, which were tightly pressed together. Anchoring myself, I cupped her breasts, squeezing them as I slid in and out of her syrupy juices. Her pussy felt so good, I had to play all kinds of mind games with myself to keep from nutting too soon.

With each down stroke, I allowed the head of my dick to caress her clit before reentering her pussy. Rayna lay beneath me with her face pressed into the pillow, emitting sounds that were a cross between singing and screaming. I'm not a selfish lover, I enjoy pleasing women. Even at a time like this when it would behoove me to bust quickly and get my ass to my appointment on time, I refused to rush. I took the time to make sure she got hers.

I kissed the back of her neck. Nibbled on her ear. "Rayna, baby. You feel so good," I whispered, meaning every word as I maintained steady strokes.

Her moans escalated in volume and her creamy pussy seemed to vibrate, pop, and spit. She was cumming, but I didn't take that as my cue to climax; I kept stroking, increasing the tempo as I intensified her pleasure. I didn't shoot off my load until Rayna had uttered a final whimper.

I'm street-wise, book smart, and I also have a sensitive side. Added to my list of attributes, is the fact that I'm well-endowed and good in bed. My heightened sensitivity and enhanced bedroom skills often give chicks the wrong message, prompting them to become attached to me.

As I eased out of Rayna's hairy pussy, I could only hope she'd take this spur-of-the-moment sex session for what it was. Nothing but two people fulfilling their lustful desires.

She turned over on her back and smiled up at me. I gently wiped perspiration from her forehead and lightly caressed her hair. "That was amazing," I said with one eye on the clock.

"Yes, it was," she agreed, lifting her mouth to mine.

I didn't have time for kissing and cuddling, and so I gave her a quick kiss, and rolled off of her.

She clutched my arm. "Wanna go again?"

"Sorry, I'm already late for an appointment. Maybe some other time."

"When? I could come back later tonight."

"Um, I don't know," I said, feeling pressured and put on the spot. "Let's play it by ear and get together the next time we're both in the mood," I said as gently as I could.

"I'm in the mood now," she said determinedly.

The chick was persistent. She had me squirming for a moment, but then I became irritated. "Yo, we both got what we wanted, so grab your clothes, get dressed, and bounce. You can come back and clean up in here later," I said harshly. I didn't want to go in on her like that, but if I hadn't, she would have kept pestering me.

My sensitive side gets overpowered by a mean streak that emerges when someone tries to back me in a corner and force my will. I had business to take care of and I couldn't allow this random, housekeeping chick to guilt-trip me into setting up a future rendezvous.

Rolling her eyes and mumbling in Spanish, Rayna gave me a seething look as she picked up her clothes from the floor. After dressing, she fussed with her hair, and then slammed the door on her way out.

I washed my dick off, dressed and left my hotel room. On the way to the elevator, I bumped into Rayna, who was pushing her cleaning cart down the corridor. Having to walk past her was awkward. "See you later," I said, not knowing what else to say under the circumstances.

"Okay, I'll see you soon," she replied, wearing a hopeful smile, which I chose to ignore.

I grabbed a cab outside the hotel and headed to University City to meet up with my man, Sharif, to get the details on a bartending job.

FONIA

I am completely submissive—the kind of woman who needs a man to totally dominate me and take control of my body and my mind. Eagerly and lovingly, I serve. I live to please, and I derive intense sexual pleasure from being physically disciplined. Nothing that draws blood or leaves me unconscious, but I do melt with ecstasy when I feel the sting of a paddle or the harsh slap of a man's strong hand against my soft skin.

I have no idea how to exist any other way. From the time I was a child, I was molded and groomed to be docile and polite—to be subservient. I'm not allowed to express my opinions or to disagree. I'm always adorned in beautiful clothes and sparkling jewelry. From head to toe, I'm the image of perfection. A pretty thing—a wind-up doll that does exactly as she's told.

2003

Before I'd ever met Mr. Lord, I sensed the influence he had over my mother, and I viewed him as a rival for her attention. She'd been hired as his personal secretary and the way she spoke his name, you'd think she was referring to God Himself. When-ever she spoke of him, her face would light up and there was reverence in her voice. Though I was only eleven years old, I had this sinking feeling in the pit of my stomach—a kind of warning. I knew on an intuitive level that nothing would ever be the same.

I recall watching my mother as she sat at her vanity table, carefully applying makeup, getting glammed-up as she excitedly prepared to leave town on a business trip with her new employer. I frowned at the sight of the open suitcase on her bed, and then sat next to her on the vanity bench, pouting and sighing audibly.

"I'll only be gone for seven days. The time will fly," she said, trying to pacify me.

"But I'm gonna have to catch two buses to get to school from Nana's house," I complained. Getting to school from Nana's house wasn't a big deal, but it was worth a try to pretend that it was.

"So, you'll get up a half-hour earlier than usual. A little inconvenience won't kill you, Fonia." She tapped the end of my nose, something she always did to get me to smile, but I maintained an unhappy expression, hoping my gloomy disposition would persuade her to cancel her trip.

"My new job pays a lot more than I've ever earned. We're going to be doing a lot better financially."

"We're doing okay," I said.

"We're going to be doing better than okay. You'll see," she said as she sprayed her neck and wrists with cologne.

"How do I look?" She stood up and gazed at me, waiting for my approval.

Wearing a tailored black jacket with gold buttons, a form-fitting skirt, and high heels, my statuesque mother looked chic and beautiful, like a beauty queen going out on a speaking engagement. I turned up my nose and shrugged; I was feeling too abandoned to dole out any compliments. This would be the first time in my life that my mother had traipsed off and left me for an entire week!

Her new job was very demanding and didn't end at five o'clock. As Mr. Lord's personal secretary, she was at his beck and call any hour of the day or night. She could be in the midst of preparing dinner or helping me with homework, but if her boss called, she'd go to her bedroom and close the door. Their working relationship seemed shrouded in secrecy.

When her bedroom door reopened, I never knew what kind of mood she'd be in. With a mere phone call, he could change her disposition from gay to morose or from controlled to erratic. A call from Mr. Lord would have my mother practically floating on air one minute and then, jumpy and nervous the next.

I hadn't met him, but I didn't like him. In fact, I detested him. At least I wanted to.

While my mother stuffed items inside her luggage, I peeked out her bedroom window and noticed a shiny Town Car pull up to the curb. "Your ride's here," I said gloomily.

"Okay, sweetheart. Nana and Poppy will be here to pick you up at seven," she said. "Lock the doors and don't open them for anyone until your grandparents get here."

"I know the rules," I whined in annoyance.

Continuing to gaze out the window of our third-floor apartment, I noticed the driver opening the back door. A well-dressed man emerged, carrying lots of large bags with impressive labels.

"Mommy," I whispered. "I think your boss is coming up to visit."

She glanced out the window and gasped. She gazed around our neat apartment, looking aghast, as if she wanted to give it an instant makeover.

I saw her boss pull out a cell phone, and the next moment, our house phone rang. My mother grabbed it on the first ring. "Hello," she said breathlessly. "Yes, Mr. Lord, please come up. It's apartment. 3-C."

She raced around plumping the pillows on the couch. "Fix your hair, Fonia. And be extremely polite to Mr. Lord. I'll have none of your sassiness. You will not embarrass me in front of my boss. Do you understand, young lady?" She had an almost crazed look in her eyes that warned of dire repercussions if I behaved inappropriately.

The doorbell rang. My mother's frantic eyes locked with mine, and I began to feel nervous too. Suddenly desiring to make a good impression on the man that was so important to her, I smoothed errant strands of hair and took a deep breath.

She opened the door and he entered with his arms laden with bags. God, he was handsome and so well-groomed and important looking in his suit and tie. He smelled good, too, and exuded a sort of masculine power that I'd never noticed in any of the male authority figures in my life. Not my own estranged father, not my Poppy, not any of my male teachers, or kindly Mr. Smithers, who owned the corner store that I frequented daily. None of the men in my life carried themselves like kings.

"You must be Fonia. And you're even lovelier than your mother described," he said in a rich baritone voice that commanded respect. "These gifts are for you, Fonia," he said, extending his arms.

It was as if someone from black royalty had entered our humble abode. As I stepped forward to accept the gifts, a curtsey seemed appropriate, but I suppressed the urge.

"You shouldn't have, Mr. Lord," my mother said, gushing with pride.

There were four bags and each was filled to the brim with gifts that any girl would die for. Juicy Couture apparel, footwear, handbags, jewelry, and an assortment of cute accessories. There were also electronic gadgets, sneakers, and a cell phone of my own.

"It's like Christmas in April," I said in awe.

"What do you say to Mr. Lord?" my mother prodded anxiously.

"Thank you, Mr. Lord," I replied earnestly.

"It's my pleasure, Princess," he said with a warm smile

that removed the negative feelings I'd held for him. "I'm sorry I have to take your mother away on business…" He paused.

"It's okay," I quickly assured him.

"My phone number is programmed in your phone. If anything comes up…if you need anything, call me immediately."

"All right." I was enchanted with Mr. Lord. He seemed like the kind of man that could fix anything. The way he'd showered me with presents and had called me Princess made me feel special. He had treated me the way I'd always wished my own father had, but he'd forgotten about me after he remarried. He and his new family lived in Seattle, Washington and I only saw him for one week every summer. Last summer, he'd tried to back out at the last minute, claiming he couldn't afford my airfare. My mother ended up paying for my transportation, determined that my father and I would have a relationship.

That visit was a disaster. My father and his wife were constantly on the go, and I was nothing more than their built-in babysitter. I felt more like Cinderella than a princess in the presence of my biological father.

Mr. Lord picked up my mother's luggage, and she gave me a hug. I watched out the window as the driver opened the car door for my mother and her boss. I gave a long sigh, but it wasn't a sigh of disapproval. I wanted a dad like Mr. Lord, and I wished with all my heart that I could join him and my mother on their business trip.

FONIA

Afew months later, we moved into a small but elegant townhouse that was located in downtown Philadelphia, in an upscale neighborhood. I was enrolled in private school, and Mr. Lord sort of lived with us...or maybe we lived with him. Our residence was beautifully decorated to suit his taste and standards.

The den was turned into his personal office. He stayed overnight approximately two or three times a week, sharing my mother's bedroom. During his overnight visits, I assumed they'd worked late and Mr. Lord had accidentally fallen asleep. Most of the time, he only stopped by for a couple of hours in the evening to check on us before going to his own home, which my mother had said was an enormous estate outside the city.

I wasn't quite sure of how to categorize my mother and Mr. Lord's relationship. He was her boss, and possibly her lover. Despite their closeness, she still referred to him as Mr. Lord. Sensing that the nature of their relationship was a sensitive topic, I didn't press her for information. He'd improved our lives drastically, and like my mother, I had also begun to believe that he could do no wrong.

Late one night, I was awakened by peculiar sounds, like someone was clapping their hands together in sporadic bursts. Curious, I crept toward the sound that emanated from my mother's bedroom and pressed my ear against the door. I heard the rumble of Mr. Lord's deep voice, but couldn't make out what he was saying. Next I heard the loud clap followed by my mother's breathy, enraptured murmurings.

What were they doing? Sex? I knew enough about sex from watching X-rated shows on cable channels to know that it was usually accompanied by moans and groans and a headboard banging against the wall. I had no idea what they were doing, and I trudged back to my room, completely puzzled.

The next morning, my mother sat down to breakfast wearing a new pair of diamond studs. "Your earrings are beautiful, Mommy," I said, trying to work up the nerve to ask about the curious sounds I'd heard last night.

"Do you like them?" she said, brushing her hair away from her face to give me a better view.

Mr. Lord put down the newspaper he was reading and smiled at me. "I didn't forget you, Princess." He beckoned me with the wave of a hand, and I leapt from my seat and rushed to him, scooting onto his lap. At this point, we'd grown close and I enjoyed the way he always swept me up into his arms, swinging me around. His lap had become my personal domain. It was my favorite spot whenever we watched TV together.

From the pocket of his robe he withdrew a gift-wrapped box. "Open it."

Grinning, I ripped away the gold wrapping paper and found a velvet box. Inside was a pair of diamond studs that were identical to my mother's, only smaller.

"Do you like them?" he asked.

My response was to wrap my arms around his neck and kiss him on the cheek, inhaling his aftershave, and pretending that he was actually my father.

"Okay, go finish your breakfast," he said, picking up the newspaper.

"You shouldn't spoil her," my mother said in a tone I'd never heard before. I looked at her, searching her face, and trying to determine if she was happy for me, but I couldn't read her expression.

Mr. Lord left the kitchen to get dressed and my mother glared at me.

"What's wrong; what did I do?"

"You're not a baby, Fonia. You'll be thirteen on your next birthday…too old to be climbing onto Mr. Lord's lap. I don't like it; I want you to stop."

But he's my father! I wanted to say, but I kept that thought to myself. Her criticism was a reminder that I was living in my own fantasyland, pretending that my mother's employer was my father.

Feeling deflated, I went to my bedroom and dressed

for school. When I came out with my backpack, Mr. Lord was giving my mother a list of duties. She held a notepad and rapidly jotted down his instructions, while repeating, "Yes, Mr. Lord," over and over.

When he noticed me, he said, "Let's go, Princess; I'll drive you to school today."

I gazed at my mother for approval. She gave me a curt head nod, but had an anxious look in her eyes.

I strapped on my seatbelt and gave Mr. Lord a smile. I felt so special, sitting up front with him.

"I understand you're scheduled to visit your father in Seattle," Mr. Lord said.

I frowned and nodded.

"What's wrong? Don't you want to spend time with your father?"

"Not really," I mumbled.

"Why not?"

I shrugged.

"Don't shrug your shoulders, Fonia. Why don't you want to visit your father?"

"I'm not comfortable around him."

"Well, I can't have my princess feeling uncomfortable. You don't have to go."

"I don't?"

"No. He doesn't pay regular child support and the visits aren't court-ordered."

"But Mommy thinks it's important for me and my father to stay connected."

An angry look came across Mr. Lord's face. "He doesn't deserve you! I'm more of a father to you than he is. I pay your tuition and I'm the one responsible for everything good in your life. Do I not treat you as if you were my own child?" he asked with anger flashing in his eyes.

"Yes."

"Good, I'm glad to know that you and I agree. The discussion is not up for debate. Your relationship with your father is over. Am I clear?"

Hit with a mixture of pride and confusion, I murmured, "Yes, Mr. Lord." To myself, I said, *Yes, Daddy.* Hopefully, Mr. Lord would make it legal and adopt me. I wondered if he'd have to marry my mother to make that happen. The thought of having my name changed from Fonia Jerkins to Fonia Lord put a smile on my face.

One evening, after my mother had prepared a quick dinner for me, she announced, "Mr. Lord is on his way over. We'll be having a working dinner and I don't want you to pester him when he arrives. He's a busy man and he doesn't have time to listen to your endless, adolescent chatter. Stay in your room and work on your book report."

"My book report isn't due until next week." I enjoyed being with Mr. Lord and couldn't understand why she wanted to shut me out.

"Start working on it, anyway."

"Can't I say hello to him?"

"No! Stay in a child's place, Fonia."

My feelings were hurt, and I could feel my lip quiver; I couldn't understand why my mother was trying to keep me away from Mr. Lord. When she'd first started working for him, she wanted me to like him, and now that I loved and adored him, she seemed to have a problem with it.

From the solitude of my bedroom, I heard my mother greet him. "Hello, Mr. Lord," she said in cheerful tone. She was usually tense and uptight when Mr. Lord was around, but not tonight. I assumed she was happy that she had me locked away in my room.

"Where's Fonia?" I heard him say.

"Oh, she has a book report. It's past due, so she'll be busy until bedtime."

Liar! Why would she lie to him, and why was she trying to keep us apart? I couldn't understand it. Refusing to be locked away like a leper, I boldly came out of my room and found the dining room table set up with candlelight and flowers.

"There's my girl," Mr. Lord said. "How's the book report coming along?"

"It's not due until next week," I said, giving my mother a look of defiance.

"Then sit down and join us, Princess."

"No! She already had dinner. Besides, she has other homework that she hasn't completed," she interjected.

Mr. Lord glowered at my mother. "What did she have for dinner?"

Mommy nervously fussed with her hair. "Hot dogs… mac and cheese."

"Don't ever feed her that kind of garbage again. Only lean meats, fruit, vegetables, and grains. No junk food! Now prepare Fonia's plate; I want her to have a proper meal." His voice rang with authority.

Mommy was furious. I could tell that by her mannerisms and the way she slammed my plate down on the table.

I felt triumphant. I hadn't started the rift between and my mother and me, but I was determined to win. That night, I realized that my mother was in love with Mr. Lord. And though my feelings were a jumbled confusion of infatuation, hero worship, and the desire for fatherly love, I refused to allow my mother's jealousy to interfere with my relationship with Mr. Lord.

Later that night, I was awakened again by those strange clapping sounds. I tiptoed down the hall and stood outside my mother's door. Overcome by curiosity, I gently turned the door handle and peeked inside the dimly lit bedroom.

Wearing a white negligee, my mother was standing with her palms pressed against a wall. Behind her, Mr. Lord wore an angry expression. He held up her negligee with one hand, and with the other he spanked her bare behind with a paddle. I thought I was seeing things, and so I stretched my eyes wide. But my eyes had not deceived me. *What did Mommy do to get Mr. Lord so upset with her?* Embarrassed for my mother, my face flushed and I quietly closed the door.

The next morning, I could barely look my mother in the eye, and when Mr. Lord didn't join us, I panicked. Maybe he was so mad at Mommy, he'd left us both. "Where's Mr. Lord?"

"He went home last night, not that it's any of your damn business," she said in a bitter tone.

"Is he coming back?" I asked worriedly. From what I'd witnessed, he'd been infuriated with Mommy, but hopefully he wasn't mad at me.

"Why are you always so concerned about Mr. Lord? He doesn't come here to see you. He comes here to see me!"

Her words felt like a slap in the face, but I came back with a cutting comment. "No, you're only his secretary, but he loves me like a daughter."

She laughed bitterly, and the sound was terrible and mocking. "You're living in a dream world, Fonia. You have no idea what I put up with…the things I do so that we can maintain this lifestyle." She waved her hand around, indicating our posh environment.

Mr. Lord loves me; he doesn't have to spank me the way he spanks you! I thought and then pulled out my cell phone and called him. I had to know that he and I were still all right.

"Good morning, Princess," he said, sounding happy to hear from me. "Is everything okay, do you need anything?"

I didn't have a plan formulated; I simply blurted out the first thing that came to my mind. "I…um, I have something to tell you. I lost one of my diamond earrings, and I've been afraid to tell you."

"Is that all? That's only a material thing—easily replaced. I'll bring you another pair when I come over tonight."

"You're not upset with me?"

"Of course not. I'm glad you were honest with me."

I gulped. The earrings were in the box they'd come in. I hated lying to Mr. Lord, and I wished I'd come up with a better story. "I'll understand if you don't want to buy me another pair," I said guiltily.

"I love showering you with gifts."

"Thank you, Mr. Lord." I hung up feeling awful about my dishonesty. Now I'd have to get rid of one of the earrings to cover up my lie. The only good thing that came out of the phone call was that I was convinced that he cared about me and thought of me as his daughter.

I gazed at my mother victoriously. "He's coming to see *me* tonight!"

JAGUAR

The meeting I'd had with Sharif had resulted in a bartending job, but I wasn't sure if taking the job had been a good decision. My shift had started at six p.m. and so far, the bar was dead. It didn't seem likely that I'd be getting the generous tips I'd counted on. I should have known better than to listen to Sharif. Sharif could spin a tale better than a bestselling novelist. During our meeting, he'd convinced me that the small bar called The Dive was raking in cash.

"It's a hole in the wall, but don't let the aesthetics fool you," Sharif had said. "There's an eclectic mix of customers: corporate executives, blue collar dudes, rich college kids, doctoral students, professors, surgeons, politicians, hood chicks, gangsters…you name it. It's the kind of environment where people working stuffy jobs and living fake lives get to hang out with the common folk. When CEO's and hood rats get to mixing it up and drinking together, all kinds of craziness starts to pop off. There's never a dull moment at The Dive, but it'll be worth it when your tip jar is overflowing with twenties and fifties.

I'm serious, Jag, you can make five or six hundred in tips on a bad night!"

Sharif's sales pitch was intriguing, and as I considered the offer, I began to imagine the possibility of not only surviving the summer, but also making a dent in the enormous debt I had accrued over the past seven years.

"So, why are you leaving? You find something that pays more?" I had asked inquisitively.

"Some associates of mine put me on with a new job—something that allows me to fully utilize my talents," Sharif had replied with a secretive smile. Sharif always had some kind of hustle going, and since I wasn't interested in anything remotely illegal, I didn't pry.

There was irony in the fact that I had recently acquired a law degree, while Sharif, who had never finished high school, was in a position to discard a job and pass it down to me.

After graduating from law school, all my college buddies had headed to Cancun for two weeks of fun in the sun. But I couldn't afford that luxury. I was deep in debt and had to find an internship that paid decent wages, but obtaining an internship that paid *anything* in New York had become an exercise in futility. Apparently, most firms were only interested in interns that would provide them free labor. It was bad enough that interns were only given grunt work, but to not even offer the minimum wage for said grunt work was reprehensible. It wasn't merely my ego that didn't allow me to accept any of the non-paying positions I'd been offered, I simply couldn't afford to work for free.

So I tossed my resume into a national database, and out of all the fifty states, the only offer for a paid internship came from a mid-sized law firm in Philadelphia, Pennsylvania—my hometown—the place I'd fled.

Blame it on miscommunication, or an overeagerness to get my career started. Whatever the case, I gave up my cramped apartment in New York and arrived in Philly with my bags packed only to discover the internship wouldn't be available until September. Finding myself in a desperate situation, I sought out Sharif.

From the time we were in middle school, Sharif had always been the go-to guy; the fix-it man. Sometimes, he was true to his word, but he also had game. Like I said, I had turned to Sharif only out of sheer desperation.

I glanced at my empty tip jar and sighed heavily. Surviving the night, let alone the summer, didn't seem likely at this point.

Many of the dudes that Sharif and I grew up with were dead, doing time, or were messed up on drugs. My main man, Curt, was serving a twisted life sentence. I couldn't even think about Curt without getting choked up.

I haven't been an angel; I've done my share of dirt. When you start hustling at age thirteen, you grow up fast. I've been around and seen a lot, and by the time I was twenty, I'd cheated death at least five or six times. The last straw for me was the day Curt almost got smoked. It sounds cold, but I can't help thinking that somehow Curt would have been better off if he hadn't pulled through.

It had been a sunny day and Curt and I were having fun, enjoying the wind against our faces as we sped along Girard Avenue on dirt bikes, laughing as we outran the cops. Zipping on and off the pavement, we gave the cops the finger as we whizzed off Girard and cut down the wrong way of a one-way street. Those lames couldn't catch us…not with our skills.

We'd bought the bikes from some South Philly dudes. Cash. No ID or paperwork required. Making back-alley deals was the way business was transacted in the hood. We were young and getting it, and if our bikes got confiscated by the cops, we'd turn around and buy four more the next day.

Flexing for the chicks that were grinning and waving at us, we felt superhuman and invincible as we zoomed through the neighborhood. The noise from the bikes was so deafening, I didn't hear the gunshots. I saw Curt pull back the handlebars, throw a leg up, and do a twelve o'clock. But when my man flew off the seat and sailed through the sky, my first thought was that there was a mechanical problem with the bike. My mind immediately began cooking up retaliation schemes for those South Philly suckers that had the audacity to sell us a defective bike. My plan was to make sure Curt was all right and then go find those suckers; leave them facedown in the same alley where the deal had gone down.

It never dawned on me that some hating-ass punks, hiding in the cut, had opened fire on Curt.

Everything became a blur after that. One minute I was stunting and doing wheelies through the streets, and the next minute, I was hovering over Curt, screaming for somebody to call an ambulance. The front of his white T-shirt was sprayed with bullet holes, and the back of his head was caved in with globs of blood and brain tissue oozing onto the asphalt. Witnesses said I lost it for a minute. They said I was rambling incoherently as I tried to scoop up portions of Curt's brain with my cupped hands. But I don't remember.

Thankfully, my subconscious blocked out that part of the tragedy. Still, after experiencing something so unimaginable, it's a wonder I'm sane. Then again, maybe I'm not. Who knows what a psychiatrist would uncover if I ever let one poke around inside my mind?

It didn't make sense for someone so young and fun loving as Curt to be laying up in a nursing home. Seeing him helpless and paralyzed, wearing diapers, and being fed through tubes made me rethink the way I viewed the world. Doctors said Curt was brain dead, that he was a vegetable, but I didn't buy it. Curt was still there. Trapped in that motionless, atrophied body, my boy was aware of his miserable situation. I could see awareness brimming in his eyes. And I was tortured by the fact that he knew what was going on. I would have felt better if he wasn't conscious of the fucked-up way his young life had been altered.

The last time I saw Curt, he was gazing at me pleadingly. Like he was begging me to help him. When the male nurse came into his room and began the process of flushing his trachea tube, Curt's eyes latched onto mine and were wild with panic. The procedure seemed painful, and Curt's watery eyes seemed terrified.

"Yo, that's enough, man," I yelled at the nurse. "You're hurting him."

"Oh, he's fine; he doesn't feel anything," the nurse replied casually, like Curt was nothing more than a house plant that he'd come in to water. Meanwhile, Curt's eyes had started rolling into the back of his head. I lost it. Something inside me flipped, and without planning, I found myself charging toward the nurse and yanking him off Curt.

Foul-smelling, milky fluids sprayed from the trachea tube and onto the walls, the bed, and on my shirt. And Curt nearly asphyxiated. Security was called and I was permanently banned from the facility.

I was a basket case after that incident, and mad at the world. I had been taking random classes at Community College, merely to keep my grandmother off my case. As long as I was in school, she didn't harass me about getting a real job, and a real job would have interfered with my hustle. But after what happened to Curt, my heart wasn't in the game anymore. I saw it for what it really was—a trap. The game was all smoke and mirrors. None of us were making any real money. We were young and gullible, and easily influenced to risk our freedom and our lives for a pair of sneakers, clothes, cheap jewelry, and a knot of cash that was large enough to impress naïve, young girls.

Through the neighborhood recreation center where I went to shoot hoops from time to time, I found out about a scholarship. That's when I decided it was time to turn my life around. Curt had gotten an unfair life sentence and I felt an obligation to make something of myself.

But after four years of undergrad in Virginia and three years of law school in New York, I ended up right back where I started, unsuccessful and broke. Working in a hole-in-the-wall bar seemed like a cruel joke.

FONIA

When Mr. Lord asked me what I wanted for my thirteenth birthday, I revealed, "All I want is you. I want you to adopt me. Please." I held my breath as I waited for him to respond.

"That's complicated. I'd have to be married to Lena, and that's not going to happen. Also, your biological father would have to give up his parental rights. He's a poor excuse for a father, but I doubt if he'd willingly sign away his rights."

"But he doesn't care about me."

"You're right; he doesn't care about you. But I do; I care about you deeply. That's all that matters. We don't need a piece of paper to think of each other as father and daughter, do we?"

I shrugged. "I guess not."

He cradled my chin between his thumb and index finger, and looked into my eyes. "Don't I treat you like you're my daughter?"

"Yes."

"Do you want to know why?"

I nodded.

"From the moment I saw you, I knew that I had to possess you—educate you in the ways of my world. I enjoy molding you into becoming the perfect little submissive," he said in a loving tone that was accompanied by a gentle stroke on my cheek.

I didn't understand what he was talking about, but his words sounded so lovely, I gave him a big smile.

"I couldn't ask for a better-behaved child. You do exactly what you're told, and I hope you never change."

"I won't change." I was flushed with pride. Having his approval meant the world to me.

He released my chin and ran his fingers over my cheek. "I'm the only man who knows what's best for you, Fonia."

"I know," I whispered, feeling mesmerized.

"That's my good girl." He stroked my cheek again and I closed my eyes, craving more of his affection. As if sensing my yearning, he kissed me softly on the cheek.

"Can I call you Dad?" I asked eagerly.

He thought for a moment and then shook his head. "No, not yet."

"Why not?" The rejection stung, and my eyes glistened with tears.

His eyes hardened a little. "You're out of line, Fonia. Never question my decisions. I prefer that you continue calling me Mr. Lord, is that clear?" he said harshly.

"Yes, Mr. Lord!" I lowered my eyes to hide my hurt feelings. Mommy frequently dropped her eyes when Mr. Lord was around. I never understood it, but now it seemed as if I had a better understanding. She felt embarrassed whenever she said or did something that he disapproved of. I was terribly confused about the nature of Mommy's and Mr. Lord's relationship. Did all bosses spank their secretaries? I wondered.

"I don't want to be out of line, Mr. Lord, but I really want to ask you something."

"Go ahead."

It was on the tip of my tongue to ask why he spanked Mommy, but fearing repercussions for snooping, I blurted, "Is Mommy your girlfriend?"

"What gave you that idea?"

"Well, uh, because you stay the night sometimes, and you sleep with her."

He released a sigh. "Lena is my employee, and we've developed a special bond. I suppose you could say we have an agreement. She's eager to succeed in the business world, and so I come over a few evenings a week to give her additional training. But in response to your question, no, she's not my girlfriend; we're not romantically involved."

I became quiet, trying to make sense of what I'd seen. Spanking an adult seemed an odd method of training, but in my eyes, Mr. Lord could do no wrong. He knew what was best for my mother and me, and I hoped she'd quickly learn her duties and responsibilities to avoid getting spanked again.

"Don't trouble yourself about your mother and me. Lena is my employee…nothing more. On the other hand, I adore you, Princess," he assured.

I felt a rush of relief, and decided on that day that I would do everything I could to stay in his good graces. Maybe one day, he'd love me enough to really accept me as his daughter. In the meantime, I would strive to please him. I'd never be like Mommy; I'd never upset him to the point where he had to spank me. I'd always be his perfect, little submissive.

2007

On my fifteenth birthday, Mr. Lord made reservations at an elegant restaurant and Mommy and I were both dressed in designer wear and were dripping in jewels. Wearing the diamond-encrusted tiara he'd given me, I felt like royalty.

He opened the passenger's door to his Bentley and when Mommy stepped forward, he said, "No, this is Fonia's special day. I want my princess to sit up front, next to me."

"Oh," Mommy uttered and quietly got in the back.

Beaming with pride, I sat next to Mr. Lord.

During our appetizers, Mommy ordered a Cosmopolitan,

Mr. Lord had cognac, and I had a virgin margarita with sugar around the rim. "This is so good," I gushed. "Wanna taste?" I asked Mommy, but she declined, wrinkling her nose.

"I'll try it," Mr. Lord said and reached for my glass. He took a small sip. "Mm, the perfect drink for the perfect little girl."

"I'm not a little girl anymore, Mr. Lord," I informed him. "I'm fifteen."

He laughed. "You're right, Princess, and we should toast to that."

Instead of joining us in a toast, Mommy guzzled down her drink and immediately waved over the waiter. "I need something stronger. Bring me a glass of bourbon."

Mr. Lord raised his glass. "To my little princess who has grown into a stunning young lady right before my eyes." And then he leaned over and gave me a soft kiss on the lips.

Overwhelmed by the joy of the occasion and so appreciative of how special he made me feel, I threw my arms around Mr. Lord's neck. "Thank you for everything; I love you so much."

"I love you too, Princess."

Mommy made a scoffing sound, and when her bourbon arrived, she guzzled the drink down.

"Are you all right, Lena?" Mr. Lord inquired.

"No, I'm not all right, but it's nothing that another drink won't cure."

By the time dinner was over, Mommy was slurring her words. When the valet brought the car around, she staggered over to it. "Oh, I forgot. I'm not good enough to sit up front. That spot belongs to my fifteen-year-old brat!" she complained in a loud voice as she climbed in the back seat of the car.

I was humiliated by her behavior. But Mr. Lord didn't seem to mind. He behaved as if Mommy didn't exist, and focused all of his attention on me. "Did you enjoy your birthday dinner?"

"Yes, it was wonderful."

"I'm sorry we didn't get to celebrate with cake and ice cream, but Lena wasn't feeling well…" His voice trailed off.

"It's fine; I had a great birthday. Besides, I think I've lost my taste for cake and ice cream," I said, angling for a compliment. Mr. Lord didn't like me to indulge in sugary food, and so I was hoping to hear, 'That's my good girl.'

Instead, he said, "Nonsense! Cake and ice cream once a year won't harm you. Overindulging in a high-fat and sugary diet and drinking too much alcohol is what makes people sick and unattractive." He glanced in the rear-view mirror and scowled at Mommy. I turned around to see what he was looking at. Mommy was sprawled out in the back, in an undignified manner.

"I'll make sure you have your birthday cake next year. I won't allow Lena to spoil your big day, ever again." His voice was low and cold; and he spoke through clenched teeth as if fighting to keep from exploding with anger.

At home, Mr. Lord helped Mommy to her bedroom and then came to my room.

I caressed the tiara that was still on my head. "I don't want to take it off."

Mr. Lord smiled at me and gently lifted it from my head. "Put it back in the box, and keep it in your top drawer."

"Yes, Mr. Lord." Everything in our home was arranged by Mr. Lord's standards. From the way the dishes were stacked in the kitchen cabinets to the way Mommy and I organized our closets. He often selected the clothing we both wore. Once when I asked Mommy why I couldn't choose my own clothes, she told me that Mr. Lord had refined taste and he wanted to make sure that we looked pretty at all times.

When he'd first entered our lives, it hadn't been easy for me to give up control. But over time, I gave in, mostly because Mommy said he knew what was best for us. Now it seemed perfectly normal for him to control every aspect of our lives. I wasn't allowed to hang out with kids my age. Mr. Lord wanted to protect me from bad influences. I didn't see much of my Nana or my Poppy anymore, either. They were my biological father's parents, and Mr. Lord didn't want them poisoning my mind, and he also feared that their unsophisticated ways might rub off on me.

"Should I put on my blue nightie—the one with the ruffles?" I asked after I put the tiara in its proper place.

"That's a good choice," he said, looking around my

room, which was decorated with Hello Kitty paraphernalia everywhere. "I think it's time to update your room with more mature decorating."

I loved my Hello Kitty-themed bedroom, and my immediate impulse was to balk at the idea of changing it, but I caught myself. I'd been taught to never disagree with Mr. Lord. "I can't wait to see the changes you make in my room!" I faked a big grin, and hoped he'd never get around to redecorating my room.

I went inside my private bathroom, washed up, brushed my teeth and changed into my frilly gown. When I stepped inside my room, he gazed at me for a long time and then said, "You look like an angel."

Mr. Lord tucked me in, and when he leaned in to kiss me goodnight, I detected a pleasant whiff of the fragrance he wore. "You smell so good, I wish could smell your scent all night."

Giving me a look of kind understanding, he removed his tie and gave it to me. "Here you are, Princess. You can sleep with this."

I eagerly reached for the silk fabric and brought it to my nose. His eyes gleamed as he watched me inhale. "Thank you, Mr. Lord."

"You're welcome. Happy Birthday, Fonia. Goodnight."

Clutching his tie, I groped for his hand. "Can you stay in here with me a little while longer?"

"Only a little while."

I closed my eyes, wishing for the warmth of his lips on my face again. I loved him so much. There was no one in the world as important to me. Except Mommy, of course. Feeling suddenly alarmed, I opened my eyes. "Is Mommy in trouble, Mr. Lord?"

His face clouded. "I'm not pleased with Lena's behavior tonight, and I'm going to have to address it when she's sober."

I gnawed nervously on my bottom lip. "Is she going to get a spanking?"

He gawked at me, shocked that I knew what he did to my mother behind closed doors. "How do you know what takes place between me and Lena in the privacy of her bedroom?"

My mouth fell open, and I became frightened that I'd displeased him by revealing that I'd been snooping. "I heard sounds one night—a few years ago," I said in a trembling voice. "I was scared, and I went to check on Mommy."

He took a deep breath and released it. "I'm a tough disciplinarian. I'm trying to train Lena, but when she disobeys, I have no choice but to reprimand her."

"Are you ever going to spank me?" I asked with terror in my voice.

He closed his eyes and shook his head as if the idea caused him great pain. "I hope not, Princess. If you remain a perfect little submissive and always do exactly as you're told, I'll never have to discipline you."

"I'll always obey you," I said sincerely.

"That's my good girl." There was love in his eyes as he smiled at me. He patted me on the head, turned off the light, and exited my room.

JAGUAR

As I wiped down the bar, my thoughts returned to Curt, and I wondered if the security staff at the nursing home still had my name and photo on the permanently banned list. Trying to shake off my gloomy thoughts, I approached the only customers in the bar, a copper-skinned woman wearing a straw fedora hat and a hefty dude with a fat, Buddha belly.

"Refill?" I asked Buddha, who was sipping on a drink that had more ice than gin.

"Yeah, hit me again. And give her another one." He inclined his round, meaty head toward the woman sitting next to him. Something about her—her demeanor and her shifty eyes—gave me the impression that she was shady. She had sharp, rat-like features and had thin lips that I suspected had never spoken a kind word. Appearing to be the spiteful, brooding type, her slanted eyes shifted constantly, as if in search of something to steal.

Though I have a law degree, I grew up on the streets, and I can tell at a glance when a female has a larcenous heart.

I turned slightly to get the bottle of Tanqueray, but Rat-Face beckoned me with a wagging finger. "Bartender, I want your opinion on something."

Sighing, I reluctantly gave her my attention. I had been subjected to the couple's asinine conversation for the past twenty minutes, and I didn't want to be drawn into it.

"What's your name, sweetheart?" she asked with her lips twisted in a deceitful smile.

"Jaguar."

"Mmm. That's sexy." Her shifty eyes ran the length of my six-two, muscular frame, assessing me.

"If you're gonna be sitting in my face flirting with the bartender, why don't you let him buy your drinks?" Buddha grumbled.

"I'm not flirting; Jaguar *is* a sexy name. I made a truthful statement; why're you making such a big deal out of it?"

These two were definitely hood rats. Nothing about them suggested they were professionals that enjoyed slumming it as a way of relaxation. And it didn't seem likely that they would be tipping generously, if at all.

"Do you watch porn?" Rat-Face asked. The question took me by surprise, but I maintained a straight face.

"Sometimes."

"I want you to meet the next big porn star…" She turned to Buddha and gestured like she was welcoming him on to a stage.

"I'm not kidding; he's got porn-star qualities."

"Stop playing," Buddha said with a burst of embarrassed laughter.

I've always heard that fat dudes have micro dicks… but maybe it's only a myth. Since I seriously didn't care about Buddha's porn star capabilities, I busied myself with the task of refreshing their drinks.

As I slapped down fresh napkins and plopped a slice of lime in Buddha's Tanqueray, Rat-Face instructed, "Take it out and show him!"

Sharif had warned me about carding patrons that looked underage, but he hadn't given me any instructions on how to deal with lewd behavior. I didn't know what I'd do if Buddha listened to this warped chick and decided to whip out his dick. The bar didn't have a security guard that I could call on, but being young and fit, I doubted if I needed any help eighty-sixing chubby-ass Buddha.

But on the other hand, if Rat-Face stayed in the bar, I'd be stuck having to listen to her ignorant and pointless conversation. It would work out best for me if I strongly encouraged Buddha to keep his dick in his pants.

"Don't be shy; show him!" Rat-Face persisted in a voice that was practically a hiss.

"I'm not showing nobody nothing," Buddha objected, which was a relief to me.

"You should be proud of your assets." Rat-Face's voice was whiny, with an annoying nasal quality. I didn't like her, and a part of me wanted Buddha to go in on her and put her in her place.

"I'm proud and everything," he said in a placating tone that disappointed me. "But see…"

Man-up, nigga! Don't let that big-mouth broad chump you like that. I thought with disgust. Rat-Face looked all right, but she wasn't anything special. Apparently, fat boys like Buddha had to work hard to get a little bit of attention from basic chicks.

"See, what goes on between you and me is personal." Buddha puckered up and leaned toward Rat-Face.

She regarded Buddha with a sneer. "You got me looking like a liar in front of Jaguar, and now you wanna be kissing on me. Uh-uh, I don't think so."

"How do I have you looking like a liar?"

Her expression softened somewhat as she mimicked a smile. "Ain't no other customers in here. It's just us. So, go ahead and show him your asset," Rat-Face softly persuaded.

"Nah, man, keep your personal business to yourself," I butted in. I wasn't trying to see that man's dick.

"I know, right?" Buddha commented.

She rolled her eyes at him. "You're corny; but thanks for the drinks." She picked up her drink and sashayed down to the far end of the bar. I'm not sure if that donkey butt she was rocking was natural or manufactured, but I suddenly knew why Buddha was so captivated.

"Women! I swear!" Buddha complained, and then wrapped a big, calloused hand around the glass of Tanqueray on the rocks. Wearing a repentant smile, he picked up his drink and waddled toward Rat-Face.

"Uh-uh. Don't come down here," she griped.

"Don't be like that; lemme buy you another drink."

"I'm good. I don't need you to buy me nothing else," she said and then turned the drink he had paid for up to her lips.

The door opened, emitting shards of sunlight and two white bikers wearing dirty leather that was covered in road dust. One was about forty pounds overweight, and the other was of average size and weight. The fat one had a scruffy, red-tinted beard and a bald head; the other had greasy, dark hair that hung to his shoulders. Looking like trouble, they strode up to the bar.

"Where's Sharif?" the big one said in a gruff tone.

"Doesn't work here anymore," I said. Wondering if Sharif had swindled these bikers out of some money, I braced myself for a disturbance of some sort.

"What happened, did all his baby mamas catch up with him?" Scruffy laughed, and there was a friendly look in his eyes that allowed me to drop my guard. "Two Heinekens," he said.

I gave him the beers and he gave me a twenty and told me to keep the change. The two bikers ambled over to the pool table in the back, and began racking up the balls. Before long, more of their motorcycle club members began trickling in, and they were such generous tippers, I felt a little guilty for stereotyping them as troublemakers.

The biker crowd was keeping me so busy, I began to lose my mental count of the tips I'd earned. With sneaky Rat-Face and her probable sticky fingers on the premises,

I thought it best to move the tip jar from next to the register and hide it among the cleaning products on a low shelf.

Both pool tables were operating and a crowd of college kids had come in. Some were seated at the bar and others gathered in front of the dartboard. The Dive had come to life and from my rough estimation, I already had more than enough money to pay my hotel bill for the week.

I was standing at the cash register with my back turned when a honey-coated voice said, "I'll have a Spunky Monkey."

What the hell was a Spunky Monkey? I'd be willing to bet all my tips that it was something that required mixing a combination of ingredients in a blender. Damn! I wasn't in the mood for that. I had been on a roll, handing out beers and pouring liquor. Shaker drinks were no problem. All you had to do was combine ingredients in a shaker, and then shake and strain, but having to concoct something in a blender was going to slow down my momentum. Aggravated, I glared at the blender that sat on an out of the way, low shelf and considered pretending that The Dive didn't have a blender. But it was my first night on the job and it was in my best interest to be nice to the clientele.

"Do I have to bust out my *Bartender's Guide* or can you tell me what goes in a Spunky Monkey?" I asked, wearing a forced smile. Sharif had given me this red book with a ton of drink recipes. He said I would only have to refer to it on the rare occasion that a customer wanted something fancy. I doubted if a drink with a messed up name like Spunky Monkey was even in the red book.

"You don't know how to make a Spunky Monkey?" She shook her head like I was a pathetic excuse of a bartender. "You make it with two shots of Kahlua, one shot of Amaretto and a half cup of milk. Pour it in the blender with six ice cubes and turn it on high," she explained with amusement in her devilish brown eyes. Her hair was shaved on one side and long and flowing on the other. Her tank top was low-cut, revealing deep cleavage and a tattoo of a yellow bee decorated her left breast.

"Nice tat," I commented before gathering up the ingredients for her concoction.

She spread her lips into a sassy smile. "I'm the queen bee; fuck with me and you're gonna get stung!"

"I'll bear that in mind." Bee-Sting had a pretty brown face and silky, long eyelashes, but she was a little off, exuding a fatal attraction quality that warned me to keep her at arm's length. Surprisingly, making her drink didn't take too long, and when I set it in front of her, she was engaged in flirtatious conversation with the scruffy, bearded biker. He paid for her drink, got another Heineken for himself, and tipped me ten dollars. Bee-Sting rose from the barstool and followed him back to the pool table area.

That was a hook-up that I hadn't seen coming. I glanced at Buddha to see what he made of the unlikely coupling, but he was busy entertaining Rat-Face, extending a tongue that was as long as the tie I'd worn to my internship interview. So *that* was his porn-like trait. I must admit, I've never seen anything like it. Rat-Face looked entranced when Buddha, who was now apparently inebriated enough to show off his asset, plunged his tongue into the glass like he was dropping an anchor into the ocean. With his thick tongue pressed against the bottom of the glass, he lapped up the remaining dregs of alcohol along with a couple ice chips.

FONIA

Mommy's drinking had become a serious problem. She kept her liquor hidden from Mr. Lord, stashing bottles inside the dishwasher and other odd places. She had tons of secret places, and wanting to protect her, I never breathed a word to Mr. Lord. On the nights that he wasn't scheduled to come over to give her training, she drank openly, stumbling around our townhouse, muttering profanities.

"Please don't drink," I'd said when she retrieved her flask from one of her hiding spots, and turned it up to her mouth. "Suppose Mr. Lord comes over tonight?"

"Fuck him!" she hissed, completely out of character. "Mr. Lord can kiss my ass," she said crudely and then took a sip from the flask.

I was stunned and appalled by Mommy's coarse language. For her to speak Mr. Lord's name in a profanity-laced tirade was practically sacrilege. I looked around, making sure he hadn't slipped inside the house without our knowing it. I couldn't begin to imagine the consequences if he'd overheard the terrible things Mommy had just said.

"You shouldn't say nasty things about Mr. Lord," I cautioned.

"Why not?" she said in a slurred voice. "He's out of town. He didn't invite you and he didn't invite me. All men are alike. I bet Mr. Lord did the same thing your real father did…went out and got himself a brand-new family. Kicked us to the curb!" Her voice was gruff and her lips were twisted spitefully. Mommy had changed a lot over the past year. She was still a stunning beauty when she was sober, but she was an ugly, vile stranger when she started drinking. "Mr. Lord has replaced you with another teenage girl, so get over it," she taunted.

"What are you talking about? Mr. Lord loves me like a daughter."

"You'll see. Mark my words. One day he's going to replace you, just like he replaced me." She pointed a finger at me and laughed maliciously. Stumbling around the family room, she continued her drunken rant, calling Mr. Lord every name in the book. In the midst of her angry outburst, I saw headlights through the curtains and was horrified to realize that Mr. Lord was paying us an unexpected visit. Terrified of falling from favor for not reporting Mommy's drunkenness, I quickly called his cell phone, pretending that I didn't know he was in our driveway.

"Mr. Lord, Mommy's been drinking. I'm scared. Can you come over right away?" I blurted in a voice that shook with genuine terror, though it wasn't Mommy I feared.

"I'm right outside, Fonia. Did she harm you?"

"No, but she's been threatening me," I said, referring to her comment about Mr. Lord replacing me.

"Go to your room and lock the door. I'll handle Lena."

"Okay, thank you," I said, feeling like a traitor, but I'd warned her that she might get caught. There was no reason why I should have to share responsibility for her misdeeds.

Mr. Lord didn't raise his voice. He simply took away the alcohol and told Mommy to go to bed. He knocked on my bedroom door and I quickly opened it.

"Is she okay?" I asked anxiously.

"She's sleeping it off," he said bitterly and I became teary-eyed, imagining that he might be so fed up with Mommy that he'd leave and never return.

"Why are you crying?" he asked.

"Because Mommy said you're going to leave us; she said you have a new family."

"That's not true. First of all, Lena is not my family... you are. I only put up with her because of you," he said, wiping away my tears. "Lena is weak and deceitful and you're nothing like her...are you?"

I shook my head adamantly. "No, I'm nothing like her, Mr. Lord." I burst into tears, feeling bad for betraying my mother, but she'd given me no choice.

He embraced me as I sobbed. "Lena promised me that she was going to quit drinking, and I believed her. I'm proud of you for letting me know the truth. I don't want you to be deceitful like your mother. Don't keep secrets from me, Fonia. Do you understand?"

I nodded.

"If I ever find out that you've been a naughty girl, you won't like the consequences."

"I won't keep secrets, Mr. Lord. I promise."

2008

On my sixteenth birthday, Mr. Lord took me to New York to shop for clothes and jewelry and he also took me to a Broadway play. Mommy was on drinking binge, so we had to leave her at home. The day after we returned home, Mr. Lord had a beautiful birthday cake delivered.

Mommy was back to her regular self, dignified and sober. It seemed that everything was back to normal and that Mr. Lord had forgiven her for getting drunk on my birthday.

We all had a slice of cake, and then Mommy had to excuse herself and do some work in Mr. Lord's office.

While she worked, Mr. Lord and I cuddled together on the couch, watching TV. "Would you like another slice of your birthday cake?" he asked.

He usually didn't allow me to have extra sweets, and I was surprised by the offer.

"Is it okay?" I asked cautiously.

"Sure, have another slice."

I went in the kitchen and cut a small slice and sat down at the table.

"Bring it in here, and finish watching TV," he called from the family room. It surprised me that he'd invited me into the room. Mr. Lord had rigid rules about eating food in areas other than the kitchen and dining rooms.

Timidly, I brought the slice of cake into the family room and sat down, very careful not to drop a crumb. Even though I had his permission, I felt anxious about breaking one of his rules.

Surprisingly, he took the plate from me and swiped icing from the cake. He poised his finger near my lips, inviting me to taste the chocolate. Feeling modest, I looked around, hoping Mommy didn't come out of the office. She became easily jealous, and her jealousy often led to drinking binges. I believed if she saw him feeding me icing from his finger, she'd react with hostility.

Though she'd gotten too drunk to celebrate my sixteenth birthday, Mr. Lord had been lenient with her, and hadn't disciplined her. But if she flew into a jealous rage, he'd march her upstairs, close the door, and give her a sound spanking.

Self-consciously, my tongue darted out and I licked a bit of the chocolate from his finger.

"I thought you loved chocolate."

"I do." I cut an eye at the door to his office, on the lookout for Mommy.

He stared at me, and I noticed an angry look in his

eyes that was usually reserved for Mommy. It was the way he looked at her when she'd forgotten to do something he'd told her, or when he had to repeat himself after giving her an instruction.

Obeying his silent command, I opened my mouth and ardently sucked the flavorful icing from his finger. After I'd licked his finger clean, he kissed me on the forehead and said, "That's my good girl. Want some more?"

I didn't want any more, but I didn't want to upset him, either. "Yes, please," I said with my hands folded in my lap while sitting perfectly erect with my knees pressed together. Sitting like the poised and well-mannered young lady that he had raised me to be.

He gazed at me and smiled warmly. "You're like clay, Fonia. Unlike your mother, you're so easy to mold."

Receiving praise from Mr. Lord inspired me, and I turned to him with my lips parted, waiting for more chocolate icing. I craved the praise that he bestowed upon me each time I licked his finger clean.

He smeared his fingertip with more chocolate and held his finger close to my lips. When I opened my mouth, he withdrew his hand, forcing me to stretch my neck and lean forward to get the icing. It was slightly humiliating, but I put pride aside and sought out his chocolate-coated finger.

He dipped his finger in the icing again, and this time, he held his arm up in the air with his finger pointed toward the ceiling. Perplexed, I gazed at him. Mr. Lord and I had never played this game and I didn't know what he wanted me to do.

"Do you want it?"

"Yes."

"You're a smart girl; figure out a way to get it. You have ten seconds." Laughing, he started counting.

Panicked, I kicked off my shoes and stood on the couch. Now towering over him, I leaned over and sucked the chocolate from his finger. Afterwards, I was mortified, and quickly resumed my position on the sofa, sitting like a proper young lady. I didn't like this game. I'd be more comfortable with it if Mommy wasn't right down the hall.

"You don't have to sit erect. Relax, Princess. He opened his arms to me and I leaned against his chest. For reasons I didn't understand, I felt like crying. Sensing my somber mood, he began stroking my hair. "You'll do anything I tell you to do, won't you, Princess?"

"Yes," I said with a sniffle, feeling degraded by the game we'd played.

"There's no reason for tears. You're perfectly obedient and I'm completely satisfied with your submissiveness."

"Thank you." Pleased by his compliment, I began to feel better. I cuddled closer to him, wrapping my arms around his waist and resting my head on chest. He nuzzled my neck. "Whose good girl are you?"

"I'm your good girl," I responded eagerly.

"And don't ever forget who you belong to," he said, brushing his lips against my neck. His mustache tickled my skin, but the warmth of his breath on my flesh was reassuring and I felt cherished. The closeness…the affection he was bestowing upon me was my reward for following his commands. No longer tense, I closed my eyes dreamily as he fed me the rest of the cake from his hand. After I'd eaten the last crumb of cake, he inserted his finger into my mouth. Like a child sucks its thumb, I sucked his finger for comfort. It was very soothing. I felt comforted. I felt safe and loved.

Mommy suddenly entered the family room, holding a few sheets of paper in her hand. She faltered in her steps and flinched as she observed the intimacy between Mr. Lord and me.

She coughed, cleared her throat, and raked a shaky hand through her hair. "So sorry to interrupt you, Mr. Lord, but the fax you were waiting for just came through," she said with her eyes focused on the floor.

Mr. Lord didn't speak right away; he looked down at me. "Are you upset, Princess?"

I nodded. "A little," I whispered, feeling like I'd been caught doing something bad.

"Are you really sorry you interrupted me, Lena?" he inquired in a cold tone.

"I would never deliberately interrupt you, but you told me to keep an eye out for this fax. I'm only doing what I was told," she said in a pathetic tone of voice.

"Don't ever interrupt my alone-time with Fonia. Unlike you, there's still hope for your daughter. Do you want to ruin her chances of succeeding in life?" His voice had risen; he was obviously perturbed. *Why did Mommy have to come into the room and ruin our peaceful, alone time?*

"I apologize, sir," Mommy said.

He didn't respond, and you could cut the tension in the room with a knife. I shot a glance at Mr. Lord, hoping he'd accept her apology and let her get back to work.

Mommy was in an awful predicament, but I was still on Mr. Lord's good side. He'd told me that I was his good girl, so I relaxed in the knowledge that although she was constantly getting herself in trouble, I knew how to behave. He'd never replace me with another girl as Mommy had alleged. I was his perfect, little submissive.

She took a few steps toward him, holding out the papers.

"Fonia and I are watching TV and you're blocking our view! Isn't that right, Princess?" he said, stroking the side of my face.

She immediately stepped out of the way. I felt sorry for my mother and wanted to help her, but I wasn't allowed to dispute Mr. Lord's words. "Yes, she was blocking our view, but I can see the TV now," I mumbled in a miserable voice.

"If you must make a nuisance of yourself, Lena, then hurry up! Bring me the papers." He waved her over to the couch, but the moment she took a step in front of the TV again, he halted her with a gesture. "What's your problem? I told you, you were in the way!" He let out a sound of frustration.

"What do you want me to do?" she said in an escalated tone.

There were two entrances into the family room: the left side of the corridor and the dining room area led into the family room. Mr. Lord pointed, indicating Mommy should back out of the room and reenter from the dining area. It took her a moment to realize what he wanted her to do. Her hesitation infuriated him.

"Never mind, you dim-wit. Get down on your knees and bring me the papers. Crawl to me."

"Mr. Lord, if you don't mind, I can do that later—in private," she said, her eyes darting embarrassedly to my face.

"No, Lena. I want you to crawl now."

She closed her eyes briefly and took a deep breath. Clutching the papers, she lowered herself slowly and crawled over to the couch. She remained on all fours with her head down as he perused the pages.

After he finished reading, he instructed her to put the papers on his desk. Still on her hands and knees, she turned around.

"Get off the floor, Lena. You move faster when you're upright." Mr. Lord observed her with disgust. Red-faced, she immediately came to her feet, but kept her eyes trained to the floor.

"Did crawling around on the floor in front of your daughter embarrass you?" he asked.

"Yes, very much," she replied.

"But it doesn't matter if you disgrace yourself and set a bad example for her when you get drunk on her birthday."

"I only had a glass of wine. I think my new medication had a bad effect on me."

"That's a flimsy excuse. You're not fit to be Fonia's mother. Do you realize that?"

Eyes downcast, she nodded. "I'm going to get help."

Mr. Lord scoffed and waved her away with an impatient hand gesture. "That's enough work for today. I want you to go to your room and contemplate how your drunkenness is impacting Fonia. I'll join you later and you can expect severe consequences."

Mommy nodded solemnly, and then went to the office with the papers. She came out of the office and headed for the staircase.

"Lena!" he bellowed. His voice was venomous and I nearly jumped out of my skin.

"Yes, Mr. Lord," she said, stopping cold.

"Come and get Fonia's plate. Wash it and make sure you don't leave it in the dish rack. Dry it and put it in its proper place."

I had nervous jitters as I listened to my mother clattering around in the kitchen. She was a wreck, and I was afraid she'd accidentally break the plate or forget to wipe every drop of water out of the sink. I wondered why it was so difficult for her to be a perfect submissive like me.

After she retired to her bedroom, I was too upset to

concentrate on what we'd been watching, and I was relieved when Mr. Lord aimed the remote and turned off the TV. "It's bedtime, Fonia." He gave me a nudge to get up, which I did immediately. "Your mother's a weak woman, and she's very deceitful. Unfortunately, I have to deal with her right now."

I nodded, but my feelings were conflicted. I loved my mother and didn't want her to be in trouble with Mr. Lord, but at the same time, I was upset with her for being so weak and deceitful.

I headed toward my bedroom while Mr. Lord strode in the direction of Mommy's room. From the corner of my eye, I saw him unbuckling his belt, and I bit down on my lip. *Mommy's really gonna get it!* I thought sorrowfully.

FONIA

2010

O ver time, Mommy's spankings became a routine part of our household, and Mr. Lord no longer kept the training sessions inside the bedroom; he openly disciplined her in front of me. He continued to praise my good behavior and rewarded me with every material item one could imagine. My bedroom closet, along with the closet in the guestroom, was filled with designer clothes, shoes, and bags. And numerous jewelry boxes overflowed with pieces of fine jewelry.

For me, the best reward was his verbal praise and physical affection. A mere pat on my head made my day sunny and bright. Curled in his lap, sucking his finger was one of my greatest pleasures in life. It soothed me like a warm blanket in the winter. But that particular form of affection was not given freely; it had to be earned.

When my eighteenth birthday rolled around, Mommy, who had been unraveling emotionally for the past few years, was being treated for alcoholism at a facility near the Pocono Mountains. Lately, she'd been in and out of mental health and rehab facilities quite frequently. Despite my mother's numerous absences from our home, I didn't act out or go through a rebellious phase. I was a model teenager. Straight A's and perfect school attendance. Due to my mother's illness and my biological father's lack of interest, Mr. Lord had been my legal guardian since I was sixteen.

I would have felt more secure if he had legally adopted me, but I didn't question his judgment. As my guardian, it was within Mr. Lord's right to make decisions regarding my education. One day when he drove me to school, he noticed a boy looking at me. On the spot, he told me to get back in the car. "You're going to be home-schooled. I've invested a lot of time molding you into becoming a perfect woman, and I won't have all my work destroyed by disgusting boys that lust after you."

I didn't say a word. When Mr. Lord became overly angry, it was best to keep quiet.

"Have you been leading boys on—making them think you're available?"

"No, Mr. Lord. I never look at boys. I don't think about them either. I'm still your good girl. I swear."

"I hope so, Fonia."

"I am!"

I was telling the absolute truth. I'd never had a high school crush; never even kissed a boy. The only male hands that had ever touched me were Mr. Lord's, and he had only hugged and kissed me in a fatherly way. Every now and then, he fed me from his finger and he gave me articles of clothing he'd worn to satisfy my obsession with his scent. But that was the extent of it. And now that I was getting older, I found that I wanted more. No boy at school could compare to Mr. Lord. He was the most handsome, the most intelligent, the most sophisticated man in the world, and I fantasized about him kissing me on my mouth, and exploring the womanly body that I now possessed.

It was a secret fantasy that would never be realized because Mr. Lord loved me like a daughter. But for me, he was father, lover, and maybe one day, my husband. He was my entire world.

His decision to pull me out of school didn't bother me in the least. In fact, I expected to be able to spend a lot more time with him now that I wouldn't be in school for seven hours a day.

But it didn't turn out that way. My online classes only took a few hours, and I had the rest of the day to myself, with nothing to do except wait for him. But his visits had started to taper off. There was always a reason why he couldn't stop by…business meeting, business trips out of town. I was stuck in the house all day and all night, and I was losing my mind with not only boredom, but I was also obsessing on the possible reasons that he wasn't spending time with me.

My mother's words haunted me: *Got himself a new*

family. Kicked us to the curb! Night after night, I cried myself to sleep.

He checked on me by phone on a daily basis, but I ached to see his handsome face. To sit and talk with him. As much as I feared being scolded by him, I'd prefer that to getting nothing at all. When a full week had elapsed without a visit, I went into a panic. Feeling desperate to see him, I called him repeatedly on his cell phone, and left messages with his secretary, pleading for him to stop by and see me.

"Not tonight. I'm busy with a new business venture," he said.

"But I miss you and I need you," I said, feeling as if my heart would break in two if I didn't see him soon.

"The desperation in your voice is making me nervous, Fonia," he said over the phone.

"I *am* desperate. Desperate to see you."

"Stop it! You sound weak and pitiful, and you're beginning to remind me of Lena."

"No, I'm not like her, Mr. Lord. I'm not deceitful. I do everything you tell me to do."

"Listen, you have to stop calling me every other hour. You've lost your phone privileges until further notice."

"But—"

"We'll discuss this further when I come to the house tonight." he said and abruptly disconnected the call.

Extremely desperate and afraid I'd lose him to another family, I put on one of my mother's negligees, which I filled out perfectly. I had no particular plan, but fearing that he was growing bored with me, I wanted him to see that I was no longer a child. I was a young woman.

When he arrived, instead of his face lighting with delight the way I'd expected, he frowned with disapproval. "Why are you dressed like that? You look like a whore!"

I winced. I thought he'd smile at me and tell me how beautiful I looked. I was stunned by his angry reaction. "I'm sorry. I wanted you to notice that I'm all grown up."

"Did I raise you to act like a trollop?"

"No."

"Get against the wall, Fonia!" he demanded in a voice that vibrated with rage—a voice that I'd only heard him use with Mommy.

"I didn't mean—"

"I said, get against the wall." He gave me a shove. "If you want to act like a streetwalker, then I'll treat you that way."

"But…" Trembling, I moved toward the wall where fine art in gilded frames hung above my head. With my forehead pressed against the cool wall, tears streamed down my face. I stretched out my arms the way I'd seen my mother do on innumerable occasions.

He lifted the negligee, revealing my naked buttocks. I squeezed my eyes closed in shame. The humiliation I felt in that moment was beyond anything I'd ever experienced. He didn't hit me with a paddle; he struck my bottom with his bare hand. Before I could recover from the first sting, he hit me again, and I cried out and began to moan. His touch was a mixture of pain and pleasure. There was moistness and a tingling sensation between my legs as I anticipated the next slap. But instead of striking me again, Mr. Lord walked away.

He went into the kitchen. I could hear the fridge open. I heard the snap as he uncapped a bottle of water. I heard the swallowing sounds as he hydrated himself. The anticipation was unbearable, and moisture trailed down my thigh.

With my back turned and my head down, I didn't see him return to the family room; but I heard his footsteps echoing as he crossed the parquet floor. Bracing myself for more harsh punishment, I gritted my teeth when he once again lifted the negligee. Surprisingly, he didn't spank me; he caressed my sore behind.

"Hopefully, this will be your first and last spanking," he murmured in a deep voice that was filled with kindness. His hand rubbed my bottom circularly in such a soothing manner; a tiny moan escaped my throat. His hand roamed between the crevice of my thighs and his middle finger found its way to the accumulated stickiness that coated my pubic hairs and smeared my inner thigh.

"What is this?" he said in a husky voice.

"I don't know," I said innocently. "Something happened while you were spanking me."

"Go clean yourself up and get out of that whore's outfit."

I walked to the bathroom with my head hung low in disgrace.

When I emerged from my bathroom, carrying the negligee, Mr. Lord was sitting on my bed. Reflexively, I crossed my arms over my breasts.

"No secrets between us, Fonia," he said in a stern voice. "You wanted me to view your maturity, so don't hide it now. Come, stand in front of me."

With my face burning in shame, I stood naked before Mr. Lord.

"Are you still a virgin?" he asked.

"Of course."

"No nasty boys have been touching you down here," he asked, patting the mound of my vagina.

"No. I would never let anyone do that."

"I never thought you'd dress like a whore, but you did."

I swallowed. "I didn't mean to. I won't do it again."

"How do I know you're telling the truth? For all I know, every word in your mouth could be a lie. Prove to me that you're still a virgin."

"How?"

"Lie on the bed and open your legs. I need to know for sure that your hymen is intact."

Though it was humiliating to spread my legs open, I did as I was told.

He touched my private parts, gently spreading open the sensitive lips of my vulva. Then a smile blossomed across his face. "Ah, so you haven't been deflowered. That's a relief," he said and unexpectedly lowered his head and kissed the mouth of my womanhood. I gasped and flinched and felt moist again.

"What's wrong?"

"I don't know," I whined, embarrassed that my body was betraying me yet again. Over the years, the feel of his kiss on my face had always warmed me, the taste of his finger had been heavenly, but feeling his lips brush against my private area sent sparks of heat coursing through me, causing me to buck and spasm as if I'd been electrocuted.

He looked me over. "Your nipples are getting hard. What do you think is causing that?"

"I don't know. It happens sometimes when I'm cold and sometimes when I'm sucking your finger," I said in a voice filled with shame.

"Hmm. I guess you can't help yourself; it's in your blood."

"No, it isn't. I'm not like my mother." I shook my head in fervent denial.

"Don't disagree with me, Fonia. If I say it's in your blood, then it's the truth. Am I right?"

"You're right."

He tapped me on the side of my head. "You don't think I know the indecent thoughts that go through your head."

Somehow he knew that I'd been having lurid and tawdry thoughts about him. Deeply humiliated, I sniffled and began to cry. "I do have bad thoughts sometimes. I don't want to, it just happens," I admitted.

"What kind of thoughts?"

"Um…"

"Dirty thoughts?"

I nodded my head and averted my eyes.

"I guess there's nothing I can do about it. Like they say, the apple doesn't fall far from the tree."

"I'm so sorry, Mr. Lord. I didn't want to be like her." I sobbed mournfully and he began to comfort me.

"Shh. Shh. It's not your fault, Fonia. You can't help what you are. The good upbringing, the fancy clothes, and private school were all a waste because you're Lena's daughter." He sighed and dropped his face in his hands, and I kept muttering how sorry I was.

He looked up suddenly. "I have a plan."

I lay on the bed, holding my breath, and waiting to hear how he planned to rid me of this affliction that I was cursed with. If he wanted to discipline me regularly, the way he did Mommy, then I had no choice but to go along with it. After all, he knew what was best for me.

"From now on," he began, "when we're out in public, I want you to continue conducting yourself in an exemplary manner. I want you to behave in the lady-like, refined manner as you've been raised. No one needs to know what you really are. Are you following me so far?"

I wasn't sure where he wasn't going with his plan, but I nodded my head.

"Once a week and behind closed doors, I'm going to allow you to act like a whore."

"Okay…" I paused, not exactly sure what he was giving me permission to do. Did he mean that I could dress up in my mother's negligees for him?

"You're eighteen…technically a grown woman and I'm

going to allow you to release some of your pent-up passion. Are you ready, Fonia?"

"Yes," I agreed readily, though I didn't know what to expect.

"Open your legs," he commanded.

I spread my thighs and closed my eyes. When I felt him insert his longest finger inside of me, I was jolted with an amazing sensation. I gasped. "Mr. Lord!" I exclaimed as he slid his finger in and out of me. Unable to help myself, I moaned and my hips moved rhythmically; I tried to stop but I couldn't control my body.

"Don't hold back. Let yourself go. Be the nasty whore that you are."

I found myself strangely aroused by the vile names he called me. My hips moved at a faster pace as his finger delved deeper inside me. I lost all sense of modesty and began gyrating and undulating. Crying out, humping and thrusting my pelvis in a terribly lewd way. My cries of passion filled my bedroom.

"Do you like acting like a dirty slut?" he whispered, coaxing me to behave with wild abandon.

"Yes, I love it," I panted, speaking the absolute truth. Mr. Lord was the wisest, most giving man in the world. He knew me better than I knew myself.

"Are you my good girl?"

"No!" I screamed as gyrated wildly.

"What are you?"

"A dirty slut and a whore." Speaking those vulgar words

out loud took me to an even greater height of ecstasy.

"There're consequences for whores," he said in a menacing whisper. "Have fun now because I'm going to whip your bare ass again, tomorrow."

With that threat, I exploded, screaming out his name as the muscles inside my vagina pulsated around his finger. I squeezed my thighs tightly, entrapping his hand. He waited until my ragged breathing had returned to normal before removing his finger.

He bent over and kissed me on the forehead. "Goodnight, Princess; I'll see you tomorrow." He clicked out my light and left. I lay still for a while, my mind spinning over the events that had transpired between Mr. Lord and me.

He'd threatened to spank me tomorrow, and I looked forward to it. I also looked forward to being able to release more pent-up passion. Our relationship had gone to a different level, and although I was still his princess, I was also a woman now. I was his woman and his whore.

JAGUAR

I don't know if there was a full moon out or not, but by ten o'clock, the place had turned into a zoo. The atmosphere had become charged with tension, and the bar was so crowded, I could barely keep up with the customers' demands. It seemed that everyone had gotten thirsty at the same time, and patrons were yelling for service. It was a pain in the ass, hearing patrons shouting, "Hey, Jag" or "bartender" and some of them mistakenly called me, "Jack."

Their annoying voices along with the loud music blaring from the touch-screen jukebox, boisterous conversations, and heated arguments had my head pounding. I'd tended bar at countless frat parties, college soirees and a couple of bachelor parties, but doing it as an occupation was a lot more overwhelming than I'd expected.

There was a pool of vomit in the men's room that I refused to clean. I wished I could identify the culprit; I would have tossed his no-liquor-holding ass out of here without hesitation. What sort of lowlife scumbag would spill his guts on the floor? Seriously, how hard is it to aim for the fucking toilet?

Adding to the chaotic atmosphere, a group of college boys were drunkenly cheering each other on as they took turns guzzling down a yard of ale. I had to get valid ID from each of them and a hundred-dollar deposit before handing over the three-foot-long glasses filled with draft beer.

A scholarly-looking, gray-haired couple had entered The Dive carrying briefcases earlier in the evening, but after one drink too many, they began to unravel somewhat, and had begun staggering around, approaching random patrons and inviting them to join them back at their hotel. From what I could tell, the customers' reactions ran the range from amused to openly disgusted. Some customers looked at me as if expecting me to handle the situation. As far as I knew, it wasn't my job to tell the old fogies what they could and couldn't say. Besides, they were extravagant tippers.

On my way to the stockroom to get a case of beer, I overheard the bikers exchanging contentious words with some corner boys who wanted to shoot pool.

"How long y'all gon' be tying up the tables?" asked one of the young thugs.

"All night!" bellowed a biker.

"All night! Yo, y'all can't monopolize both tables. You gotta give up one of 'em."

"This is our monthly tournament; we're using both tables, so get lost."

"Yo, where's Sharif at? I'm about to start spazzin' out on these bikers."

"Sharif doesn't work here anymore; take your problems to Jag, the new bartender."

Having overheard the exchange, I groaned at the prospect of having to play mediator between disgruntled bikers and neighborhood thugs.

On my way back to the bar, Rat-Face came slinking out of the Ladies Room. "Hey, Jaguar," she said in a slurred voice. "If I wasn't with him…" She nodded toward the area where Buddha sat and giggled maliciously. "If I wasn't getting with the porn star, I'd fuck the shit out of you right on top of the bar." She gave a smirking smile.

Rat-Face had taken me off-guard with her bold proposal. Big ass or not, I didn't like her, and I wasn't interested in the least. "Yeah, some other time, I guess," I said, not knowing what else to say.

"Without a doubt. Mmm-hmm. I want some of that," she said leeringly as she eyeballed my crotch. I could feel my dick beginning to shrivel in retreat. She proceeded to join Buddha, and I made my way behind the bar. Feeling perplexed and somewhat violated, I began filling the cooler with Budweiser.

"Bartender," someone called. I turned around and faced a chubby Ivy Leaguer. "Somebody puked out their guts in the restroom," he complained with his mouth turned down in repugnance.

"Yeah, I know," I said, my face scrunched in revulsion. "Maintenance will be here soon," I lied and stole a glance at the clock. It was only ten-twenty, and the janitor didn't begin his four-hour shift until midnight. Meanwhile, the old couple was becoming a public nuisance, going from one customer to the next, still trying to get someone interested in a ménage à trois. The last thing I felt like doing was giving the horny, old fogies a stern talking to. And my feet, hands, and back had started bothering me from all the constant walking, bending, and pouring drinks. Additionally, the air conditioning didn't seem to be doing much and it was too hot for me to exert the energy required to physically throw them out.

The Dive needed a couple extra bartenders, a bouncer, and a cleaning person that worked throughout the shift.

Sharif called to check on me while I was in the midst of making strawberry daiquiris for a pair of hot twins that were celebrating their birthday. As much as I detested fooling with that blender, the girls were eye candy, reminding me of my long-time fantasy of a ménage with identical twins.

"What's up, man?" I said over the whir of the blender and the cacophony of background noise.

"It sounds busy; you all right?"

"I'm good, man. I'm holding it down." If he'd called a half-hour ago, he would have caught me in a foul mood, but I was feeling a lot better, so I didn't complain.

"Just wanted to give you a heads-up, the owner is gonna send someone over around closing time to count your register."

"Who's he sending?"

"Not sure. Probably Harvey. You'll recognize him easily.

Light-skinned dude, always dressed in a suit and bow tie. He tries to front like he's the boss, but he's nothing more than a flunky."

"All right, I'll keep that in mind," I said, cutting a lustful eye at the twins and scheming on a way to get both of them back to my hotel room. "Yo, thanks again for putting me on with this gig," I said to Sharif before hanging up.

I placed the frozen drinks in front of the twins. They took sips of the pink-colored libation that reminded me of a 7-Eleven Slurpee. Both girls smiled and gave the "thumbs-up" sign.

"Happy Birthday, ladies; your drinks are on me, tonight." I flashed a smile and hoped my charm, good looks, and generosity would score some points with them.

"Thank you," the sisters said, and then squealed in unison as if I'd bestowed them with keys to matching, exotic cars.

"You must be new here; we've never seen you before. Hope you're not just filling in for the night; you're too cute for us to let you get away," said the frisky sister, whom I assumed was the dominant twin.

"No, I'm not filling in. I'm here for the summer."

"Oh, good. Hey, why don't you give me a birthday thrill and unbutton a few of those buttons?" said the other twin, who apparently was as feisty as her sister. Guess there didn't necessarily have to be a dominant twin, as I'd heard.

"As stuffy as it is in here, you should open up your shirt

so that smooth, chocolate skin can breathe." The girls slapped hands and laughed.

"I'm Najah and this is my sister, Nona. And you are…?"

"Jaguar. Friends call me Jag."

"Hi, Jag!" they said at the same time, both wearing identical, teasing grins, and leading me to believe that my cherished, sexual fantasy was within the realm of possibility.

"Jaguar is an unusual name. Is that your fake, bartender name or is it on your birth certificate?" Najah inquired. She lifted the straw from her drink, and licked the frosty-pink end of the straw.

"Jaguar's on my birth certificate," I said in as calm a voice as I could manage, considering that she had my dick throbbing each time her tongue flicked out of her mouth.

"What's your last name?" Nona wanted to know.

"Jackson." Some people don't like giving out their government name, but I had nothing to hide.

"Jaguar Jackson. Sounds like a porn-star name."

When the word "porn" entered the conversation, I immediately shot a look down the end of the bar where Buddha had been sitting, but he and Rat-Face had gone. I hoped they were gone. I didn't want Rat-Face to come scurrying out of some corner at closing time, demanding to ride my dick.

"Can I get a birthday cherry in my drink?" Nona asked. I immediately obliged, dropping three Maraschino cherries into the daiquiri. Holding the stem, she pulled one of the cherries from her drink and placed it on her tongue. Then she seductively puckered her lips around the cherry, sucking it for a few seconds, and then pulling it out of her mouth, and began the process all over again. Watching a woman do anything that involves the usage of her lips and tongue gives me freaky images of fellatio and I automatically want to get my dick sucked.

Tauntingly, Nona repeated the dick-teasing demonstration until I winced from the desire to stick my dick into something wet, like her mouth or her sister's pussy.

Closing time couldn't come soon enough. I was physically attracted to the twins and they were obviously feeling the same. If Najah and Nona were dressed in the same outfit, I wouldn't have been able to tell them apart, and I wondered if I'd be able to distinguish one from the other once I had their naked asses in bed.

I was about to suggest we continue the birthday celebration at my hotel when some clown bull carrying a beer in one hand and a glass of Hennessy in the other, sidled up to Nona and started busting it up. I heard him introduce himself as Lamario. *Lamario! What kind of a fucked-up name is that?* She tossed him a smile, welcoming the intrusion. Dude was in violation and I felt like eighty-sixing his ass for that stupid name and for interfering with my fantasy.

Najah finished her drink and said, "I'll have another."

"Me too," Nona chirped in.

Call me petty, but I didn't want to give Nona any more drinks. I felt like I had the right to withdraw my offer of buying her drinks all night. I felt like suggesting that since Lamario was taking up all her time, he should have been paying for her drinks. Not wanting to appear childish, I kept my petulant thoughts to myself.

I made another batch of the pink slush and begrudgingly set Nona's drink in front of her. It's a wonder smoke didn't blow out of my nostrils when she had the audacity to offer Lamario her glass, saying, "Taste it; it's delicious."

To his credit, he declined. "Nah, I'm good," he said frowning at the slushy concoction before taking a healthy swig of Henny that he chased down with beer.

"Are you from Philly, Jag?" Najah asked, pulling my attention away from her sister and Lamario.

"Yeah, I'm originally from here," I muttered sullenly, unable to adjust my bad attitude.

"What part of Philly?"

"The bottom."

"Oh." There wasn't much else for her to say about the bottom, being that it was such a bad part of town.

The natives were getting restless, and so I returned to my bartending duties. Whenever there was a lull, I halfheartedly continued my conversation with Najah. Don't get me wrong, Najah was the business, but I had my heart set on getting with both her and her sister, and it had seemed possible until Lamario interfered with my plans.

Najah was starting to feel the liquor; I could tell by

the way she kept touching me. Each time I stopped to chat with her, she would reach out and caress the top of my hand or run a finger over the veins in my arm.

Sitting next to her, Nona was also feeling a pleasant buzz. Lamario was sitting at the bar with his eyes closed and a smile on his face. I looked down and noticed that Nona was running her hand over the bulge in the front of his pants.

"We should take this outside," he said dreamily, in a whispered voice that he thought was confidential, but both Najah and I had overheard.

"Outside…where?" Nona asked.

"My car…in the lot."

"Okay," Nona readily agreed, and then rose from the barstool.

Najah grasped her sister's wrist. "Nona, I know you're not going anywhere with him!"

"You can come, too!" Lamario said, cutting his eye at me and laughing, as if he and I were in on a private joke. I mean-mugged him. The shit wasn't funny. This bozo had invaded the territory that I had already pissed on, stole one of my chicks, and was now plotting on the other one. Pussy can turn a civilized man into a savage, and I probably would have swung on that bull if Najah had decided to take him up on his offer. But unlike her sister, Najah was loyal.

"My place or yours?" she said with a soft smile when I placed her third drink in front of her.

"Whichever is closest? I'm staying at a hotel near the airport; what about you?"

"I'm much closer—Powelton Village."

"Sounds good," I said without much enthusiasm. I wasn't all that interested anymore, but I'd probably have a change of heart by closing time.

Najah scrawled her address and phone number on the back of a business card that promoted a hair salon. "Drop by when you get off. I have to get my sister; have to make sure she didn't run off with a serial killer." She pulled out her phone and tapped on the screen. "Meet me at the car, Nona," Najah said firmly. Maybe Najah was the dominant twin, after all. And maybe there was still a chance for me to get with both sisters. But after some thought, I had to ask myself if I really wanted to indulge in Lamario's sloppy seconds. Hell no!

FONIA

B y age twenty-one, my relationship with my mother had completely dissolved. Alcohol consumed her life and she had abandoned her parental duties a long time ago. Now-adays, she didn't have a stable environment; she drifted around and only contacted me when she needed money.

I met with her secretly and winced when I saw how haggard and disheveled she'd become; she was nothing like the beautiful woman she'd once been.

"What do you want?" I asked, looking over my shoulder, afraid that Mr. Lord or one of his employees had followed me.

"I got kicked out of the place on Larchwood Avenue, and now I'm ready to get myself together. I'm going into a treatment center, upstate. The next time you see me, I'll be clean and sober."

I'd heard that before. Mr. Lord had sent her to six or seven treatment centers, but since she'd finally taken the initiative to get help on her own, I hoped that this time the treatment would work. I shoved six hundred dollars into her hand. "You can't go on like this; you look horrible and you reek of alcohol," I scolded.

"I said I'm going to get treatment. Why do you always have to act so high and mighty?" she said, sticking the money inside a pocket. "He always tried to make you think that you were better than me, but you're not," she spat. "He used me from the very beginning, pretending to be interested in me so he could get to my little girl."

"You should be grateful that he intervened and helped you raise me. Had it not been for Mr. Lord, I wouldn't be the well-bred young woman that I am."

My mother sneered at me. "You think you're on his level? Ha! That's a laugh. He's a sick man, you know. He's a member of a secret society that enjoys hurting and degrading people."

"Mr. Lord would never hurt me. He disciplines me when I require it, but he loves me."

"Oh, he's disciplining you, now? In other words, he finally got around to whipping your behind?"

"Because he loves me and wants what's best for me!"

"You better get away from that man, Fonia. Bringing him into our lives was the biggest mistake I ever made. And I took his abuse in exchange for what I thought would be a better life, but I paid a high price for that upgrade. You need to get away from him before you end up being a drunk like me."

I scowled in repugnance at the very thought of ending

up like my mother. "Mr. Lord loves me, Mommy; he's going to marry me one day."

"Oh, he loves you all right. He loves what he's turned you into. But when he's ready to settle down, it won't be with you. He's going to marry a society girl. He'll keep you on the side until he gets tired of you, and then he'll throw you out to the wolves, the way he did me."

"You became a hopeless alcoholic. He had no choice but to throw you out; he was afraid that you were setting a terrible example for me. He didn't want your bad influence to rub off on me."

"Well, who do you think turned me into a drunk? Your precious Mr. Lord, that's who!"

"He didn't put the bottle up to your mouth; you did."

"It was the only way I could escape from the sick things he did to me—"

"What sick things? He only spanked you when you deserved it," I blurted, defending Mr. Lord.

"He did more than that. He forced me to go to secret parties once a month. And the things that he and his friends did to me at those parties are too disgusting to think about without needing a drink."

"What secret parties? You're drunk right now, and you're talking nonsense."

"Drunk mind, sober tongue. Isn't that what they say?" She laughed bitterly. "Most of the guests at those parties enjoyed being humiliated, beaten, and urinated on, but not me. I hated all of it."

Urinated on? Clearly, my mother had lost her mind.

Then she gazed at me and I saw lucidity and for a brief moment, and I also saw a glimmer of a mother's love in her eyes. "Don't let him take you to any of those parties, Fonia. Once that happens, you'll slowly start losing your mind."

"I don't know what you're talking about. You need help, Mommy, and I hope the treatment will work this time around," I said sincerely. "But you really have to stop contacting me. You know I'm not allowed to communicate with you."

"Aren't you going to help me get on my feet when I get out of the facility?"

"No, I can't. You're on your own now. Please don't contact me again."

A smirk formed on her lips. "When he gets tired of you and gets himself a new family, you're going to end up exactly like me."

Driving the Lexus that Mr. Lord has given me for my twenty-first birthday, I sped through traffic lights trying to get home. I was only supposed to leave the house to run errands. I had no idea how I would explain the mileage on the odometer, which he checked regularly. I decided to shop for groceries at Whole Foods in Wynnewood. There was a Whole Foods that was closer to our home, but it didn't carry the special caviar that Mr. Lord enjoyed. Driving to Wynnewood would explain the extra mileage.

When I arrived home, I was surprised to find his car

in the driveway, but was relieved that I'd had the insight to come up with a good excuse. Carrying a Whole Foods shopping bag, I entered the house.

Mr. Lord was in his office, and I immediately went to greet him.

"I didn't know we needed groceries," he said. He kept tabs on every item in the house and knew which groceries needed to be replenished.

"I wanted to surprise you with one of your favorites."

"And what might that be?" he asked, eyeing the bag suspiciously.

"Your favorite caviar," I said, reaching into the bag to show him proof. "I drove all the way to Wynnewood to get it."

"Put it away, and then come have a seat. I want to talk to you." His tone was stern.

I went to the kitchen, wondering if he somehow knew that I'd been communicating with my mother.

In his office, I stood with my hands folded in front of me, bracing myself for a scolding.

"There's no easy way to tell you this, Fonia…"

"Tell me what?"

"I'm getting married."

Shocked and devastated, I sank into the chair across from his desk. Unable to believe what I'd heard, I could hardly breathe.

"I've been backed into a corner financially and the only way to survive is to join forces with a very powerful family. My marriage will be nothing more than a business arrangement, and I expect the arrangement between you and me to continue."

The room was starting to spin; this couldn't be happening. My mother's prediction was coming true, and my worst fear was being realized. Mr. Lord was getting himself a new family. He was leaving me. "How can we continue if you're getting married?" I asked, feeling dazed.

"Leave that up to me. My wedding is in three months."

"Who's the lucky woman?" I asked with bitter tears filling my eyes.

"Her name is Sylvia Chessman. She lives with her family in Phoenix, Arizona. The ceremony will take place there, and of course, I'd love for you to be there, but my fiancée wouldn't understand our special relationship.

"She wants to honeymoon in Bermuda for a week, and I've agreed, but I can't have you out of my sight and on your own for that length of time. Your passport is up-to-date and I'm going to book a flight for you from Philadelphia to Bermuda on my wedding day. I'll reserve a suite in the same hotel as Sylvia and me."

My head was spinning with a million questions that I was afraid to ask for fear of appearing impudent.

Despite the fact that my world had collapsed around me, I uttered, "All right," responding as obediently as ever, while hoping with all my heart that he was only joking. It had to be some sort of test to see if I'd stick with him through the most bizarre circumstances.

"You're pouting, and that's unbecoming," Mr. Lord chastised. "You're not a child anymore; surely you realized that sooner or later I'd marry a worthy young lady."

"I don't understand why you're not marrying me. I did everything you ever asked; I thought I made you happy. Please don't marry her, Mr. Lord. I'll correct whatever mistakes I've made. I can make myself worthy if you give me a chance." My words came out in short, frantic bursts.

"You did nothing wrong. My marriage to Sylvia is a marriage of convenience...nothing more." He glanced at his watch. "I'm going to be spending a lot of time flying back and forth to Phoenix for the next few months. In fact, I'm flying out tonight. But I'm going to squeeze in some time to buy you a new wardrobe for the Bermuda honeymoon." He gave me a smile, but I couldn't return it. Profound pain enveloped my heart, and all I could do was stare at him through teary eyes.

"Fonia," he said with patience in his voice. "We've never needed a piece of paper to define our relationship, have we?"

"No."

"And we don't need one now. Sylvia will be my wife in the eyes of the law, but you're the wife of my heart. Sylvia nor any other woman could ever please me the way you do. I want you to think of the trip to Bermuda as *our* honeymoon. Reality is not always what it appears to be. People see what they want to see. Do you understand?"

"No, Mr. Lord, I'm sorry, I don't understand."

He sighed and then gave me a patient smile. "When Sylvia and I leave for Bermuda, the guests at our wedding will see newlyweds, happily beginning a new life together, but in reality I'll be actually starting a new life with you. Are you ready to finally give yourself to me completely?"

"Of course. I've been waiting to give myself to you since I was eighteen."

"Your wish will soon come true. When we return from Bermuda, you won't be a virgin anymore. I've devoted years to molding you into a decent and malleable young woman, and I can't think of a better time to deflower you than on *our* honeymoon."

"Why do we have to wait? I'm ready now." It was true; I yearned for a deeper level of intimacy. For years I had been experiencing strong sexual desires that weren't being met. At night, I often touched myself, imagining that Mr. Lord was making love to me in a traditional way…penetrating me with his penis instead of his finger.

"What do you mean, you're ready now? Do you know how disgusting and perverted you sound? Don't you dare question my decision to wait another three months." His voice shook with rage and he pointed his finger at me angrily. "I tried to raise you to be decent and pure, but you're no better than your mother. You're nothing but a whore."

I swallowed guiltily.

"If you don't think you're capable of waiting until my

wedding night, then feel free to walk away from the life I've provided for you."

"I can't walk away. You *are* my life, Mr. Lord."

"Then don't disagree with me."

"I overstepped my boundaries, and I won't do it again."

He shook his head regretfully. "Maybe it's not a good idea to keep you in my life."

"I'm sorry. Please take me with you on your honeymoon. I mean…*our* honeymoon." I felt horrible. Mr. Lord rarely lost his temper with me, and I wanted to be back on his good side. I gave a half-hearted smile. "I'd be happy and honored to give you my virginity on your wedding night."

"Do you mean that or are speaking words that you think I want to hear?"

"I mean it with all my heart. Your pleasure is my pleasure, Mr. Lord."

"That's my good girl." He stood up and opened his arms. I rushed into them, basking in the reward of his affection and warmth. "I won't forsake you, Fonia. I'm aware that you can't exist without my guidance."

Choking up, I nodded my head in agreement. "I don't want to exist without your guidance. I'm nothing without you. The thought of losing you scares me."

"You're not going to lose me. I don't know how I'm going to do it, but I'm going to figure out a way to work you into my married life. I could move you in under the guise of being part of the cleaning staff…or you could be Sylvia's personal maid."

I gasped inside. But when he began to caress my face, making me feel warm and loved, I realized I would do anything to be close to him. I'd even move into his home and become his wife's maid.

"On second thought, moving you in my home may not be a good idea. Sylvia's a smart girl and she'd catch on." He looked off in thought. "I'm not sure what I'm going to do about you, Fonia, but whatever I decide, you'll have to trust that I know what's best for you."

"I do trust you, Mr. Lord," I said. But inside I was terrified. I felt as if I'd already lost him. He was going to throw me to the wolves, like my mother had prophesied.

JAGUAR

The stench of vomit drifted into the atmosphere every time someone opened the door to the men's restroom. Customers were so tipsy, they'd stopped complaining about the funk, but I was getting nauseous. Watching the clock, I anxiously awaited the cleaning dude's arrival.

The janitor, a middle-aged man named Ben, finally arrived a few minutes before midnight. Ben was slightly bent over with missing teeth in the front. He scowled a lot, and every few minutes, he removed his hat and raked his fingernails across his balding scalp. Scratching and digging in his head, he frowned like he couldn't quite get to the itch.

Slapping his hat on his head, Ben stood in the doorway of the restroom with his mouth turned down, solemnly observing the foul mess. Grunting in displeasure, he yanked his hat off again and scratched his head harder than before. He gathered the cleaning supplies and began to work slowly and methodically, taking an extremely long time to clean and disinfect the men's room.

Chaos and confusion ensued as Ben slow-poked through the cleaning task. Men who were badly in need of relieving themselves had the choice of either going outside to take a leak or using the ladies room, which had a perpetual, long line.

Drinking Red Bulls all night, I couldn't hold my piss any longer nor could I abandon the bar and go outside. Being the big dog in charge, I pulled rank and jumped in the front of the line that had formed outside the ladies' room. There were two stalls inside, and I hurried to the first one that became available. The chick using the stall next to me was releasing an endless stream of urine, the kind that gushes out violently after a night of heavy drinking.

She was still peeing after I'd finished relieving myself. I shook my dick off, zipped up my pants, and was standing at the sink washing my hands when she finally exited the stall. With all that heavy pissing, I expected to see a burly, unattractive biker chick. But she was cute and petite, wearing washed-out jeans and a halter top. Her honey-colored hair was curled in ringlets that hung down her back. She looked pleasantly surprised when she spotted me at the sink washing my hands.

"Hey, handsome, what are you doing in the little girls' room?" she asked as she joined me at the double set of sinks.

"The men's room isn't operating at the moment."

"Lucky me," she said, smiling as she looked me over. "So, you're the new guy, huh?"

"Yeah, my name's Jaguar."

"Betty," she said, giving me a flirty look. After washing and drying her hands, she pulled a tube of lip gloss out of her purse. I had no reason to linger any longer, but watching a woman apply lip gloss is another act that gives me inexplicable, freakish pleasure. When she realized I was watching her, she stroked the wand against her lips slow and teasingly. Then she stared at my crotch and licked her lips, giving the impression that she was offering to give me some head.

I can't blame my behavior on alcohol since I'd only been drinking Red Bull. But something innate—some primal urge took over my sense of decency and decorum, and the next thing I knew, I was unzipping my fly. Betty dropped to her knees and I began stuffing the swelling head of my dick between her luminous lips.

The slippery dick-glide those glossy lips provided was incredible. Overwhelmed by her skillful, head game, I grabbed handfuls of her hair while she gripped my ass, pulling me closer, encouraging me to shove my dick further down her throat.

I grunted and groaned while she made noisy sucking sounds. Our combined sound effects were loud and insane, and I got extra boisterous when I shot my load. I tried to muffle my moans and groans by clamping my lips together, but to no avail. Despite my attempt toward discretion, I lost my cool and shouted, "God-damn!" in a strangled voice that sounded like I was in the throes of a violent death. If that wasn't bad enough, I yanked the girl's hair so hard, I pulled out tufts of her honey-colored, spiral-curls.

Betty rose from her knees and spit my jism in the sink, and I frowned in disapproval. I felt offended that she hadn't swallowed my seed. I don't know why it bothered me, but it did. I guess I can be a jerk sometimes. I've never been proud of the selfish and egotistical aspects of my personality. But it is what it is.

After my heart rate calmed down, I instantly became disgusted with myself for participating in a sordid, sex escapade during working hours. If I planned to continue earning wages, I'd have to garner some restraint and decline getting blowed inside my place of employment.

I felt bad for Betty, though. She didn't get anything out of the impromptu quickie. I'm the type of man who likes to satisfy my partner, but in this extreme situation, reciprocity wasn't an option.

"Uh, thanks," I muttered, barely able to look Betty in the eye. She smiled at me and gave me a pat on the shoulder as if to say, "Good job." And that's when I noticed her wedding ring.

How fucked up is that? A married woman gave brain to a total stranger in a public restroom! Oh, well, I couldn't undo the act. As I quickly exited the restroom, I glanced guiltily toward the pool tables, wondering if Blowjob Betty was married to a rowdy biker.

Fifteen minutes later, I noticed Betty tongue-kissing a guy who was wearing a backpack—a geeky guy who had ordered a bottle of cheap champagne right before

I'd gone into the ladies' room. The guy seemed soft, not the type who was looking for a fight. It was a relief that I wouldn't have to worry about getting knifed or shot, but I couldn't help grimacing as I witnessed Betty and her husband engaged in a passionate kiss.

Blowjob Betty was a devious chick, deliberately feeding her unsuspecting husband the sediments of the cum-shot she'd received from me. When the kiss ended, they made a toast and their friends shouted, "Happy Anniversary!"

A little after one in the morning, things had finally started to slow down and I was able to sit for a moment and catch my breath. The door opened, and a sepia-toned goddess walked inside the establishment. She was wearing a pale blue dress with a thin black belt below her bosom. She carried a clutch bag and was wearing heels. Very elegant attire for a place like The Dive. She was so gorgeous, so regal, my jaw literally dropped. As I gawked at her, I searched my mind for my best pick-up line. As she approached the bar, I felt a strong pull that went beyond her extraordinary looks. And my increased heart rate wasn't a result of the immeasurable amount of Red Bull that I'd been drinking all night.

Instead of walking like a mere mortal, she seemed to glide. With her head held high, she gave the impression of royalty. In contrast, her eyes were slightly lowered, holding a glimmer of bashfulness. She was powerful and demure all at once, and whoever she was, I felt an inexplicable desire to make her mine. And not for a quick fling. I'm talking, let's move in together—tonight. No! Fuck shacking up. Let's get a marriage license and tie the knot!

The lady in blue had me completely captivated.

I've done a lot of living in my twenty-seven years. Been around the block a couple of times. Women have always gravitated toward me and I've had more than my share. I've had relationships with females of various ethnicities, been in love with career women as well as hood chicks with several baby daddies, and I've been involved with women who were old enough to be my mother. I've experienced a lot, but I've never been aware of a first encounter that was remotely similar to what was happening in this moment.

I glanced at her again. And in her eyes I saw something tender and inviting.

As much as I detested fucking with the blender, the beautiful mystery chick could get a frozen drink or anything else she wanted. Straightening my shoulders and affixing a smile on my lips, I mentally prepared to put my heart and soul into any girly drink her heart desired.

But a group of rowdy college boys suddenly appeared out of nowhere, blocking my view as they ordered a round of tequila shots.

I set up the shot glasses and filled them with Patron, and when I finished pouring, I didn't see my sepia angel.

In a panic, I scanned the bar room, and literally breathed

a sigh of relief when I spotted her blue dress. She was sitting at a table near the window. There were no waiters at the establishment, and customers were supposed to order from the bar and take their drinks back to their table, and so I decided to play the role of waiter.

Hoping she wasn't waiting for a date to join her, I stepped from behind the bar and approached her table. I had no idea what I was going to say to her, and though I felt awkward and self-conscious, the swag in my walk suggested complete confidence.

"Can I get you a drink?" I asked, deliberately making my voice a little deeper than it actually was.

"I'd like white wine, please. Skinny Girl, if you have that brand." She had the refined vocal quality of the upper crust.

"I'll check and see. But, I doubt if we have it. I do know that we have Moscato."

"Moscato is fine."

"Be right back."

I returned with a chilled glass of Moscato and placed it in front of her. She went inside her handbag, and I told her the drink was on me.

"Oh, you don't have to."

"No strings attached," I assured with a smile. "Enjoy your drink."

"Thanks," she murmured.

I wanted to ask her name, but the fear of appearing desperate sent me heading back to my post behind the bar.

JAGUAR

The way I was sweating that chick was completely out of character for me. Oddly, my confidence had taken a hit, which made no sense considering I'd gotten my knob slobbed in the restroom, and an innumerable amount of women had been hitting on me and practically throwing their panties at me all night.

The college boys were on their fourth round of shots when the lady in blue stood up and gathered her purse and the empty wineglass. My heart rate accelerated as she weaved through the crowd, and glided toward me.

Anticipating her desire for another glass of wine, I grabbed the bottle of Moscato.

Out of nowhere, a short, bow-tie wearing, light-skin dude joined me behind the bar. The boss's flunky, I assumed. Damn, his timing sucked. So much had occurred since Sharif's phone call, I'd completely forgotten that Harvey was supposed to come through at the end of the night.

"You should have announced "last call" ten minutes ago," he said, moving purposefully toward the register.

"Been busy; it slipped my mind," I responded, looking over his head to locate my future wife.

"I guess Sharif forgot to mention that I'd be stopping by to count the drawer and to close up," he said in an authoritative voice that demanded I give him my full attention. "You should start settling your tabs," he said firmly.

"Right." I put the bottle of wine down, planning to refill the pretty girl's drink as soon as I collected from the patrons that were running tabs.

I dashed around, gathering cash and credit cards and ringing up receipts. I was in such a rush to get back to the mystery girl, I could no longer be bothered with keeping a mental tab of my tips. At last count, I had made around three hundred. As badly as I needed money, getting more tips wasn't at the forefront of my mind.

She wasn't standing where I'd last seen her. Hoping to catch a glimpse of her blue dress, I scanned the barroom, but she was nowhere to be found. Disappointment hit me like a punch to the gut.

Maybe she'd gone to the restroom. I tried to keep an eye on the ladies rest room door, but Harvey kept distracting me, giving me a list of chores like I was his apprentice or something. I wanted to smash that cocky, little, half-pint in the face, but I couldn't afford to lose my job. Besides, he looked like the corny type of dude that would involve law enforcement and press charges. I couldn't afford that. Even a minor arrest could ruin my law career before it got started.

"By the way," Harvey said. "The boss wanted me to check out your bartending skills before I made my presence known."

"He told you to spy on me?"

"You could put it that way. I noticed you abandoning the bar to serve one of the patrons sitting at a table. This is an informal establishment, and we don't provide table service here."

"I'll keep that in mind," I told Harvey, wishing he'd shut up and get out of my face.

Every time someone went in or out of the ladies' room, my head whipped in that direction, looking for my baby, but she was nowhere to be found. Finally, Ben turned up the lights, brightening up the place with an unpleasant glare that announced the evening had come to an end. I felt a rush of relief, eager to get back to my hotel room where I could lick my wounds in private.

A few people sat around mumbling that they hadn't heard "last call," while others reluctantly began to trickle out the door. It seemed that no one was ready to call it a night. Some wore sad expressions and others were belligerent, cursing and rolling their eyes as if it they were being kicked out hours before closing time. One young woman was actually crying as she exited; dark mascara ran from her eyes and streaked her cheeks. I had no idea what that was about and I didn't want to know.

With a mop and bucket nearby, Ben was ready to get to work. Trash bags draped over his arm, Ben stood by the door shaking a huge keyring filled with jangling keys.

"It's time to get up out of here!" Ben hollered gruffly, attempting to speed along the stragglers that were still sitting around, nursing the last dregs of their drinks.

Why'd she leave without even a hand wave? I wondered. I sulked as I cleaned my work area. Harvey was getting on my nerves, chattering as he took an inventory of the liquor. "You had a busy night," he said. "We're running low on Seagram's 7."

"Yeah, I guess," I replied without interest.

"And we're low on Smirnoff. It was a really good night, and the boss will be pleased. But in the future, you should keep a list of what's running low. A good bartender always keeps track of his inventory. Also, a good bartender…"

Man, count those bottles and shut the fuck up. I didn't give a shit what a good bartender did, so I tuned him out. I supposed I should have been keeping track of the liquor stock, but I hadn't had an opportunity. Pouring drinks and interacting with customers had kept me super busy.

"I hear you're only going to be with us for the summer," he said, making more unnecessary small talk.

"Yeah," I muttered, refusing to say more. If it weren't for this little interfering midget, I would have at least gotten the young lady's name and possibly her number.

"I've also been told that you're a lawyer."

"Not yet."

"Oh?"

Mind your business, lil' yellow-ass muthafucka.

"Oh, so you haven't taken the bar exam yet?"

"Nah." Busy stacking napkins and straws for the morning shift, I kept my responses down to a minimum.

"I've heard that some of *our* people..." He brushed the top of his high-yellow hand as if he and I shared the same complexion. "Well, they say that it isn't uncommon for some our folks to have to take the bar exam four or five times. Just giving you a heads-up," he said with a smirk. "I have a friend that's a lawyer. He works for the DA's office, and only makes fifty-eight thousand a year. After all those years of education and he's barely above the poverty level."

I refused to explain my future plans. Hoping to deter him from engaging me any further, I decided to switch to heavy, street vernacular, which I was certain would offend the pompous, little, sawed-off jerk and dissuade him from engaging me further. "Yo, Harvey, some people gotta make it do what it do. Personally, I'm on some, 'it-is-what-it-is'-type shit, cuz I'ma get mine any way it comes. You know what I'm sayin'?"

"No, I don't. I have no idea what you just said." Harvey looked at me with repugnance as he moved a few feet away from me.

I noticed that Ben had started to haul out the trash, and so I decided to pitch in with the clean-up process, leaving Harvey behind the bar, tallying up receipts. I straightened up the pool table area. After that, I sprayed the front of the jukebox with Windex, and wiped down all the mirrors.

I'm not a fan of manual labor, but doing chores was less aggravating than listening to Harvey as he basically told me that I'd chosen the wrong profession.

An hour later, we all exited The Dive. Ben pulled down the cage and locked it with one of the keys from his giant key ring. Harvey strode toward a late-model SUV. Scratching his head, Ben shuffled over to an old Plymouth.

I had Najah's information in my pocket, and I briefly considered stopping by and seeing shorty, but I was mentally and physically tired. I'd had enough sex for one day. I probably could have mustered up some energy if Najah convinced her sister to join us in a threesome, but Nona had hooked up with ole boy, ruining my freaky plans.

Accustomed to riding the New York subways, it didn't bother me that I didn't have any wheels. I headed in the direction of the Market Street El. I'd take the El to Thirtieth Street, and then take a shuttle back to my hotel.

A car horn honked and I looked toward the sound, and I couldn't believe my eyes. There was my baby, sitting behind the wheel of a dark-colored Lexus. I could have acted cool and took my time crossing the street, but I wasn't playing any games, and so I hustled over to her. I wanted to break into a full-on run, but didn't want to look like a sucker. I had a little bit of swag as I dipped low while trotting toward her.

"Hi, again," she said. She was parked under the street light, and I got an even better look at her face. She had a flawless, dark toffee complexion and the cutest nose that turned up at the tip. "I hope you don't mind that I waited for you to get off."

"It's fine."

"I, uh, I wanted to apologize for leaving abruptly while you were in the midst of preparing me another drink. It was rude of me," she said, lowering her eyes bashfully.

"It's cool. You don't owe me any explanations." This chick was really different. Had an innocent quality that I found appealing.

"I didn't want to leave without giving you an explanation. I'm really not as discourteous as I appeared; I was raised better than that. But, I thought I saw someone I knew, and I sort of had a panic attack."

"An old boyfriend?" I asked curiously, looking over my shoulder and ready to defend myself if some nut bull came running out of the shadows.

"No. I wouldn't refer to him as a boyfriend."

"I get it; it's complicated."

"You could say that." Her lovely face clouded over as if a bad memory had appeared in her mind.

"Well, thank you for the drink, Mr....?"

"Jaguar. You can call me Jag."

"Thank you, Jag. I was feeling really down, but your kindness brightened my evening."

"Glad I could help...uh...Ms....?"

"Fonia."

"Can I get your number, Fonia?" I pulled out my cell, ready to lock her in.

Her brows furrowed together. "I'm sorry; I can't give it out."

"Seriously?"

She made an apologetic expression. "I can't give you my phone number."

Why can't she give me her number? She must be married. I glanced at her ring finger and it was bare. There were sparkling jewels on several fingers, and on both wrists and her ears. But there was no wedding band or engagement ring. I supposed she was in some sort of serious relationship, and the thought bothered me immensely.

"Would it be okay if I stopped by again tomorrow? You don't have to…well, I don't expect you to buy my drinks or anything. I like the atmosphere in the bar," Fonia said.

"Yeah, you're welcome to come through anytime you like," I said casually, though I was eager to see her again. The sooner the better. If it were up to me, we'd be going to my place or hers. We didn't have to do anything, either. We could simply talk. I wanted to know everything about her, and I was willing to put my guard down and share the important events in my life.

"Well, I have to go," she said.

Disappointment hit me hard; I wasn't ready to say goodbye.

She gave me a sad smile. "I'll see you soon. I mean, if it's really okay with you. I wouldn't want to impose."

"You won't be imposing. I look forward to seeing you

again," I said, and I really meant it. She was a good-looking woman but there was something else about her. She was so fragile and delicate. It seemed as if she needed to be protected from something, but I had no idea what.

"Well, goodnight," she said, fluttering her fingers. Her eyes began to dart about nervously again, and before pulling off, she took a quick look over her shoulder. Fonia was clearly very nervous about the dude she thought she'd seen in the bar. Maybe the bull she was concerned about was a stalker. Pretty girls like her were like magnets that attracted the crazies.

I imagined someone antagonizing Fonia and my blood started to boil. If a stalker showed up at The Dive, trying to fuck with Fonia, I'd probably leap over the bar, with some ninja moves and I've never had a lesson in Karate or Kung Fu.

As I strolled along Market Street, I thought about the way I'd reacted when Fonia walked in the bar. There had been this powerful emotional tug that pulled me over to her table. I had no control over it, and our meeting seemed like destiny.

FONIA

While away in Phoenix, Mr. Lord seemed to have forgotten that I existed. I wasn't allowed outside without his permission, but a combination of loneliness, depression, and cabin fever sent me out for a late-night drive. I'd been shielded from the seedy side of life and as I drove around the West Philadelphia area, I noticed people of different ethnicities drifting out of a bar called The Dive. I'd never walked inside such a place in my life, but for some reason I was drawn to it. I sat in my Lexus watching people, and everyone that emerged from the bar seemed happily intoxicated, without any troubles or cares.

I realized that alcohol wasn't the solution for resolving problems. Watching how my mother had declined was proof that hard drinking ruined lives. But I was so sad and lonely; I simply wanted to sit anonymously in an atmosphere where I wouldn't be judged. I could put my elbows on the table if I wanted, use the wrong utensils, and no one would notice that I wasn't behaving like a proper young lady. In a seedy place like The Dive, I wouldn't have to be concerned about bumping into anyone who knew Mr. Lord or me.

I noticed a small group of people leaving the bar and the sound of their laughter filled the air. I seldom laughed anymore. Hadn't cracked a smile since Mr. Lord had revealed his wedding plans. Though I had the best of everything that money could buy, I realized that I actually had nothing at all. No friends. No family. No career. No hope for future happiness.

I'd been kept completely sheltered and now that Mr. Lord had left me, there was a huge void in my life. Without him controlling my daily activities, I didn't know what to do with myself.

As unbelievable as it might seem, I was technically still a virgin. My sexual experiences were limited to encounters with Mr. Lord's finger. Wanting to keep me pure, Mr. Lord was staunch in his beliefs that my hymen should remain intact.

Though I'd never admit it to him, I thought the idea of a honeymoon that included his new bride and me was rather bizarre, but I so craved his attention that I actually looked forward to being with him in Bermuda.

I yearned for companionship. Someone to talk to. Male attention. Preferably someone with a take-charge disposition like Mr. Lord. Feeling insecure and vulnerable, while at the same time, feeling defiant, I turned off the engine and boldly walked inside the bar.

It was a crude environment, filled with an interesting mix of people. Conversations were loud, and the smell of liquor was pungent in the air. Overwhelmed by the noise level and the odd intermingling of scents that rushed to my nostrils, I searched the crowded bar for a seat and found one by the window.

I'd been to countless five-star restaurants where alcohol was served, but I'd never been in the presence of a large group of inebriated people. The atmosphere was charged with sexual tension. Wearing sensual expressions, bodies swayed rhythmically in time with the music, while others kissed and groped each other openly. These loose and uninhibited people were fascinating to watch.

I wondered what I should order to drink...a virgin margarita or a virgin mojito. Maybe a Shirley Temple? I felt flustered. Mr. Lord always ordered my beverages in public, but due to my mother's addiction, he didn't allow me to consume any alcohol whatsoever.

But Mr. Lord was away in Arizona, visiting his future wife.

Though the thought of him being married caused me a great deal of pain, and though I tried to have faith in his promise that his pending nuptials wouldn't change our close relationship, I couldn't help hearing my mother's warning in my head.

Sitting in the seedy bar, I was trying to take my mind off my suspicion that Mr. Lord had grown tired of me and would soon banish me from his life exactly as he'd banished my mother.

In the midst of my thoughts, a man appeared at my table and asked what I was drinking. I'd never personally ordered a drink before, and it seemed childish to request a Shirley Temple or any other virgin cocktail.

Recalling an advertisement I'd seen, I asked if they had Skinny Girl wine, thinking that it might be the closest thing I could get to a virgin drink. But the bartender offered me something I'd never heard of, and I accepted. Then he offered to pay for it. I tried to decline the offer, but he firmly insisted.

The drink was delicious. Made me feel very warm and tingly. I wanted more, but decided that one glass was enough. I returned the soiled glass to the bar, but I couldn't seem to get his attention. As I stood at the bar, I saw someone that reminded me of Mr. Lord's driver. In a panic, I raced out of the bar. When I made it to the safety of my car, the man came outside to take a smoke, and I realized with relief that he wasn't Mr. Lord's driver.

I sat in my car for quite a long time, waiting for the bartender, and when he finally came out, I thanked him properly. He asked my name, and I told him, and I discovered that his name is Jaguar.

Jaguar asked for my number, and though I dared not give it to him, I did ask permission to see him again tomorrow night. He agreed.

Excited and happy to have someone to talk to. Elated that I'd made a new friend, I smiled during the drive home. It was the first time I'd smiled since Mr. Lord gave me the devastating news of his impending wedding.

JAGUAR

Looking forward to seeing her again, I was hype as shit the next day. I went all the way to the North-east, chasing behind Jerome, my barber who'd been cutting my hair for like, forever. Barbers tend to roam from one shop to the next, and having to chase them down can be frustrating, but Jerome hooked me up—the trip was well worth my time.

But she didn't come through, and that messed with my head.

Anticipating her arrival, I had been unable to concentrate behind the bar for three nights in a row. Spending too much time staring at the door, I mixed up orders, gave customers too much or too little change. Luckily, the customers were forgiving and didn't hold my absent-mindedness against me.

I couldn't help wondering if something had happened to her. Nah, it was time to stop making excuses for her. She played me. Probably a rich girl who got bored with the high-class establishments she was accustomed to and decided to spend a few hours slumming it, purely for kicks. She'd admitted that she enjoyed watching the patrons. Perhaps she was a student—an anthropology major—and had been given an assignment to observe the behavior of intoxicated, ghetto natives, I thought cynically.

Around eight o'clock, the bar got crowded and I was rushing around like crazy, and so I had to pull my eyes away from the door and give my full attention to pouring drinks and ringing up orders.

Sharif had led me to believe that the average patron only wanted basic drinks. He'd said they didn't go for fancy cocktails. So why did a group of chicks request six different kinds of martinis? And one of the members of the group asked for a cocktail called Red-Headed Slut, a drink that I learned was comprised of one ounce Jägermeister, a half-ounce of Peach Schnapps, and cranberry juice. We didn't carry Jägermeister, and so after referring to my handy *Bartender's Guide*, I found out I could substitute the expensive German liqueur with Peppermint Schnapps.

I wasn't with all those crazy-named drinks. Sometimes the customers could tell me what went into their specialty drinks, but in most cases, they expected me to know. I mean, yeah, I could fix a basic cocktail like an Apple Martini, a Long Island Iced Tea, a Black Russian, Whiskey Sour…drinks that I'd heard of. But when customers requested cocktails called Dumpster Baby and Slippery Nipple…well, that required research, and having to look up recipes was time-consuming and aggravating. I felt like cussing Sharif out every time I had to thumb through the *Bartender's Guide*.

While I was busy shaking up the ingredients for a chocolate-cherry martini, someone had the audacity to ask for a strawberry daiquiri. In this hectic atmosphere, the last thing I needed was to have to slow down to make a freaking blender drink! Masking my scowl with a smile, I looked toward the voice. To my surprise, one of the twins was sitting at the bar. I wasn't sure if it was Najah or Nona, but I was hoping it was Nona since I'd stood Najah up on the night of their birthday.

"Hey," I said, not knowing which girl I was greeting.

"Save your phony smile. All it would have taken was a phone call to let me know you weren't gonna make it. Standing someone up is uncouth and rude. I thought you had more class than that."

So, it was Najah after all, and she was irate. Her voice was louder than necessary, and I hoped she wasn't on the verge of making a scene. I searched my mind for a believable excuse, and came up with a great explanation.

"I wanted to get in touch with you, but I didn't have your number. You only wrote down your address. I'm sorry, but I had to stay a few hours later than I'd expected after the bar closed. I didn't want to pop up on you in the wee hours of the morning." She had included her phone number along with her address, but I figured she'd been too tipsy to remember.

Najah pondered my words for a few moments, and then said, "I'm free tonight; what about you?" She spoke softly now, and fussed with her hair. The angry spark had left her eyes and was now replaced with a flirtatious glimmer.

Instead of responding, I turned away. I had to think about the risk involved in going to bed with a chick that didn't mean anything to me.

Contemplating my dilemma, I pulled out the blender and began making her drink. It had been three days since I'd last gotten my dick wet. Three days is a long time for a young man in his prime to go without sex. The last time I'd had intercourse had been with the maid at my hotel, and now each time I encountered her, I would greet her politely and she would look at me with anticipation, as if expecting me to signal her to follow me to my room. When I kept it moving, she'd sigh and roll her eyes and mutter in Spanish. The tension between the maid and me had prompted me to think about relocating from the hotel to an affordable apartment.

Bathroom Betty, the chick that sucked me off in the ladies' room had given good head; she was the kind of woman that would let you run up in her windpipe with no-strings-attached. But she was off limits from now on. I would never get with her again, not after seeing how she played her husband. That chick was treacherous.

In a perfect world, there would be more women who enjoyed sex in the moment and didn't expect a repeat performance on a regular basis. But since we don't live in a perfect world, I'd been handling my own sexual needs. Jerking off these past few days had been preferable to dealing with a female that I didn't have an emotional connection with.

Being honest with myself, I had to admit that although Najah had a hot body and a pretty face, I didn't have a connection with her. Plus, she seemed somewhat unstable. The fact that she'd had gone from boiling mad to purring like a kitten in a matter of seconds had definitely put up a red flag.

I set the daiquiri in front of her and pondered the kindest way to turn down her invitation. Yes, I'm a jerk from time to time, but I'm not ruthless. I wouldn't deliberately break a chick's heart.

Najah puckered her lips around the straw, took a sip, and then looked up at me. "So, are we hooking up tonight?" she asked, batting her eyelashes.

"Nah, I'm good."

"You're good? What does that mean?" she asked with her voice escalating. "I didn't ask you if you needed to relieve yourself. I asked if you wanted to spend some quality time with me…get to know me better. But you know what…" She smacked the drink, toppling it, and spilling pink slush all over the bar top. "Go fuck yourself, Jaguar!"

Najah had taken shit too far. Going into character and looking as if I'd lost it, I gave her my crazy-eyed look, combined with flared nostrils, panting, and a heaving chest. I'd seen lots of loony niggas in my time, and it was easy to mimic them. "Yo, take your nutty ass out of here before I toss you out." I scrunched my lips together tightly, and approached her, breathing like a dragon.

Najah wasn't totally crazy; she had enough sense to recoil in fear. She scrambled off the barstool and then hauled her ass out of the bar.

"You all right, Jag?" a male customer asked. I nodded. "You can't let a female get to you like that. You gotta learn how to let shit go…just brush it off," he said, finishing off a glass of Johnny Walker.

"Yeah, you're right," I agreed, though my display of out-of-control rage had merely been an act. I wiped up the mess Najah had made, relieved that I'd had the insight to recognize a kook before I went to bed with her.

I looked at the door, once again, yearning for Fonia to cross the threshold. I took back all my earlier thoughts. She wasn't a spoiled brat. She was only being cautious, protecting her heart.

I'm not a hopeless romantic; I keep it real. But there was something going on between Fonia and me that I couldn't explain. A special spark that she had to have felt too. I could only hope that she'd fight through whatever fears she was struggling with and come back through.

FONIA

The night I was supposed to go back to the bar to see Jag, I'd gotten dressed in a Chanel ensemble and was ready to walk out the door when the phone rang. It was Mr. Lord, checking in. He asked how I'd been spending my time, and seemed concerned that I might be depressed in his absence.

"I was depressed," I admitted. "But I'm starting to feel a little better now. I've been keeping busy."

"What exactly have you been doing to keep yourself occupied?"

I relayed a list of activities that began from the time I woke up to the time of his call. I listed all my chores and other activities in the order that I had performed them. "I had a light breakfast, worked out on the treadmill, twice. I did a load of laundry, and prepared a seven-hundred-calorie dinner. Oh, I almost forgot, I went to the hair salon," I added.

He was quiet for a moment. "Your next hair appointment isn't scheduled until next week."

"I know, but I've been doubling my workout routine…

you know, getting my body ready for the beach in Bermuda. With all the sweating, my hair had started to look a wreck."

"In the future, you need to consult with me before you change your routine or any of your appointments. I don't want you leaving the house without getting my expressed permission. Is that clear, young lady?"

"Yes, Mr. Lord."

"Sylvia and her mother are going out to consult with a wedding planner, and I'll have some free time this evening." His brusque tone had softened. "You and I can Skype. No clothes. I want to see you in the nude. I'll check back in an hour or so."

He disconnected the call and I went to my bedroom and disrobed. I wouldn't be able to spend time with Jag after all. *Maybe tomorrow*, I thought sadly.

But Mr. Lord kept an electronic leash on me the next day and the day after. At the conclusion of each Skype session, he would insist that I lie back on my bed, open my legs, and expose myself. He wanted to see for himself that my virginity was intact. Though it was degrading to open my vagina in front of a computer, the humiliation was always accompanied by a peculiar thrill.

"Are you wet?" he asked, already knowing the answer.

"Yes," I murmured.

"Are you ready to act like a whore?"

"I am." My voice quivered with excitement.

"Use your finger; pretend it's mine."

I did as he instructed. Only I didn't pretend that Mr. Lord's finger was lodged inside me. As I probed my moistened interior, I imagined that Jaguar was lying on top of me, kissing me and telling me that I was beautiful while he slowly penetrated me.

While in Arizona, Mr. Lord didn't call me at scheduled times; his calls came in at random times of the day and night. Sometimes he woke me up at four, five, or six in the morning, at other times, he didn't call until nine or ten in the evening. I noticed that he never called between midnight and three. Deciding to put that block of time to good use, one night I began to get dressed after I hung up from Mr. Lord at eleven-thirty.

I could no longer blame my desire to see Jag on loneliness. Mr. Lord kept me occupied with his phone calls and Skype sessions. The fact was, for the first time in my life, I was attracted to someone other than Mr. Lord. I had memorized the features of Jag's handsome face, and had fantasized about him so often, I was certain that I knew how his lips would feel against mine. How his mouth would taste.

I'd never experienced the kind of kisses I'd seen in movies and on TV. Mr. Lord only gave me quick pecks on the lips, and I was ready for a real kiss. The intimacy that I shared with Mr. Lord left me yearning for more.

Most people become rebellious in their teens, but I was a late bloomer. Now, at twenty-one years old, I found myself craving love, romance, and affection, and nothing could stop me from going after what I wanted.

I put on the exact outfit that I had planned to wear last week when I'd tried to sneak in a rendezvous with Jag. I applied lip gloss and arranged my hair. Standing in front of the mirror, I scrutinized my reflection. I liked what I saw and hoped Jag would too.

When I reached Forty-second and Sansom Street, I began to lose my boldness. A case of nervous jitters had me circling the block over and over instead of pulling into a parking spot or the lot in the back of the bar.

After securing a place to park, I began to have second thoughts and considered going back home. *Suppose he's married or has a girlfriend. What will I do if she's there with him tonight?* Somehow, I managed to push through my fears, and convinced myself to get out of the car and walk inside the bar.

He was standing behind the bar, mixing drinks, and he was better looking than I remembered. Tall and dark with scrumptious, kissable lips. He moved behind the bar with the physical ease of an athlete. Beneath his clothes, I could see the play of muscles as he went about his duties.

Finally, our eyes met and his welcoming smile immediately put me at ease. He held up a finger and mouthed some words that I interpreted as, 'Give me a minute.'

I found a seat and waited patiently while Jag served drinks. I couldn't take my eyes off him. Nor could any other woman in the bar. I watched with fascination as various women engaged him in flirtatious conversations as he mixed their drinks.

After a while, a bolt of hot jealousy coursed through me so suddenly, I was startled and somewhat ashamed of myself. Though he was the object of my sexual fantasies, it was foolish of me to feel territorial over a man I hardly knew. But I couldn't control the emotion. I didn't want him smiling or talking to any of those women at the bar. I wanted him all for myself.

I saw him pointing in my direction, and then a patron of the bar, a big guy with a barrel belly, ambled over to my table.

"The bartender wanted you to have this." He set a napkin in front of me and placed a wineglass on top of it.

I thanked him and when I looked over at the bar to extend a smile of gratitude, Jag was distracted…laughing and talking with a group of women that were sipping from martini glasses.

Sipping very slowly, I wondered if he planned on coming over and talking with me for a few minutes. I glanced around. The place was extremely crowded with people laughing and having a good time. It seemed that everyone was enjoying themselves except me.

My thoughts began to drift, and I wondered if maybe I should leave. It was presumptuous of me to assume he had free time to spend with me while he was working. Well, he actually seemed to be having more fun than actually working, but this was his place of employment and I shouldn't have popped up out of the blue.

Deciding to discreetly exit, I took one last sip.

"How are you, Fonia?" said a husky male voice. I looked up and was staring at Jag.

"Oh, hi." I broke into a big smile. "Sorry for the spur-of-the-moment visit. Something came up last week, and I couldn't get away."

"You don't owe me an explanation; I'm happy to see you." He looked me over. "You look nice. I practically did a double take when you walked through the door. I thought Naomi Campbell was gracing the place."

I lowered my eyes, pleased yet embarrassed by the compliment.

"It's really good to see you, though," he repeated with a slight smile.

"It's good to see you, too. And thanks for sending me the glass of wine."

"My pleasure. I had to look out, and make sure I took care of you." The brilliance of his beautiful smile seemed to light up our area, and I also noticed that he had the most beautiful dark brown eyes.

He glanced over his shoulder. "The natives are getting restless. I have to get back to my workstation. How long are you gonna be here? Can you wait around until we close?"

"Sure."

"I'll send you more Moscato."

"Can you send me bottled water instead? One drink is more than enough for me."

"Water? You sure?"

"Positive."

Suddenly, my phone began to vibrate inside my purse. It could only be one of two people: my mother or Mr. Lord. Hearing from my mother was usually something I dreaded, but at the moment, I preferred a call from her than a call from Mr. Lord. I opened my purse and glimpsed at my phone, hoping to see one of the many unfamiliar numbers my mother used when calling me. No such luck. Mr. Lord's name appeared on the screen, and the letters seemed to vibrate with urgency and impatience.

Normally, I'd pick up immediately. But I couldn't. Not while inside a bar, at almost one in the morning. He'd think I'd gone off the deep end if he knew I was out in the streets mingling with common people at this hour of the morning.

Panicked, I pushed the IGNORE button and stood up abruptly. "I have to go."

Jaguar looked surprised and then a scowl formed on his face. "You're leaving already?"

"I'm sorry; I really have to go," I said and hurried out of the bar.

JAGUAR

Being a good guy doesn't get you anywhere. People think you're soft when you act like a gentleman.

Fonia finally came through, looking as radiant as ever. I was in the midst of filling orders for a group of fine-ass women that were visiting the city for a conference, but I took the time to make sure Fonia was all right. I sent a drink—free of charge—to her table. I couldn't serve her personally, but I sent my man, Buddha. Reminded him to keep his tongue in his mouth. Ever since that Rat-Face chick had pumped him up with the idea that he had porn-star capabilities, Buddha had started flashing his tongue on the female customers whenever he had a little too much to drink.

Providing table service in a joint like The Dive is unheard of; it's a privilege. I don't give that kind of personalized attention to any of the customers, but I did it for Fonia. I wanted her to know that I wasn't harboring any grudges, despite the fact that she'd left me hanging last week.

As soon as I had a few minutes to spare, I went to her

table to check on her personally—to make sure she had everything she needed. Even though my feelings were a little bruised, I played it off like getting stood up was no big deal. No sooner had we agreed to hook up after closing when I caught her stealing a glance at her phone. Then she jumped up and said she had to leave. I didn't know if she thought she'd spotted her stalker again or what. One minute we were making plans to see each other later, and the next minute she was gone. She left me standing at her empty table wondering what happened. Left me feeling like a sucker.

That's it! No more Mr. Nice Guy! The next time she shows up, she can walk up to the bar, order her own damn Moscato…bottled water or whatever, and pay for her drinks like everyone else. I won't be extending anymore special courtesies. All she's going to get out of me is, *Hey, what's up?* I'll be keeping it short and sweet. No more chitchatting or extended dialogue for that wacko chick.

I had started to catch feelings, and since I didn't know anything about her—never so much as kissed her—I realized I was allowing my emotions to get out of control. Good thing I had enough sense to rein myself in. I've always been good at hiding my feelings, and the next time she walked her fine ass up in the joint, I planned to show her a totally different side of Jaguar Jackson.

The next day, Sharif strode into The Dive soon after I arrived. There were only a few customers, and I had time to kick it with my man. Though he was dressed casually, it was obvious that he'd had a come-up. His T-shirt alone looked like it set him back around two or three hundred. And his watch, an exquisite timepiece with a face that had the direct resemblance of the dashboard of a luxury car had to have cost a lot of stacks. The piece around his neck had so many diamonds, it lit up the dim bar room like a light show.

"Looks like somebody is moving up in the world," I commented.

"Yeah, my money's up; I'm doing all right," Sharif confirmed.

"Put me on, man. I make good tips here, but working this bar five nights a week is back-breaking."

"I don't know, man. You might not have the stomach for what I'm into."

"You think I'm soft?"

"All those years in school probably softened you up," he said, laughing.

I eyed him suspiciously. "I hope you weren't stupid enough to get back into the dope game."

"Do I look crazy? I don't believe in going backward in life."

"Well, what's up? What are doing? Murking muthafuckas for profit?" I laughed a little, but I was dead serious.

"Nah, nothing like that," he said with a smile. "If I tell you, you gotta keep it to yourself."

"For sure."

Sharif leaned in and spoke softly. "I'm working for a network of people—"

"The mob?" I asked with a scowl.

"Nah, man. Are you gon' let me talk or you gon' keep interrupting me?"

"Go ahead." I went into listening mode, reminding myself not to ask any more questions until Sharif had finished talking.

"So, this network is comprised of millionaires…hell, some of them might be billionaires. They're all a part of this secret society that gets together for freak events…"

Sharif paused and I was ready to fire some more questions at him, but I caught myself. *Just listen*, I reminded myself again.

"They're into some sexually deviant shit. You have never seen or imagined the freaky activities that go on at their events."

I couldn't keep quiet any longer. "What kind of freaky activities?"

"A little bit of everything. They indulge every fetish you've ever heard of. Mind-blowing. Kinkier than anything I've ever done."

"What do *you* do at these fetish events? You know, what does your job entail?"

"When I first started out, I only tended bar; but now I'm much more involved in the inner workings."

"Doing what?"

"I set up the scenes; have everything organized when the guests arrive. The members fly in from all over the country and some come from outside the States."

"You set up scenes? What does that mean?"

"The fetish events are big productions, and I have to make sure that everything is flowing perfectly. It's hard to explain, but I'm sort of like a party planner for the S&M crowd."

"Okay," I said, starting to get the picture. "So, you're the one that binds a chick to a bedpost so a sadistic freak can beat the crap out of her?" Somewhat disgusted, I turned up a corner of my top lip.

"Don't judge, man. All the players are consenting adults. Nobody is getting their asses whipped unless they want to."

"But why would somebody—"

"Don't know; don't give a fuck. I'm paid, nigga. And what I do is legit."

"I'm trying to get an idea of what it is that you do."

"I make moves."

"What kind of moves?"

Sharif sighed. "You chose the right profession. Listen to yourself, asking a million questions just like a lawyer. But anyway, I do a lot of shit. I'm a multitasking mutha-fucka. I make sure that all the fetish equipment is on hand."

"Fetish equipment?" My curiosity piqued, I raised a brow.

"Floggers, blindfolds, ropes, cuffs, nipple clamps, cages, and racks...shit like that. I'm responsible for hiring the caterers, the car service that picks up guests from the airport. I'm also in charge of the security team."

"Why do they need security?"

"Lots of reasons."

"Such as?"

"People try to escape from time to time."

"Can't they leave if they want to?"

"Not if they're there for bondage and discipline. Look, it's hard to explain. Most of the people are there to live out a fantasy. If they paid to be enslaved, then it's the club's responsibility to keep them in bondage. They don't really want to go anywhere; trying to escape is part of the fantasy."

"Damn," I muttered. "You're a fantasy-event planner. It must pay very well since you gave up your full-time, regular gig."

"The money is crazy. A couple of the regulars here at The Dive got me involved."

"No shit?"

"Fact. This old, gray-haired couple. They look like they should be home enjoying retirement or taking care of their grandchildren, but they're two old-ass freaks. Rich as hell."

I wondered if Sharif was referring to the gray-haired, old couple that I'd met my first day on the gig. The old geezers that had been harassing the customers, trying to get someone to go back to their hotel for a threesome. They were big tippers but didn't appear to be rich. In fact, they looked a little scruffy. I thought they might both be professors at the university—a pair of brainiacs that were too eccentric to care about their appearance.

"Do they carry old, beat-up briefcases?" I asked.

"Yeah, that's them."

"Wow. They have to be up in age. They look to be in their seventies," I said, shaking my head.

"Ol' boy uses Viagra," Sharif responded. "I don't know what the old lady is on."

"Are they members of the freak society?"

"Founding members."

"Wow." I shook my head again. "Since they have access to all sorts of kinky behavior, why were they in here trolling for sex? I watched them going around hitting on both men and women…trying to get someone…*anyone*…to go back to their hotel. I was embarrassed for them."

"The events are held twice a month, and that old couple likes to get kinky on a regular basis," Sharif explained.

"If they're so rich, why can't they hire call girls…call an escort service? Why go through the aggravation of trying to pick up people in a bar? The patrons were disgusted, and I was about to physically eject the old kooks."

"I don't know what makes people tick; nor do I care. I'm getting paper. Tax-free dollars. You won't hear me complaining about Mr. and Mrs. Meyers." Sharif frowned.

"Damn, I didn't mean to blurt out their names. Keep that shit to yourself."

"Man, you don't have to worry about me mentioning their names. They're good tippers, but on some real shit, I hope they stay the hell out of here." I grimaced like I had a nasty taste in my mouth. "Those two elderly sex fiends turn my stomach."

"That's age discrimination, man. That ain't cool."

I smirked. "They had their time to shine; they should be ready to shut shit down by now."

"In other words, because they're past their prime, you feel they shouldn't have a sex drive?"

"It's okay if they keep it behind closed doors. At this point, if they still have a sex life, it should be their private business."

"But it would be cool…you know, the lifestyle they lead would be acceptable if they were, like, thirty years younger?"

"That's not what I'm saying." I gave Sharif an irritated look. "Man, I'm not going to stand around and debate with you. Dude needs to be sitting in his rocker on the porch and his wife should be knitting a sweater or something."

"I didn't know you were so narrow-minded, man."

"I'm not. But this feels a little personal."

"How's that?"

"Ol' girl is as old as my grandmother was around the time she died. I'd hate to think that my Mom-Mom would ever have been hanging out in a bar, pestering the patrons for recreational sex."

Sharif burst out laughing. "Excuse me for laughing. But that visual of your Mom-Mom soliciting customers for sex really fucked with my head." Sharif cleared his throat and took on a serious expression. "Dig it, man. If you want to get that money, you're going to have to loosen up. You have to accept that times have changed. People are living out their fantasies, and folks of all ages are embracing their sexuality. If I put you down with a bartending gig at one of the events, you can't be turning up your nose while you're mixing drinks."

"I wouldn't let my personal beliefs interfere with my work," I said, feeling a little ashamed of how I'd maligned the couple's sexual behavior based purely on their perceived age. With all the dirt I'd done in my life, I had a lot of nerve, preaching about what was morally right or wrong.

Customers began to trickle in. The regulars greeted Sharif warmly, asking if he was guest bartending tonight. Sharif embraced and bumped shoulders with a couple of his old customers, and then said to me, "It's time for me to get up outta here. I'll hit you up in a couple of days about the bartending position. Give it a lot of thought, Jag. That scene might be too much for you."

"I'm good; I can handle it."

"All right, man. I'll holla at you."

FONIA

I didn't respond to Mr. Lord's persistent calling until I was back at home with my face washed clean of makeup and wearing pajamas. In case he wanted a video call, I had to appear as if I'd been asleep. I answered in a drowsy voice. To my surprise, instead of being perturbed with me for taking so long to answer his call, Mr. Lord seemed concerned about my well-being.

"Fonia, are you okay?" he'd said anxiously.

"What's wrong? What time is it?" I rasped, intentionally sounding disoriented.

"Sorry to wake you, Princess. There's been a change in my wedding plans, and I wanted to discuss it with you."

"Oh?"

"But we can talk about it tomorrow. Get your beauty rest."

"Okay. Goodnight." I hung up, feeling confused and conflicted. Though I was attracted to Jaguar, I realized my loyalty toward Mr. Lord was as strong as ever. Hearing the warmth in his voice reminded me of why I'd grown to love him back when I was only eleven. Despite being a demanding man and a stern disciplinarian, he had a loving and caring side. Whenever that aspect of his personality emerged, my heart would melt.

My conduct lately had been risky and absolutely scandalous. I chastised myself for lurking in a seedy bar late at night and deliberately attempting to initiate a relationship with another man. Mr. Lord had always been above board and honest with me. He would be so disappointed if he knew that I'd been sneaking behind his back and flirting with a strange bartender.

From the tone of his voice, I could tell Mr. Lord wanted to discuss something very serious with me. I convinced myself that he had decided to call off the wedding, and I couldn't blame him. A marriage of convenience wasn't worth ruining what he and I had built over the course of ten years. After spending the past few weeks in Arizona with his fiancée, he probably came to realize that I was the only woman that truly understood his needs and desires.

And he understood me. He knew me better than I knew myself. Not Jaguar or any other man would ever be able to fully please me. Only Mr. Lord could give me the structure and discipline that I required. I vowed to push thoughts of Jaguar out of my mind and focus totally on being the perfect submissive for Mr. Lord.

When he called the next morning, I was eager to hear the details of his cancelled wedding, but the news he imparted staggered me. I had to grasp the arm of a chair and take a seat.

"Sylvia doesn't want an elaborate wedding; she wants to elope. She feels her mother is taking over the wedding planning and she's extremely upset. Her parents only have themselves to blame for her fiery temperament and rebelliousness. She won't be such a volatile young woman once I've turned her over my knee. A good, forceful spanking that turns her buttocks a flaming red will put a stop to her theatrics. But in the meantime, I have no choice but to go along with her demands. It's in the best interest of my business."

My heart dropped. The wedding was still on, and even worse, he planned to introduce his new bride to our lifestyle—to the special intimacies that I thought were reserved for me.

"When are you going to spank her?" I asked in a voice barely above a whisper.

"I'm not sure. I'd love to throttle her on our wedding night, but I'm afraid that she'd run off and ruin the business arrangement between her father and me. Unfortunately, I'm going to be stuck with a wayward wife for a while. Having you in my life is such a comfort. I miss you, Princess, and I'm looking forward to spending time together."

So, the wedding was still on, and I was nothing more

than his concubine. I dropped my head and sighed. "May I be honest with you?"

"Of course."

"After we spoke last night, I convinced myself that you had changed your mind about marrying her."

"Why would you think that? You know the success of my business is dependent upon the relationship I've been establishing with Sylvia's father."

"Wishful thinking, I suppose," I said solemnly.

"You sound sad and there's no reason to be. You're number one. You'll always be. By the way, I do have some good news to share with you."

"What is it?"

"Sylvia has decided that we should wed the day after tomorrow—merely to annoy her mother. Her parents have spoiled her rotten, and I find myself in the awkward position of having to indulge her childish whims. We're still honeymooning in Bermuda, and I took the liberty of changing your flight. Sorry that I won't be able to select a new wardrobe for you; you'll have to rely on your own taste. You'll make me proud, won't you?"

"Yes, I'll make you proud." I whispered, feeling sick to my stomach.

"A car will take you to the hotel from the airport. Once you've settled in, you can order room service, but do not leave your room under any circumstances. I'll come to you when I can. Do you understand?"

"Yes."

"Good. I'll see you in Bermuda, Princess."

After our phone conversation, I cried for hours. I'd never understood what exactly had been going on between Mr. Lord and my mother, but now that I'd grown up, I realized that Mr. Lord's spankings aroused sexual desires in women. The idea that he'd even want to spank his bride was troubling. If their marriage were only one of convenience, why would he want to give her the kind of pleasure that he gave me?

For so long, I'd followed his every command, but expecting me to share him with his wife was asking too much of me. It was time for me to start thinking for myself. It was time to sever the relationship between Mr. Lord and me.

I'd have to figure out a way to support myself, but in the meantime, I had money put away. Enough to break away from him and make a new start.

I left Mr. Lord a note, telling him goodbye and requesting that he not look for me.

Taking only my personal possessions, I moved into a one-bedroom apartment in a complex near Seventy-ninth and Lindbergh Boulevard. Living without Mr. Lord's approval and guidance was scary and thrilling at the same time. Determined to start fresh, I changed my cell phone number. Doing whatever I wanted, whenever I wanted without having to give a report of my daily activities was liberating. For the first time in almost ten years, I was free.

Knowing how determined Mr. Lord could be, it wouldn't surprise me if upon his return from Bermuda, he hired a private investigator to locate me. It didn't matter. No one could force me to return to him.

Living on my own was an eye-opening experience. It was clear to me that Mr. Lord had begun brainwashing me at a very early age, persuading me to believe that our unnatural union was perfectly normal. From the time my sexual passion had begun to assert itself, he had manipulated me into confusing physical pain and emotional humiliation with sexual gratification.

My ties with my mother had been completely destroyed. I had no idea if she'd gotten sober or if she was still a hopeless drunk. Hopefully, I'd be able to forgive her one day for allowing Mr. Lord to control and manipulate me.

I pushed thoughts of my mother out of my head. I'd been emotionally imprisoned for so long, all I wanted to do was bask in the freedom I'd been deprived of for ten long years.

In time, I would be ready for a genuine sexual experience with someone who loved me as much as I loved him.

JAGUAR

B en, the cleaning man, had been complaining about finding an inordinate amount of condoms in the small cubby area behind the restrooms. He'd asked me to keep an eye out and ban anyone caught having sex back there.

"The things they do in this bar are indecent. It's so crude the way they drop used condoms on the floor. It's only a matter of time before this place gets shut down," Ben cautioned with a furrowed brow and a wagging finger. "You should patrol that area several times throughout the night."

Ben's warning had gone in one ear and out the other. After getting my dick sucked in the bathroom, I was no model of decent behavior. I damn sure wasn't going to start policing the place, searching for whom was fucking whom in the shadows.

The bar was busy, and I'd been holding my piss for an eternity. Rushing to the restroom, I saw a flutter of movement in a far corner. Somebody was getting in a quickie between drinks. I laughed to myself and continued inside the restroom, unzipping my pants and yanking out my dick as I hurried toward the urinal. After relieving myself, I figured I should say something to the copulating couple. If I didn't want to hear Ben's complaining about used condoms, the least I could do was urge the patrons to be responsible and dispose of their condoms in a trash receptacle.

I eased up on the pair and saw a woman's shapely, round ass gyrating slowly. A pair of jeans hung at her ankles, dragging the floor. Intertwined with the jeans were white lace panties. Her long, chestnut hair fell around her shoulders, obscuring her face. Her glossy, dark hair bounced against her tanned skin as she worked her softly curved body.

I couldn't see the guy who was banging her, and when I heard soft moans emanating from the person who was backed into the corner, I lifted a brow. Was she getting banged by a man or was she freaking another woman? Though my brain couldn't quite process what was going on, my dick didn't require specific details. Responding to the soft, feminine moans and the sensual roll of womanly hips, my dick stiffened immediately.

After a closer look, I realized that two women were in the corner, kissing and bumping pussies. The imagery was highly erotic, and I stood there leering at them. Aching to get in on the action, my dick fattened up like it had been injected with steroids.

The dominant chick…the one that was pumping like she possessed a dick, looked over her shoulder and smiled at me. I remembered her pretty smile. I'd served her 100 Proof, Old Grand-Dad earlier tonight. It had seemed odd for a fresh-faced, young woman to order a glass of strong whiskey, which she drank straight.

Her thinly strapped, red top showed off her toned upper body but concealed her tits. From what I could see, the rest of her body was slim but curvaceous.

"Wanna join us?" she asked, her hazel-green eyes glimmering with mischief.

Do I? Hell, yeah!

"Don't stop," her partner, a blonde with a more athletic build, urged breathily as she pulled the slender brunette closer. The top of her dress hung to her waist, exposing her boobs. Her areolas were quite large with plump nipples in the center. Breast size had never mattered to me, but there was something about big-ass areolas and nipples that gave me a monstrous hard-on.

As badly as I wanted to get into the middle of that sex sandwich, I couldn't. I had a bar full of thirsty people and a cash register filled with the owner's money. I couldn't recklessly fuck around on the job again.

"I'm busy right now, but I'm free after we close. Can we can get together later?" I said in a hopeful tone. I was damn near salivating as I imagined beating up the brunette's pussy while I licked those saucer-sized areolas and sucked the protrusive nipples.

"You wanna get with him, babe?" the brunette asked the blonde.

"I don't mind," the blonde murmured, groping for the other girl.

They went back to kissing and grinding, and I wrote my number on the back of an old business card that someone had given me. I dropped the card on top of her white lace panties and headed back to the bar.

I hoped the girls were serious about a threesome. Wild, uninhibited fucking with no strings attached was exactly what the doctor had ordered to take my mind off a certain, dark-skinned beauty who liked to play mind games.

ơơ◦↟═

The brunette's name was Michelle and she referred to the blonde as Blondie, so I called her Blondie, too. Michelle had requested that I bring some whiskey to the sex party. The liquor stores in Philadelphia were closed after I got off from work, and so I had to figure out a way to steal a bottle from the bar and sneak the liquor past pain-in-the ass Harvey's prying eyes. It was no easy task, but I managed to hide away two small bottles, thanks to my camouflage pants with their deep pockets.

We got together at Blondie's crib, a large, sparsely furnished apartment on Spruce Street, only a few blocks from The Dive.

"I haven't been here long," Blondie said, explaining the lack of furniture. There was only a futon in the bedroom, which wasn't going to support the three of us, and so the girls spread a blanket and a sheet on the floor.

While Michelle uncapped one of the bottles of liquor I'd given her, I got busy pulling Blondie's dress over her head. She wasn't wearing a bra. Her tits, high and soft and with taut nipples were on display and waiting to be fondled. My mouth went straight to those nipples that were ripe with desire. I sucked the right one for a few moments and then hungrily switched to the left.

Hard as concrete, my dick was pushing and straining inside my pants, eager to be liberated. I took it out of bondage and guided Blondie's hand downward. I let out a groan of pleasure the moment her soft hand touched my hot erection. Inside her palm, she lightly stroked my pulsing shaft and, with the same hand, she teased the sensitive head using circular motions with the pad of her thumb.

Pretty soon, she coaxed out a dab of pre-cum and began shining up my knob with the slippery substance. It felt so good, I squeezed my eyes shut and gritted my teeth, unable to concentrate on sucking Blondie's plump breasts.

I opened my eyes and noticed Michelle had been stripping out of her clothes. Naked, she sidled up to Blondie, caressing her face and kissing her neck. She did me a huge favor when she took over the titty-sucking aspect of the ménage à trois. Now I could concentrate on the tingle and zings that rocketed through my body with each dick stroke. I was on fire and my dick had spurted out enough pre-cum to provide a substantial lubricant for the hand job Blondie was giving me.

Seeing Michelle's lips wrapped around Blondie's fat tits was taking me close to the edge. I was grunting and the hand-fuck I was getting felt like I was penetrating a hot pussy.

After a while, the hand job was starting to get old, and I was ready to fuck one of the two girls. It didn't matter which one. I grabbed the girl that was closest, and that turned out to be Michelle.

We'd all been standing, but I needed to be lying down or kneeling in order to fuck the way I wanted. I was ready to go hard—to be all up in it.

Blondie was making sexy little noises as Michelle lathered her nipples with her tongue. More than ready to slide into the tight clutch of warm pussy, I tugged Michelle's wrist, trying to persuade her to disengage her lips from Blondie's tits and drop down to the floor with me. But Michelle was attached to Blondie's tits like a starving baby.

Making the best out of the situation, I eased my dick out of Blondie's grasp and got down on the sheets and blanket and watched the two girls while jacking my dick. Blondie's bright eyes gleamed with excitement as she watched me masturbate. I thrust my dark, veiny erection in and out of my fist, flaunting it…enticing her with its sizeable length and width.

Blondie grasped Michelle by the shoulders, nudging her away as she followed me down to the floor. The patch of damp pubic hair let me know she was ready to get banged with something more substantial than a clit. That pussy was craving some male meat. She pounced on top of me, reaching down and positioning my dick at the mouth of her pussy. She pushed down, taking in my throbbing erection until it was buried to the hilt. She slid up and down my pole, moaning and yelling almost hysterically.

I let her ride me like that for a while, but then I took control. I cinched her waist and proceeded to lift her up and down as I bucked upward, driving my dick in and out of her hole. Sweat was pouring off my face and running down into the crevices of my neck, and I'll be damned if Blondie didn't start lapping up the sweat. The chick was kinky as fuck, and I loved it. Feeling her tongue licking my sweaty neck took me to a new level of passion. I wanted to fuck her brains out like my dick was a power tool, but I began to slow it down, pulling my dick out slowly and then reentering her smoldering pussy with measured gyrations.

This brother was putting his thing down, and Blondie couldn't handle it. She was throwing her head back, panting, moaning and starting to make those whimpering sounds along with a tantalizing, high-pitched, "Ohhh!"

She couldn't help her loud reaction; I was killing the pussy.

Then she changed the game, and began to whisper provocative words in my ear. The freaky shit she was talking prompted my dick to thump and my body shuddered with arousal. I never thought that hearing racial slurs would bring out the freak in me. I guess I don't know myself as well as I thought I did.

"You're a black-ass Mandingo and I'm your white-bitch slave," she moaned.

Damn! Okay, then. I can get down with that, I guess. She had taken "dirty talk" to a level that I was unfamiliar with. The way my dick was leaking semen as it pulsed and spazzed out of control, I had to assume that it enjoyed the sleazy, slave references.

"I only fuck black motherfuckers, but I like to eat white-girl pussy," Blondie confessed.

"Damn, Blondie, baby…why don't you eat black-girl pussy?" I asked in a husky, lustful voice, encouraging her to fuel my passion with more twisted, race talk.

"Michelle gets jealous every time I stick my tongue in black snatch."

"Oh, okay," I grunted, trying to sound understanding.

"But she likes to watch me eat out black girls whenever she gets drunk."

This fuck-fest was amazing, and I was glad Michelle didn't view me as a threat. I looked over at Michelle, wondering if she was drunk enough to let Blondie eat some African-American pussy. I could probably scroll through my phone and come up with a willing participant. Freaky chicks gave me their numbers on a daily basis at the bar, and I was sure quite a few of them would agree to getting some late-night head. My dick was busting at the seams at the very thought of watching some multi-cultural, same-sex cunnilingus.

Michelle had been watching us and listening as she took swigs from the whiskey bottle. Aroused by the way her girl was getting dicked-down, Michelle moved toward us, swallowing liquor and rubbing her clit with every step she made.

I thought Michelle was going to join in, but instead, she remained a spectator, stuffing two fingers between her legs, attempting to bring herself to an orgasm.

While Blondie rode me and spoke provocatively in my ear, my hand wandered over to Michelle, substituting her thin fingers with my thick, sturdy digit. I finger-fucked Michelle until she spread her legs wide, moaning while her pussy drippings splattered onto my hand.

Blondie pumped up and down for a while, but when she took notice of the pleasure I was giving Michelle, she grasped my wrist and pulled my finger out of Michelle's hot pussy. Initially, I thought Blondie was being unreasonably jealous, but when she began to suck Michelle's juices from my finger, it dawned on me that she was serious about loving white pussy.

Using my hand like a lifeless, sex utensil, she repeatedly stuffed my finger in and out of Michelle's pussy, licking the cream from my finger and moaning, "Mmm," as if Michelle's pussy drippings tasted like melted candy.

Blondie's freaky, pussy-eating activities had the potential of making me bust a premature nut. So, in an effort to take her mind off of pussy and make sure she concentrated solely on my dick, I turned her over, pulled her to her hands and knees and plunged dick into her from behind.

Fucking Blondie doggy-style gave me a deeper thrust. My thrust was so deep, Blondie and I were both shouting obscenities that bordered on racial slurs. "Take all this big, black dick," I heard myself demanding, caught up in the moment.

"I'm your cunt-whore; fuck me like I'm your white-trash, bitch-slave," Blondie screamed, throwing the pussy at me so hard, I was practically delirious.

"Whoa. Calm down, Blondie," I warned. "The shit you're talking is about to make me skeet."

At that point, I'd forgotten about Michelle, but the sound of her chugging down liquor reminded me of her presence.

Blondie said she wanted me to splash her face with cum. Hearing those freaky words got the best of me; I couldn't hold back any longer. I pulled out, and I groaned like a wounded animal when I shot my load in her face.

Two seconds later, Michelle was on top of Blondie. They bumped pussies while kissing passionately. Neither seemed to mind that their faces were splattered with sticky semen.

FONIA

Having unlimited leisure time has been a new experience for me. My daily routine was regimented for so long, I'm surprised that I've been able to relax at all. But I have. I've spent the past few days lounging around my apartment, watching reality shows, movies, and sitcoms for hours and hours, like a TV addict.

Taking a break from worrying about my appearance has been heavenly. I had been eating, sleeping, and lounging in designer sweats, treating my expensive apparel as if it had the value of something purchased from a second-hand store.

It's been ingrained in me to always look my very best, in and out of Mr. Lord's presence, but lately, I've found that I get a morbid sense of enjoyment, imagining his reaction if he saw how unkempt and slovenly I've become.

The furnished apartment wasn't equipped with pots and pans, dishes or flat wear, and I used that as an excuse not to cook. The trash bin in my kitchen was filled with fast food containers, paper plates, and plastic utensils.

Having never had the luxury of ordering take-out food, I've been overdoing it.

Mr. Lord obsessed over my weight, terrified that I'd lose my youthful physique if I strayed from the strict, low-fat diet that he'd tailored for me.

Today, instead of having food delivered, I decided to get some fresh air and sunshine. Clad in wrinkled, Chanel sweats that were splotched with food stains, I drove to the deli that I usually called to deliver my junk-food delights. I had a taste for a big, sloppy cheesesteak—something I hadn't tasted since I was a young girl.

Habib, the Middle Eastern guy who usually delivered my food, waved at me as I stood at the counter, placing my order. "Why didn't you call in your order; I would have brought it to you?" he said with friendly smile.

"I've been cooped up too long. Needed to get out."

"I see. Well, it's good to see you, Fonia," he said as he loaded packages into a box.

Not long after Habib left, my order was ready. Carrying a brown paper bag filled with an assortment of fatty treats, I drove back to my apartment complex. As I parked, I noticed Habib getting out of a nondescript car.

"Hi, again," he said with a hand wave. "As you can see, I make deliveries at this complex many times a day."

I offered a polite smile, and then noticed him looking at me in an odd way. I knew I looked a wreck, but I was completely un-apologetic. "What are you staring at?" I said, feeling a lot like the feisty girl I used to be before Mr. Lord redefined me.

"Nothing. I wasn't staring." Habib looked stunned by my harsh tone.

"I don't care about your opinion of me. So what if I look a mess; it's my life!" I said in a hostile tone.

"But you don't look a mess, and if I was staring, it's because I think you're very beautiful," he said, surprising me.

I mumbled an apology and hurried away from the parking lot.

The next day, I woke up yearning for fried egg, sausage and cheese on a garlic bagel. Eventually, I would get myself together and buy groceries as well as cooking utensils, but I was on strike against everything that was deemed correct and socially appropriate.

I called my favorite deli and placed my order.

Twenty-five minutes later, Habib arrived with my food.

"I'm really sorry about the way I yelled at you yesterday."

"No problem. I'm sorry for staring at you. To make up, I put a large coffee in with your order."

"That was sweet of you, but I'm not allowed to…" I caught myself before I said I wasn't allowed to drink coffee. I could do whatever I wanted, but letting go of my old programming was more difficult than I'd realized. I'd never tasted coffee, but I was willing to give it a try. "Thanks for the coffee." I took a sip and it wasn't bad.

"Do you work around the clock, Habib? You're the only person from the deli that delivers my orders."

"I'm on summer break from school."

"Oh. Where do you go?"

"I'm a grad student at Drexel University. Working double shifts helps pay for my education."

"That's great." I felt a pang of regret. I had been a good student. I could be in college or enjoying a career had I not been brainwashed into believing that my only purpose in life was to please Mr. Lord.

Habib looked at me closely. "What's wrong? Your eyes look so sad right now."

"I had a sad thought for a moment, but I'm okay." I gazed at him and realized that I hadn't ever really looked at him before. He was a good-looking guy with intense, wide eyes and thick black hair that he was constantly pushing out of his face. He was slim but muscular, and super hairy. The first few buttons of his shirt were undone, and I could see chest hairs peeking through the opening of his shirt. Surprisingly, his hairy chest, as well as the silken hairs that covered his arms, appealed to me.

When Habib looked at me again, he saw a different look in my eyes; he saw the look of lust.

Intuitively, he drew me into his arms. "Is it okay if I kiss you, Fonia?"

I nodded and let out a soft moan. Being that close to him allowed me a whiff of his male scent. He didn't give off the cologne fragrance that was Mr. Lord's scent. His odor was a combination of perspiration and pure masculinity.

Our lips touched and he parted mine with his tongue. This was my first tongue-kiss, and I closed my eyes, enjoying the sensual way his tongue lashed against mine as his hand groped my breasts. My nipples hardened the way they did whenever Mr. Lord spanked me. Using one hand, Habib stuck his hand beneath my top and masterfully undid my bra.

"Ahh," I cried out when his hands claimed my breasts. With each gentle squeeze, I felt tension knotting up between my legs. I had to fight the urge to rip his hand away from my breast and stuff it where I needed it most.

His lips traveled to my neck, and he delivered a flurry of soft kisses. His lips made their way to my chest, and my back arched the moment he cupped one of my breasts, covering the rigid nipple with his warm kiss. His other hand meandered down to the crotch of my sweat pants. Through the fabric of the sweats, his middle finger caressed my clit.

Warm moisture quickly pooled between my thighs, and my body writhed with desire. Mr. Lord would have told me that I was acting like a whore, and in his world, I was only given sexual release once a week.

"Oh, Habib," I murmured, as I became lost in the different sensations that flooded me. "Habib," I repeated breathlessly. "I want to act like a whore."

Habib went still. His lips fell away from my body, and

he stopped stroking my clit. "What do you mean?" he asked in a voice filled with alarm. "Do you want me to pay you?"

"No, just give me permission."

"Okay," he said, looking perplexed. "You can act like a whore."

I snatched my sweat pants down, while pulling Habib toward my bedroom. Panting, Habib helped rid me of my sweat pants and panties. I collapsed on the bed and he followed me. I reached for his hand and guided it toward my hot spot. Until now, I hadn't realized how much I missed my weekly orgasm.

But Habib didn't slide his finger deep inside me the way I expected. He caressed the outer area of my vagina briefly and then unzipped his pants and removed them.

"What are you doing?" I asked in horror, my eyes glued to his erect penis.

"We're going to have sexual intercourse…isn't that what you want?" He stroked his shaft, which was much bigger than a finger. His burgeoning manhood frightened me.

"I don't know if I'm ready." I eyed his throbbing member with fascination.

"I have a condom." He began groping through the pockets of his discarded pants.

"But, I've never done it before; I'm scared."

"You're a virgin?" He looked at me incredulously.

I nodded my head.

"I'll be gentle," he said. "I'll take my time with you."

"Okay," I said in a nervous whisper. I was supposed to lose my virginity to Mr. Lord on his wedding night. I had never imagined giving this precious gift to a stranger, but I felt compelled to do so. If I had one wish, it would be for Mr. Lord to witness how recklessly I was squandering the prize that he had planned to claim for himself.

Habib entered me and it didn't feel good at all. I yelled in pain as he tried to ease it inside me.

"Relax. It always hurts the first time."

I squirmed in discomfort as he forced himself inside me. I wanted him to stop, but motivated by my desire to defy Mr. Lord, I withstood the pain. Finally, Habib's body shuddered and his breath came out in rough gasps.

He lay on top of me panting for several minutes. He gazed down at my face. "Was it good for you?"

I hadn't reached an orgasm and I felt completely let-down. I'm sure my disappointment was visible on my face. "It wasn't what I expected," I admitted.

"You'll feel pleasure the next time," he promised as he got dressed. "I have to get back to work, but if you'd like, I'll come back when I finish making my deliveries."

"What time is that?"

"Eleven o'clock tonight. Is that past your bedtime?"

"No, I'll be up." I didn't have a lot of faith that Habib could give me that rush of immense pleasure that Mr. Lord gave me, but I was willing to give him one more try.

Habib left and I felt downhearted as I changed the blood-smeared sheets, but a wicked thought put a smile on my lips. Instead of throwing the sheets in the hamper, it occurred to me that I should neatly fold them and mail them to Mr. Lord's office. But it was only a thought; I'd never do anything that crude.

JAGUAR

Back at work, my customers were showing their appreciation for good service by keeping my tip jar jammed with money. I couldn't complain about the kind of money I was making at The Dive, but living in a hotel was starting to hurt my pockets. In addition to paying my student loans, I wanted to get an apartment, and save up to buy a car.

Sharif had never gotten back to me about the underground sex club job, and it bothered me that he thought I was too judgmental to mix drinks for a bunch of freaks. Hell, after my liaison with the twisted lesbians, I was certain that I could rock with any sick scenario without blinking an eye.

Engaging in wild sex with a stranger is like getting drunk to forget your problems. The frenzy of meaningless sex gives you a high that makes you briefly forget about your problems. But after you've climaxed, whatever you were trying to escape is still lingering in your mind.

After my tryst with Blondie and Michelle, my problem seemed to have intensified, and I felt worse than ever.

I had fun with the girls, but after the rush of illicit sex was over, I crashed…felt like I had hit rock bottom. When it was all over, I wanted to hurry out of that unfamiliar environment and return to my hotel.

While I washed up, the girls were still cuddling and making out. They both had cum smeared over their faces, and when I stepped back into the bedroom, smelling the co-mingled fumes of pussy and semen, I felt sickened, and I felt ashamed for participating in racially-charged dialogue.

Blondie wanted to go for another round, but I declined. I couldn't get out of the crib fast enough. She thought she was going to cuddle with both Michelle and me, but I could hardly look at her cum-stained face without cringing.

Hit by a feeling of deep despair and loneliness, I realized that random sex hadn't taken away my desire to be with Fonia. More than ever, I wanted to get to know her better and gaze into her beautiful, brown eyes.

Having such strong feelings for Fonia is crazy. I don't know anything about her, yet since the day I first set eyes on her, I haven't been able to get her off my mind.

I've been fucking since I was thirteen, and I've had more pussy than I could begin to count. But I might as well turn into a monk…a priest…or something because meaningless sex isn't doing it for me, anymore. I crossed clingy women off my list of sex partners, thinking that no-strings-attached sex situations would work for me.

But now I've come to realize that self-medicating with meaningless sex isn't working at all. The aftermath of sticking my dick into miscellaneous pussies and mouths has left a blemish on my soul.

My heart knows what it wants. It wants Fonia, and no one else can fill the void.

Being realistic, though…if Fonia isn't the one for me, then I'll have to accept that. But I've decided to steer clear of future sexual encounters with people I barely know and have no kind of emotional connection with.

I'm not saying that the next time I have sex, I'm going to take a trip down the aisle. What I'm saying is, I've grown weary of fucking for the sake of busting a nut. I need to have genuine feelings for my partner before I get that intimate again. It's time to take my dick out of the game and put it on hiatus. I decided to become celibate until I met someone whom I believed I could build a future with.

My plan to become celibate seemed a little hypocritical since I wanted to work with Sharif at the sex club. A celibate dude in a highly charged sexual environment was like an ex-addict trying to make a living selling drugs.

But I could do it; I knew I could. My will has always been strong. My inner strength is what got me out of the hood and into undergrad school while my friends were dying and going to jail. My belief in myself got me through law school. If an ex-thug like me could turn my life around through sheer will and the desire to overcome my circumstances, then I could certainly give up pussy for a while.

I wondered if being celibate meant no sexual release at all. Nah, fuck that; if I didn't jack off at least once a day, I'd probably lose my mind.

Reaching for a bottle of Absolut, my back was turned when I heard my man, Buddha exclaim, "Look who's here! What's good, mamma?"

"Don't front; I'm not even speaking to you, anymore," said the annoying voice of Rat-Face.

I let out a sigh. I had been a having a good night up until that point.

I turned around to pour liquor for two neighborhood regulars and acknowledged her with a curt head nod. No words. No smile. I didn't even ask her what she was drinking. She hadn't done anything to me, personally, but there were certain people that I simply didn't like, and she was one of them. I didn't know her real name and didn't want to know it.

Buddha's real name was Calvin, but with his big, round belly, he'd always be Buddha to me. "Get my girl, Myeesha, a drink," Buddha said, revealing Rat-Face's name.

"Don't be trying to make up with me now," she said, shaking her head.

"Don't be mad, Myeesha. Have a drink with me," he soothed.

"I don't want anything from you." She held up her hand, positioning it so close to his face, I felt personally disrespected and offended as a man, but Buddha was steadily smiling like the shit was cute.

"How you doing, Jag?" she asked, looking me up and down and trying to undress me with eyes that were narrowed into slits. With her eyes squinted like that, she looked more like a rat than ever.

"I'm good," I said in flat voice. "Whatchu drinking?"

She licked her thin lips. "I'd like to gulp down a tall, thick chocolate milkshake." Again, she gazed at me through squinted eyes—a look she presumed was seductive.

"I don't make milkshakes," I said tersely.

"Humph. From where I'm sitting, that creamy milkshake has already been made. It just needs somebody to suck it up." She ogled me like I was edible. "Never mind on the milkshake. I want a hot chocolate sundae...bananas, a couple cherries...I want it all." She licked her lizard lips again, and I felt like giving a loud groan of exasperation.

I glanced at Buddha and he looked hurt by the way she was openly flirting with me. I was irked with this chick and her sexual innuendos. She was crazy if she thought I was going to go along with the spiteful game she was playing. "Tanqueray?" I asked, remembering what she'd been drinking the last time.

She nodded and gave me a lingering gaze. "With ice," she said. "And stir it with your finger...sweeten it up for me."

Damn, can't you be original, I thought in irritation. I heard some version of that line about five times a night.

Some of the female customers seemed to think that telling me to stir their drink with my finger was a unique expression. From time to time, I obliged them. It depended on my mood. But there wasn't a chance in hell that I was going to indulge Rat-Face's request.

"Put her drink on my tab," Buddha said, trying to get on her good side.

"I can pay for my own drinks," she snarled.

"Look, we got off on the wrong foot; let's start over."

"Uh-uh. You burned me once, and I'm through."

As much as I couldn't stand Rat-Face, I was very curious about what a good guy like Buddha could have done. "Why you being so hard on my man?" I asked.

She took a swig of gin, smacked her lips in an obnoxious way and told me how she'd booked a videographer to film Buddha's long tongue while he gave her head.

"You can get all the head you want, baby," Buddha interjected. "But I can't get involved in porn. I'm active in my church and I'm involved in my community. Sorry, but I can't put myself out there like that."

"You should have said that in the first place," she whined.

"I didn't think you were serious about filming me."

"Whatever…" She held her hand up again.

Buddha leaned in and spoke in a lowered tone. I overheard him say that he wouldn't mind giving her oral sex all night, but he couldn't do it in front of a cameraman.

Giving my man the privacy to plead his case, I went to serve customers at the other end of the bar.

About twenty minutes later, Buddha held up a finger,

gesturing for more drinks. I reluctantly worked my way back to where he and Rat-Face were sitting. I grabbed the bottle of Tanqueray and tried to pour without looking at her face.

Buddha excused himself to go to the restroom, and Rat-Face didn't waste any time harassing me with all kinds of sexually explicit comments.

"Calvin's going back to my place with me. You should come with us."

"I'm working."

"After you get off."

"Nah, I'm good."

"You scared of me or something?" she queried with her head tilted to the side.

I gave a bitter laugh. "Do I look scared?"

"If you're not scared, what's the problem?"

"There's no problem; I don't get down like that."

"Oh! You think Calvin's gay!" She laughed. "Believe me, he's all man; you don't have to worry about anything happening between the two of you. I wanted you to stop by so you and I could get busy. I already ran it by Calvin and he doesn't mind watching."

"I'm not into that."

She smiled at me indulgently. "I take it in the front and the back."

I shook my head. "Nah, I'm all right."

"Do you want me to get rid of Calvin?" She refused to take no for an answer and was totally unaware that she made my flesh crawl.

She wouldn't let up and so I had to get honest with her. "I'm not into you like that," I admitted.

A look of disbelief spread across her face and she tossed back her drink. "You don't wanna fuck me?"

"No, I don't."

"We could do something else, then." Her eyes roved down to my crotch. "I'd love to wrap my lips around that." Her tongue flicked out and brushed her lips. "As good as you look, I know you got a big, juicy dick. Let me tell you something, Jag," she said in a conspiratorial whisper. "I'm a bona fide freak in the sheets, and you don't have to work your back if you don't want to. I got you, boo." She smiled broadly and confessed, "I lick balls, baby. I guzzle the whole nut sac before I go to work on the dick. All you have to do is lie still while I suck the cum out of that chocolate stick."

Coming from any other woman, that kind of dirty talk would have had my dick pulsing, but my dislike of Rat-Face was so intense, I could feel my dick shriveling up in disgust.

From the corner of my eye, I saw Buddha returning from the restroom. He had allowed his girl to talk him into a co-signing on a twisted proposition, and he had a guilty look on his face.

Buddha sat down and looked at Rat-Face questioningly. She held out her hands and shook her head.

I put down a fresh napkin in front of Rat-Face and poured her another drink. "This one's on me; I hope you and Calvin have a good time tonight."

As I busied myself, taking care of other customers, I heard Buddha say, "I knew I shouldn't have gone along with that shit you were kicking. I can't believe I let you mess up my friendship with Jag."

She said, "Your friend, Jag, ain't normal; I offered him pussy, ass, and brain. He didn't want anything. Watch yourself around Jaguar; I think he's gay."

I laughed to myself. Turning down Rat-Face had been easy, but I was curious to see how firmly I held my ground if someone less obnoxious offered the options that she had.

FONIA

I showered and changed into a different pair of designer sweats. Time was ticking by slowly. It was only two in the afternoon, and I was getting antsy as I impatiently waited to get together with Habib at eleven o'clock.

I didn't have a personal interest in Habib, but I wanted the sexual pleasure he'd promised.

The person I was truly interested in was Jaguar, but I'd ruined my chances with him. I didn't dare go back to the bar where he worked. The furious way he'd looked at me when I told him I had to suddenly leave warned that he wasn't the kind of man that put up with a women who appeared to be playing games. My intentions had been sincere, but my erratic behavior told a different story.

Too wired to sit around doing nothing, I put on some lip gloss and dark shades, and then grabbed my handbag. It was time to get some groceries...buy some cookware. I also planned to grab a bottle of wine to share with Habib.

I checked out my reflection in the mirror. My hair was piled in a high ponytail, and although I didn't possess the polished look of my past, I didn't look half bad, either.

The camel-colored sweats hugged my slim body, showing off my curves. The fabric of the dark brown stretch-top clung to my firm breasts, revealing a bit of cleavage. I felt very sensual and I exuded a sense of confidence as I moved up and down the aisles of the Wine and Spirits store. Women looked at me with envy and men stared at me with desire. I noticed that one customer kept appearing next to me as I browsed the selections. He was an extremely tall, light-skinned man with curly hair that was mixed with salt and pepper at the temples.

"How you doing, pretty?" he said, flashing a bright smile.

I returned the smile as I picked up a bottle of Moscato. He was a nice-looking, distinguished man who appeared to be in his early to mid-forties.

"My name is Eddie," he said, staring lustfully at the swell of my breasts.

His hot gaze urged my nipples to harden beneath the delicate, cocoa-colored fabric. Blushing, I lowered my eyes and murmured, "Fonia."

"Do you have a man, Fonia?"

I shook my head.

"No? That's hard to believe, but listen…" He took on a serious expression. "A pretty thing like you needs to be with a man like me."

"And what kind of man are you?" I asked with a playful smile.

"The kind of man who knows how to treat a woman

right. The kind that won't stop until you're screaming with pleasure."

His words aroused me and I could feel desire knotting up inside me. Habib had left me yearning for release, and this kind stranger was offering to give me what I needed.

"Is that all you're getting?" he asked, nudging his head toward the bottle of wine I was holding.

"Yes."

He reached for it. "I'll pay for it. Are you sure this is all you want?"

"I'm sure. I don't drink much," I said and then walked with him to the cashier. He paid for my wine and the three bottles of liquor that he'd been carrying in a basket.

Outside the liquor store, he walked me to my car. "I don't live far from here. Do you want to follow me to my home?"

"Sure," I said, unable to resist his offer to give me sexual pleasure. As if I was under a spell, I followed Eddie without question. He drove to an attractive neighborhood of new houses that were all identical. He pulled into a garage and I parked in the driveway.

Inside his nicely decorated home, I noticed a glass case filled with basketball trophies. "I used to play pro basketball," he said.

"What do you do now?"

"Relax on my boat and enjoy retirement." He pointed to the staircase. "Go upstairs and get comfortable; I'll come up and join you shortly."

"Okay." Although I was rebelling against Mr. Lord, a

part of me still appreciated being told exactly what to do. Eddie was nothing like Habib, and I had a good feeling about hooking up with him.

His bedroom was very masculine, decorated in earth tones. His bed, much larger than a king-sized bed, must have been custom-made. I slipped out of my Christian Louboutin sandals and hoisted myself on top of his high, massive bed.

Hearing his footsteps as he climbed the stairs filled me with a rush of excitement. Eddie entered the bedroom carrying a tray. A mixture of pleasant scents filled the room. "I'm going to start you off with a sensual massage," he told me, setting the tray on the bedside table. "Let's get you out of those clothes." He gently pulled down my pants. "Take those pretty panties off for me," he said, gazing at me hungrily. "It arouses me to watch a woman take off her panties."

Starving for passion, I peeled off my panties. Feeling bashful, I pressed my thighs together.

His breathing was deep and ragged. "There's no reason to be shy when you're with me. Open your legs," he urged. "Show me that pretty pussy."

A surge of desire shot through my system. Hit with a yearning so deep, my nipples tightened and a painful pulsation throbbed between my legs. I feared that evidence of my arousal had seeped out, glazing the plump lips of my vagina.

"Don't hide it from me. Open those smooth brown thighs, and let me see all that sweetness," he coaxed.

His words were mesmerizing and the sound of his voice sent a chill up my spine. As if hypnotized, I obeyed him, slowly pulling my legs apart. I squeezed my eyes closed as aching knots of need began to build in my pelvis, leaving me breathless.

"Oh, yeah. I knew you'd have a pretty pussy. And I can see that you're nice and wet already," Eddie said with approval. Mr. Lord usually chastised me and called me a whore whenever passion poured from my loins, but Eddie seemed to like it. He swiped a finger between my pouting lower lips and I began to pant. My body was on fire and I raised my hips invitingly.

"Is your pussy begging me?"

I nodded briskly.

"Tell me what your pussy wants?"

"Um…"

"Don't think about it. Let your pussy freestyle."

I didn't know what he wanted from me. I was in sexual agony and he wanted me to make up sexual rhymes. "I can't. I don't know what to say."

"Let me help you along." His finger found my clit and he began to stroke it tenderly, smearing the quivering flesh with my steaming juices.

"Please," I uttered, thrusting upward, as I felt the slow rise of an orgasm building. "Please, fuck me."

"We don't have to rush this. I still have to give you your massage."

"No!" I shouted. "Fuck me!"

Desperately, I pulled him on top of me. Preparing to

fulfill my need, his hands reached down to fumble with the opening of his pants. I helped him as he shoved his pants down his thighs.

"Get naked," he said as he tore off his shirt.

Following his lead, I lifted up and ripped off my top.

"There's no need to rush, darling," he said softly.

"I can't help it; I want you to fuck me," I said, throwing my legs around his waist. "Fuck me, hard." Using the F-word made me feel naughty and liberated.

Finally, giving me what I desperately wanted, Eddie pressed the cap of his dick against the entrance of my pussy. Feeling him slowly sinking inside was exquisite pleasure, and my pussy muscles automatically clenched around his shaft as my inner walls sheathed him.

Eddie's hands glided over my body, cupping the mounds of my ass. Digging his fingers into my flesh, he drew me close, filling me with his swelling shaft and giving me slow, sensual strokes. I arched into him, accepting his deep thrusts. Suddenly, he released the hold on my ass and stopped moving.

"What's wrong?" I asked in a panic.

"Nothing's wrong." He stretched his arm out, reaching for something on the bedside table. He rubbed my ass with scented oil and gradually resumed the rhythm of his strokes. My knees dug into his sides as I strained for sweet release. Taking me off guard, he slipped a lubricated finger into my anus.

Jolted by the suddenness of the dual pleasure, I became briefly tense. Seconds later, I began to shake uncontrollably as the tremors of an orgasm rocked my body. Cries of appreciation tore from my lungs as I gasped and tried to catch my breath.

Eddie let out a rough cry as he reached a climax. He slumped forward, resting his forehead on my shoulder. With his chest pressed against mine, I could feel the frantic thumps of our erratic heartbeats.

"Oh, my God, that was the biggest orgasm I've ever had," I said breathily. "I want more."

"You're a little firecracker, aren't you?" he teased, whispering in my ear.

"I've been sex-deprived," I said with a smile. It pleased me that I had found a sex partner that was so giving and willing to fulfill my needs.

"You've got me now. Whenever that little pussy gets hot, bring it over here so I can take care of it."

His words were thrilling. My pussy was always hot and I was happy that he would fulfill my needs. Anticipating daily orgasms, I closed my eyes as we lay together in post-coital bliss. I stroked his curly hair as I waited for him to give me some more dick.

"Eddie! Whose damn car is in your driveway?" a woman's hostile voice interrupted the serene atmosphere.

"Oh, shit, what's she doing here?" Eddie yanked his arm away from around me and bolted upright.

I sat up also. Pulling the sheet up to my neck, I tried to cover my naked breasts. "Who is that?" I asked in a panic.

"That's Wanda—my fiancée. Get your clothes on, baby. You have to get out of here."

Before I could search through the tangled-in-the-bed linen for my underwear, I heard footsteps pounding up the stairs. Then, a woman who would have probably been attractive if her face wasn't creased in rage, stormed into the bedroom. Her short haircut was stylishly maintained with lots of gel and I was particularly focused on the gold bangles and earrings that she began to remove as she advanced inside the room. She slammed her jewelry on top of the bureau.

"Hold up, Wanda; it's not what it looks like," he said, quickly sticking one leg in his pants while Wanda raced toward him, swinging balled fists. Eddie was so tall, her blows all landed in his midsection and below the waist.

He grunted as he tried to block the punches. "Cut it out, Wanda; she's just a friend."

"You dirty dog. Every time I turn my back, you're sticking your dick into another so-called friend."

"I didn't put my dick in nothing; we were only talking," he said weakly.

"Shut up, liar. That whore is naked and your drawers are right there." She pointed to the floor where Eddie's briefs lay in a crumpled heap.

Wearing a shocked expression, he stared at his underwear as if he had no idea how they'd landed on the floor.

Wanda turned her anger on me. "You're about to get fucked up, bitch." She pointed a finger at me, and I noticed that her nails painted a silvery metallic were filed into dangerously sharpened points that resembled small daggers.

She lunged for me, and I recoiled and cried out in fear, imagining my face being mutilated by those weapon-like fingernails.

Eddie grabbed her. Holding Wanda in a bear hug, he subdued her while she fought to break free.

"Get your ass out of here," he spat, glaring at me. His kind eyes had changed into smoldering circles of fury. I whipped the sheet off and jumped out of bed.

"Let me go, Eddie," Wanda yelled. "That bitch needs some consequences for trying to fuck up our relationship."

"No, she's not worth it!" He spoke soothingly, caressing her and subduing her with kisses on the side of her face and her neck.

I kept a watchful eye on Wanda as I put on my sweat pants. Trying to dress as quickly as possible, I frantically searched for my top that had also gotten lost in the covers.

"Why does this keep happening? Our wedding is in two weeks and you're still fucking around," she said, erupting into tears.

"Shh. Shh. Don't cry, babe. I'm gonna make it up to you."

"No, I'm tired of your shit," she said, shaking her head, crying, and trying to push him away.

"Calm down, baby. Don't push me away; let me give you what you need."

By the time I had slipped my top over my head, Eddie had guided Wanda over to the bed.

He gently nudged her, encouraging her to lie atop of

the sheets that had been crumpled during our steamy lovemaking. I stared in fascination as he raised her dress, slid down her thong and buried his face between her legs. Soothing her with his tongue, he murmured. "I'm sorry, Wanda. It won't happen again. Do you forgive me?"

"I can't," she said between gasps.

"Please forgive me, baby. It won't happen again." He licked between her thighs and she cried out.

Arching up to him, she whispered, "Oh, yes. That's it."

"Do you forgive me?"

"Yes, I forgive you, Eddie. I have to. Can't nobody eat pussy the way you do."

Eddie plunged his tongue inside Wanda and slurped loudly. I tore my eyes away from the bizarre, yet erotic scene and rushed toward the open door. As I bustled along the hallway, I could hear Wanda moaning. Sounds of passion echoed as I trotted down the stairs and out the front door.

Inside my car, I let out a long breath. After being threatened by fingernails and after the panic of having to dress hurriedly, my heart was thumping. I glanced in the overhead mirror, and wiped away the sheen of perspiration that covered my forehead.

Backing out of driveway, an image of Eddie licking between Wanda's legs flashed across my mind. I heard her loud moans in my head. I'd never experienced oral sex, but my vaginal muscles clenched involuntarily as I imagined how good it probably felt.

JAGUAR

I met up with Sharif and some bulls I didn't know to shoot some hoops at a basketball court in North Philly. Since working at the bar, I had gotten a little out of practice and the other team whipped our asses. I ripped off my shirt and mopped perspiration with it.

"I see you're hitting the gym at your hotel," Sharif commented.

"Don't be checking me out. You turned sweet or something?"

"Nah, nothing like that. I was wondering if you're ready to make some real money. You know, bartending a party."

A smile spread across my face. "I'm more than ready, man."

"I'm gonna hire you on a trial basis. Try you out at a small get-together at a private home."

"When?"

"On your day off—tomorrow. The hostess requested that you wear black pants...and she wants you to go shirtless."

"Why do I have to show skin?" I asked with a frown. "I'm not participating in anything freaky."

"Chill, man. She wants some male eye candy behind the bar. There'll be more than enough freaks to satisfy her urges."

"So, where's the party being held?"

He gave me a King of Prussia address and I winced as I mentally calculated what a cab ride outside of Philly would cost. I needed a car ASAP.

"You're expected to get there at eight. That's an hour before the guests start to arrive. She wants to make sure you have your bar set up and that you're looking hot with your torso slathered with oil."

"Huh?"

"Yeah, I forgot to mention that part."

"Bare-chested and oiled-up—like a male stripper?" I asked, scowling.

"You'll get used to it. I've had to do it, back when I was tending bar at the parties and events."

"Who's going to apply the oil?"

"Probably one of her servants."

"Damn, man, is there anything else I should know about this job?" I grumbled.

"Nothing comes to mind. I won't be there, so you'll be pretty much on your own."

"What! I thought you were the head honcho...the man that put it all together?"

"I did put it together. A small event like this doesn't require my presence. You'll be all right, Jag. And if it doesn't work out, at least you'll be well paid for your time."

"Yeah, all right, Sharif." I rubbed the bridge of my nose, wondering what I was getting myself into.

ᴏᴏᴕ▄▄

The cab's navigation system was outdated and the cab driver was struggling to find the address I'd given him. I pulled out my phone, tapped the screen, pulling up the GPS. I spoke the address and we were given clear directions.

Far from the any main streets, the large, colonial-style home was hidden away in a private setting and surrounded by many acres of woods. I paid the driver and looked around. The sun had gone down, and the quarter moon wasn't providing much light. I'd hate to be held captive trying to escape this place at night. I watched the cab drive away and I resisted the urge to chase it down and jump back in.

A man dressed in formal attire opened the door. "I'm Jaguar Jackson; here to bartend the party."

"Good evening, Mr. Jackson. I'm Madam's butler. Come in," he said, admitting me inside the house.

I'd never been admitted anywhere by an actual butler before, and I could barely keep an amused smile from my face. He steered me to the room where the bar was located. Atop the glass shelves was an impressive inventory of top shelf liquor and expensive wine.

"You'll find everything you need in the kitchen." He

pointed to the area where the kitchen was located. "The fridge is well-stocked with a variety of fruit for garnishing the drinks. Juice, soft drinks, and other beverages are in the pantry. Any questions?"

I had a few questions in mind, but the butler wore a stoic expression that didn't welcome unnecessary chatter. Since he hadn't mentioned anything about removing my shirt or being oiled, I didn't bring up the subject, either. Maybe Sharif had given me the wrong information.

"No questions," I said. "I guess I'll get to work."

"Very good, sir." He bowed slightly and exited the room.

Very good, sir! Was that guy for real? And what was up with the theatrical bowing. Dude took his butler responsibilities way too seriously.

From the fridge, I gathered oranges, lemons, limes, and mint leaves. Noticing celery among the vegetables, I broke off a few stalks to garnish the drink of anyone who ordered a Bloody Mary. I never made the drink at The Dive, but I figured someone in this highbrow crowd was certain to want one. After getting jars of olives, maraschino cherries, and an assortment of juices and soda from the pantry, it took less than twenty minutes to prep the garnishes and stock the bar with mixers.

With time on my hands, I sat on a stool behind the bar and began fooling around with the apps on my phone.

Out of nowhere, the butler reappeared. "Pardon me, sir. If you've finished prepping, would you please follow me?"

"Uh, sure. Where are we going?" I asked, not one to blindly follow someone's command.

"I'd like to escort you to a changing room, if you don't mind, sir. A servant girl will help prepare you for tonight's festivities."

I thought I'd dodged that bullet, but apparently I was going to get oiled-up, after all. "No problem," I said, though I didn't like the idea at all.

The butler left me inside an elegant, small room with smoky-mirrored walls, white plush carpets, a white leather, wing-back chair, and an octagonal-shaped glass coffee table with a centerpiece of bright red roses contained inside a white vase. The mostly white room had an elegant and austere appearance.

I sat down. Watching the door, I fidgeted in the chair and tapped my finger against the arm of the chair. The suspense of waiting for the servant girl was more nerve-wracking than I imagined taking the bar exam would be. The reminder that I'd eventually have to take that damn exam made me groan.

When the door opened, I took in a sharp breath. The tall chick that entered the room had sable-colored hair with streaks of golden honey. Bangs brushed her eyebrows and a long ponytail trailed down her back. She was wearing a sheer, black baby doll negligee with a matching thong beneath. The see-through thong revealed a shaved mound and a fat clit that poked into the delicate fabric.

Her pussy distracted and excited me, and I shot my

gaze down to her bare feet and concentrated on her gold-polished toenails long enough to get my heart rate under control. Stealing another quick glance at her puffy, shaven mound and thick clit, I forced my gaze up to her face, which was partially concealed by a mask. She carried a tray with baby oil and a white hand towel.

"Greetings, sir, my name is Lilliana. Madam wants me to prepare your body."

"Hi," I replied, staring at her lush, red lips. Imagining the things she could do with that mouth, my eyes lingered there for a while, and then journeyed down to the full breasts that were visible through the sheer fabric. My appreciative gaze drifted to her taut tummy, settled at her crotch again and dwelled hungrily in that area until I was practically drooling. I scanned her firm thighs, which I yearned to part in order to get to the treasure that lay between them. She was one hot-ass servant-girl, and I hoped my dick would act civilized while she applied oil to my upper body.

"Would you remove your pants, please, sir?" she asked in a shy voice.

"My pants? Uh, look, there must be a misunderstanding. I agreed to work without a shirt, but I wasn't told that I was expected to be stark naked while I mixed drinks." I stood up. "You people better hire yourselves another bartender."

"I understand, sir. Forgive me if I sound forward, but I don't think Madam intends for you to work in the nude."

"So, why are you asking me to take off my pants?"

Lilliana's thick lashes fluttered as she lowered her eyes bashfully. With her eyes downcast, she murmured, "I was told to give you a lower body massage. To relieve any stress you might feel while working in a highly sexual environment."

Nervously, she nipped at her lower lip, and then glanced up at me. "Do you want me to relieve you of stress, sir?"

Is she asking if she can suck my dick? I wondered, feeling more aroused than before. Why did I have to decide to go celibate right before taking a job with such tempting fringe benefits? Wanting to be clear of her intentions, I asked, "What do you have in mind?"

"Anything you desire, sir. I'm here to serve you…to fulfill your needs."

The way she spoke—so soft and shy—was extremely arousing. And the way she kept referring to me as 'sir' was having a tremendous effect on my groin. My dick had awakened the moment she walked in the door, but this current topic of serving me and fulfilling my needs had me breaking out in a cold sweat.

"What would like, sir?"

I'd like to fuck, get sucked, lick that sweet-looking cat, and bust a massive nut. But I couldn't indulge. I'd made up my mind to stop whoring around and I had the strength of will to stick to my guns.

"Would you prefer manual release, sir?" she suggested.

Hmm. A hand job was probably a harmless activity.

Yeah, I could let her jack me off without breaking my vow of celibacy, I convinced myself. "Yeah, that'll work," I said, unzipping and lowering my pants.

After I'd stripped out of my clothing, Lilliana set the tray down next to the flower arrangement. She neatly folded my pants and shirt and placed them on the other side of the bouquet of roses. I stepped out of my drawers and before I could pick them up from the floor, she bent down. "Allow me, sir," she said softly.

At The Dive, I busted my ass for hours, waiting on drunken muthafuckas. This was the life and I could get used to the King's treatment I was receiving from Lilliana. I watched in fascination as she gently folded my underwear, treating the cotton fabric with reverence, acting as if my drawers were made from spun gold.

My dick responded by lifting up. The swollen head knocked impatiently against my stomach before it lowered itself, standing erect with its lone, weepy eye, focused on slipping past the thin material and filling Lilliana's luscious pussy.

She treaded toward me and I took a fortifying breath. She squeezed baby oil into her palm. "Would you like to have a seat?" she asked as she took my huge erection into a loose fist. She stroked tentatively, looking at me, waiting for my response.

"Yeah, I'll have a seat," I muttered in a husky, lustful voice. With my heart racing a mile a minute and my dick thumping and quivering, I was beginning to feel light-headed. It was best to sit before I collapsed.

She released her hand as I eased into the chair, and then she daintily lowered herself down to her knees. At eye level with my dick, she moistened her mouth and then bit down on her lip as if to restrain herself from giving me head. Her lubricated hand went into action and a harsh moan escaped my lips. My breathing was ragged and hoarse.

It was a slow, agonizing burn as her oiled hand stroked me leisurely. Craving release, I panted as I sped up the tempo, urging her to work faster, prodding her to keep up with my pace.

"Yeah, that's right," I groaned, my face scrunched in a grimace. My balls tightened and my whole body buzzed with energy. That tingling sensation was the familiar precursor to busting a load. I groaned as she picked up speed. Her oiled, fisted hand sheathed my dick like a warm pussy, and I began to murmur incoherently.

Sensing that I was about to explode, Lilliana offered, "Feel free to use my mouth or pussy as a cum receptacle."

"Damn!" I bellowed and humped her hand even faster. Had she really asked if wanted to used her mouth or pussy as a cum receptacle? *Fuck, yeah!* I wanted to cum inside her mouth *and* her pussy. I wanted to squirt half my load in her mouth and then deposit the rest of it inside her plump, hairless pussy. It was fucked up that I had chosen to torture myself with abstinence. Well, it was a type of self-restraint. Letting her jack me off was sort of like a vegetarian that occasionally ate fish or poultry.

"Madam wants you to use me as your personal cum-slut tonight," she whispered.

Oh, goddamn! Lilliana had taken dirty talk to the next level, and I couldn't take any more. I gripped her by her shoulders and with my face contorted like a crazed beast, I growled as I shot the biggest load ever. Hot cum splashed into her palm and dribbled over her hand. She held onto my erection until I'd shot out the last drop of cum.

She cleaned my dick with the warm, white towel on the tray, oiled my chest, arms, and back, and then held out my drawers, followed by my pants, inviting me to step into them.

I could get used to being catered to like this. Having a servant girl waiting for me after a hard night at the bar would brighten my life.

FONIA

I couldn't get the image of what I'd seen Eddie doing to his fiancée out of my head. Her cries of pleasure echoed in my mind.

Mr. Lord had kissed me in my secret place before, but it hadn't been a lingering kiss. His tongue hadn't touched me at all, but I could recall the warmth of his breath and the soft texture of his lips as it touched my most intimate body part, giving me an electrical jolt. He'd only given me that special kiss once, and I'd yearned for him to repeat the gesture ever since. Only I wanted him to kiss me longer, more passionately, and much deeper.

Touching myself, I gazed at the clock. Only forty minutes before Habib got off from work. I was eager to feel the thrill of oral sex and I hoped Habib was as good as Eddie seemed to be. My body ached for it and I didn't want to be disappointed by reluctant lips or an inexperienced tongue. I hoped Habib performed with the same enthusiasm that Eddie had while eating Wanda's pussy.

I showered, sprayed on my favorite cologne and put on a childishly frilly nightdress. I would have preferred slipping on something sexy, but Mr. Lord forbade me to dress like a whore, and I only owned two-piece pajamas and boring nighties. But now that I was on my own, I could wear whatever I wanted. *Tomorrow, I'll go shopping for provocative lingerie*, I thought with a wicked smile.

I poured wine into a paper cup. Sipping Moscato, I noted that wineglasses had to be added to the growing list of items I needed for my apartment.

The doorbell rang and I rushed to open it.

"You look pretty," Habib said.

"Thanks. Would you like some wine?"

He frowned. "No, thanks; I don't drink."

"Oh." I shrugged and took another sip, enjoying the warm feeling that was flowing through me. "I guess we should go to the bedroom."

"You don't beat around the bush," Habib said with a smile.

"I'm trying to make up for a lot of lost time."

He put his arm around me as we walked to the bedroom, but I didn't have romantic feelings for him. I wanted a thick erection pulsing inside of me, but more than that, I wanted an enthusiastic tongue to bring me to a shuddering orgasm. Once again, images of Eddie and Wanda popped into my mind.

Feeling hot and bothered, I turned to Habib. He bent down and captured my mouth. Still reflecting on the hot sex scene I'd witnessed today, I opened my lips to Habib, kissing him with a mouth that was hungry and demanding.

"You taste sweet," he whispered in my ear as his lips brushed along my jawbone and down to my neck. I wanted him to go much lower, but he stopped kissing me as he focused on slipping his hands beneath the hem of my nightdress, and cupping my ass.

Pressed close to him, I could feel his hardness and I began groping at the front of his pants, my fingers moving swiftly to unclasp his belt. Habib pulled his shirt over his head and tossed it on the floor. He unzipped his pants and shoved them down. Following his lead, I shed my frilly gown and let it float down to the floor and settle next to his shirt.

Habib kissed me again while smoothing his hands over my curves. His naked body pressed against mine felt good. We were close to the same height and I could feel the heat of his erection pushing against my creamy center. Excited, I ran my hands down the length of his back.

The ache between my legs was agonizing. "Fuck me, Habib; fuck me now," I urged, thrilled by the freedom of speaking openly in such a vulgar manner.

Holding his dick, I guided him to my slick opening, and this time he slid in easily. Habib began speaking in his own language. I didn't understand a word he said but judging by the tone, I knew that he was enjoying the feeling. It seemed like a perfect time to make my request.

"Habib?"

"Yes," he said in a raspy moan.

"Do you like oral sex?"

He stopped moving and looked at me oddly. "If you want to, I don't mind. Do you want me to wash myself off?"

I frowned. "No, that's not want I meant."

"I don't understand."

"What I'm asking is if you'd put your mouth on me. You know, down there."

He looked at me with horror in his eyes. "I can't do that. It's filthy; my religion forbids it!"

"But it's okay if I do it to you?"

"I would never force you to take me inside your mouth."

"But you wouldn't turn it down," I said, nudging him and squirming away from him.

"Please, Fonia. Don't be upset with me. I'm very religious."

"I'm disappointed, Habib. I can't pretend that I'm not."

"Let's finish what we started. Let me take your mind off of oral sex. It's not a nice thing for a young lady to think about."

I sat up and sighed. "I really want it, Habib, and if you won't do it, I'll have to find someone who will."

"But if you don't finish me off, I'll get blue balls."

"Sorry, Habib. I'm not in the mood anymore." I eased off the bed and stooped to get his shirt.

"Fonia, it's not that I don't want to. It's my religion. I'm not allowed to."

I tossed him his shirt and pants. "Please leave, Habib. I'm really not in the mood anymore."

Looking forlorn, he dressed. I walked him to the door. "Can I call you tomorrow?" he asked. He looked at me with large, sad, puppy dog eyes.

I shook my head. "I know what I want and you won't do it; there's no point in wasting each other's time."

Habib left and I locked the door. Back in my bedroom, I stimulated myself with my fingers. I'd been a very bad girl today and if Mr. Lord knew how whorishly I'd been behaving, he'd spank me until my bottom was numb. The very thought of a severe spanking caused my heart to race. I imagined Mr. Lord kissing me tenderly after spanking me, and then soothing me by lodging a warm tongue inside my pussy. I moaned and writhed on my finger as pleasure began to build to a nearly unendurable peak. As if a dam had broken open, my body vibrated with sensations.

"Ahh!" I cried out as orgasmic spasms rocked my body so hard, I nearly fell off the bed.

JAGUAR

After being relieved, cleaned, and rubbed down with body oil by Lilliana, the butler knocked on the door and informed me that it was time to begin my bartending duties.

My first two customers were masked, shirtless men wearing only loincloth that was made from what appeared to be soft calfskin. One had dark hair and the other's hair was pale blond. They looked like gladiators...very buff...very tan with muscles that glimmered from sparkled body oil.

"Evening, sir, Mistress would like a Bloody Mary," said the light-haired man, whose bronzed body starkly contrasted his pale hair. He spoke with a foreign accent that I couldn't make out. Russian, maybe, but I wasn't sure.

"Coming right up," I said and then acknowledged his dark-haired counterpart. "What would you like?"

"Master is having a glass of cognac, sir. He only drinks Rémy Martin XO." Looking behind me, he scanned the shelves.

"I have it," I reassured him, turning and reaching for the bottle.

"Good! Master will be pleased," the dark-haired guy commented in a deep voice. There was nothing the least bit feminine about either guy, and even if one of them was the sex toy for a male, sexual dominant, it was none of my business. I was there to mix drinks, not to judge anyone.

At least I didn't want to judge anyone, but working around half-naked, muscle-bound dudes was a little disconcerting. They were super polite and seemed perfectly normal, except for the loincloth, which I found distracting.

Intent on keeping my eyes focused on their faces and not the fabric that covered their groins, I poured the cognac and set it on a small, silver tray. But when the pale-haired man picked up the tray, and turned to leave, my gaze shifted downward—by accident— and I got an eyeful of muscled man-ass. I wasn't very happy about that.

Busy mixing a Bloody Mary, I noticed three young ladies approach the bar. All three were masked and dressed in sheer lingerie similar to Lilliana's. "I'll be with you in one minute," I said, stealing glances at them.

Through the sheer fabric they wore, I was able to view three different sets of breasts, and a swift southward glance revealed a variety of shaven pussies. Thanks to Lilliana's administrations, I could enjoy the view without the discomfort of an erection. My dick wasn't dead; it pulsed in response to the trio of bare pussies, but it didn't go berserk, tenting my pants or oozing pre-ejaculate.

The atmosphere was calm with soft jazz playing in the background. Unlike The Dive, there were no yelling or boisterous arguments. Everyone was in a pleasant mood—all smiles—as if being the personal property of another person was a great honor.

The girls chatted softly among themselves while they patiently waited to place their orders. I wasn't trying to eavesdrop, but being in such close proximity, I couldn't help catching bits and pieces of conversations that seemed to be focused on their Mistress's or Master's likes and dislikes.

Replete with a stalk of celery, I gave the Russian guy the Bloody Mary and when he walked away, I kept my eyes fastened on the faces of the girls.

This was a pleasant bunch of people. No one appeared to be the crazed, sexual deviants that I imagined would be in attendance. Not only were they polite and easygoing, they all spoke to me respectfully, referring to me as "sir," and making me feel somewhat uncomfortable and important at the same time.

"Master would like a double shot of Grand Marnier," one masked beauty said, and I detected a French accent.

"And you?" I asked an Asian chick who stood in the middle of the other two. She spoke perfect English, but I could see the slant of her eyes through the eyeholes in the mask.

"Mistress would like a vodka and tonic," she said.

There were French and German accents and an Asian female. This was like the freaky version of the United Nations, I noted.

The third girl had a Southern accent, and she ordered white wine for her mistress.

So far, the group that I'd served were all extremely friendly and cheerful...almost giddy with joy. Perhaps the members of the secret sex society were on to something. Maybe choosing to live out your most bizarre fantasy with a consenting adult was the key to happiness.

After about an hour, I had gotten comfortable behind the bar and had gotten a groove going as I mixed drinks that were elaborately garnished with curled lemon and peelings, and skewered fruit.

So far, my impression of the party was that it was pleasantly bizarre. I had yet to see any of the Masters and Mistresses. I supposed the dominants didn't have to be bothered with ordering or carrying their own drinks when they had a house full of willing servants to do their bidding.

Making sure the bar top remained glossy and clean, I wiped it down for the umpteenth time. My head lowered, I rubbed the wood briskly, bringing it to a brilliant shine. As I toiled, I caught a glimpse of a shadow, and then a reflection appeared in the polished wood. Startled, I jerked my head up and found myself staring into the intense, ebony eyes of an ebony-hued woman.

A black leather mask, trimmed in black lace, concealed the upper part of her face. What I could see—gleaming dark eyes and bright red lips—was very attractive. The mask matched her dramatic leather and lace bodysuit. Thigh-high stiletto boots completed the dramatic look that displayed a firm body with curves in all the right places.

Judging from her attire and the quiet strength she exuded, this woman was a dominatrix—possibly the hostess of tonight's event.

"Good evening, Miss." I'd never interacted with a dominatrix before. Mildly amused by the participants of what seemed to be a costume party, a slight smile played at the corners of my mouth.

"Good evening, *Madam*," she corrected sternly.

Inwardly, I balked at addressing her as Madam, but decided that a little role-playing wouldn't kill me. "Good evening, Madam," I said politely.

"You must be Jaguar." She had a deep voice for a woman. The husky quality was tantalizing. More than likely, a very attractive face was obscured by the mask, and though her lean, toned body appeared youthful, I suspected her physique was crafted from long hours at the gym or working with a personal trainer. Something in her voice and in her eyes spoke of a mature woman—someone in her mid- to late-forties—maybe early fifties. Someone who, over time, had grown accustomed to giving orders.

"Yes, ma'am, I'm Jaguar Jackson," I responded respectfully.

"I'm Madam Midnight," she said, extending her hand

as she sized me up with an appreciative glint in her eyes. "How do you like my party, so far?"

"Very nice. It's different, that's for sure," I added with a chuckle. "Your guests appear to be having a good time."

"My guests?"

"Uh, yes. The guests who've been ordering the drinks tonight."

"They're not guests...they're servants. Like Lilliana." She fell quiet, monitoring my reaction. Under the scrutiny of her penetrating gaze, I could feel my face flush.

"Did Lilliana take care of your needs sufficiently?" she asked.

"Uh, yes, she did. Quite sufficiently," I added with more nervous laughter.

She didn't return the laughter. She didn't crack a smile. Maintaining a serious expression, Madam Midnight stared at me as if my response had been rude and disrespectful.

I wiped the smile off my face and mirrored her somber demeanor. "Lilliana was an unexpected treat. Thank you, Miss...I mean, Madam."

It's unusual for me to stumble over my words or to become visibly flustered, but due to the nature of the conversation, I couldn't help it. There was no respectful way of saying, *Thanks to your servant girl's mad, jack-off skills. I unloaded a half-gallon of backed-up cum.*

Madam Midnight turned slightly and beckoned someone. With her chin raised and her head held high, she was regal and utterly commanding. In an instant, the butler stepped into the bar area. He bowed as if to a queen.

"At your service, Madam," the butler said, his gloved hands folded in front of him.

"Make sure that the bartender gets his break at the appointed time. I think he'll be comfortable in the solarium."

"Yes, Madam," the butler replied.

"That'll be all," she said and shooed the butler away with a dismissive gesture.

She returned her attention to me. "You seem to be working out. I'll let you know if I'll require your services after tonight. Now, if you'll excuse me, I have to get back to my guests." She turned around and took a few steps, and then stopped. "By the way, during your break, feel free to sample some of the hors d'oeuvres that are being served. Or…if you'd like, you can sample another servant." She gave a wry smile and strode out of the room.

En route to the solarium, the butler guided me along a long corridor. We passed a number of rooms with closed doors. Interestingly, those doors were painted in various colors: gold, purple, bronze, metallic blue. As we approached the room at the far end of the hall, I noticed that the rust-colored door had been left ajar. A gruff male voice could be heard.

"Kiss it," the man inside the room implored. His command was followed by a woman's pitiful sobs.

Curious to see what was going on, I slowed my stride and peeked inside the room. A masked man dressed in black spandex pants and vest made of linked chains was wielding a paddle while a servant girl was bent over a bench with her enflamed and welted buttocks exposed. The man whacked her across the ass so hard, her svelte body lurched forward.

"Kiss it!" he demanded, bringing the wood paddle close to the lips of the weeping girl. Crying softly, the servant kissed the instrument of torture.

It's a normal, human response to try to help someone in distress, and I impulsively stalked across the threshold of the room, prepared to defend the damsel in the distress. The butler caught me by the arm. "This is no concern of yours. Everything that occurs at Madam's parties is strictly consensual."

The brute wearing the chain vest glowered at me, and whacked the girl even harder. Again, he implored her to kiss the paddle. Whimpering and sniffling, she complied.

Scowling and shaking my head in bewilderment, I reluctantly walked alongside the butler as we made our way to the solarium. "There's no way that girl was enjoying herself. There's nothing sexy about getting the crap beat out of you," I groused.

"You'd be surprised by the multitude of people that have embraced S&M and have discovered the pleasure in pain."

"That's crazy," I said tersely. "That girl wasn't discovering pleasure. There was fear in her eyes and she was crying from the pain and humiliation."

"She was crying tears of joy," the butler said. "For a masochist, physical punishment is a powerful aphrodisiac. Couple that with humiliation and it's the ultimate erotic adventure," he explained.

I responded with an excessive frown.

We reached the solarium, which was a moderately sized, oblong room, and the butler gestured for me to take a seat on a velvet couch that was bordered by huge, potted plants.

"Food and libations will be served shortly."

I nodded, but food and drink were the last things on my mind. I wanted a better understanding of what made these weirdoes tick. "If the beat-freak was giving that girl pleasure, why was she crying?" I asked again.

He gave a wry smile. "Receiving an invitation to serve at one of Madam's parties is considered an honor. The servant that you witnessed being spanked—"

"Spanked? I wouldn't call that a spanking. That was an ass-whooping—a beat down," I interjected passionately.

"I've been Madam's butler and confidante for many years, and I know that the young servant has been waiting for several months for the privilege of being disciplined by a Master Dominant. I can guarantee that she'll be angling to get an invitation to the next event."

I found that hard to believe. "Oh, well…to each his own," I said in a nonchalant tone of voice, but inside I felt contaminated by having witnessed the brutal scene. I thought about Lilliana and the numerous servants that had ordered drinks from the bar. They'd all seemed like such a cheerful group, their eyes wide with excitement and anticipation. I couldn't imagine any of them suffering at the hands of a crazed sadist.

In my mind, all the participants, including Lilliana and Madam Midnight had been merely role-playing, and having harmless fun. But I now realized that there was a much darker side to this gathering.

I'm no saint. I've done my share of ass smacking and hair pulling during the throes of passion, but to beat the shit of somebody for sexual gratification seemed insane, and the debauchery I'd witnessed made my stomach churn.

I briefly considered retrieving my shirt and walking off the job. But I was out in the boonies with no way of getting back to civilization until the cab driver returned to pick me up after midnight.

Somehow, I'd have to get through the rest of the night, tending bar for a party full of lunatics. I knew one thing for certain: the chain-wearing sadist would be wise to stay away from the bar area. There was no telling how I'd react if I saw him face-to-face. It would be interesting to see how much of a tough guy he'd be if he had to go up against me. I've got skills. Spent most of my life brawling. With my fists as well as gunfights.

The sound of heels clicking against the floor sounded

in the distance. "Your food has arrived. Enjoy your meal." The butler bowed slightly and exited the solarium.

Wearing a shy smile, Lilliana entered the room, carrying a tray of fancy finger foods. Beside her, another young lady dressed similarly was also balancing a tray.

"Here you are, sir." Lilliana spoke sweetly and her eyes radiated joy. A part of me had feared that she'd been the girl bent over the sadist's bench, and it was a relief to see her looking cheerful and well.

"Thank you," I muttered, though I had no appetite.

"It's my pleasure," she replied, and then glanced at the other servant, a petite, waif-like young woman. "This is Madilyn. We're both here to cater to your desires."

I nodded, acknowledging Madilyn, and then glanced at Lilliana. "Thanks, but I'm good; I don't need anything."

"All right, we'll leave you in private."

I had grown weary of this fantasy world where nothing was as it appeared…everyone was pretending. My thoughts turned to Fonia. I hadn't gotten to know her, and yet I missed her. In this environment of decadence and debauchery, someone as innocent as she appeared would be like a breath of fresh air.

I never touched the food that was beautifully displayed and smelled delicious, and when the butler suddenly materialized, he glanced at the uneaten hors d'oeuvres.

"Wasn't hungry," I explained.

"I've come to escort you back to the bar," he said.

I could have found my way back, but I suppose the

hostess didn't want me wandering around unsupervised and possibly stumbling upon other acts of depravity.

The rest of the evening was uneventful. Somehow, I managed to keep a smile plastered on my face while I mixed drinks. I didn't see Madam Midnight again nor did I see the masked sadist that deserved the same ass kicking he had delivered to that helpless woman.

The butler gave me a thick, black envelope. The silver seal on the back was scripted with double MM's for Madam Midnight. The hostess was really into her pseudonym.

In a somber mood, I settled in the back of the cab. I broke the seal and peeked inside the envelope. I was surprised to see an impressive stack of hundred-dollar bills. I'd expected to earn a thousand, but I suppose the hostess thought I deserved a generous bonus. As badly as I needed extra cash, the money didn't lift my spirits. Oddly, the crisp bills made me feel worse. I was relieved that neither Madam nor the butler had spoken to me about working any parties in the future.

I wondered how Sharif was able to tolerate such an insane, make-believe world. Big bucks or not, I doubted if I'd accept any more alternative-lifestyle gigs. Clearly, I didn't have the stomach for it.

Times like this, it would have been nice to have someone to go home to. Again, I thought of Fonia. I thought about her expression when her phone had vibrated in her purse. Something scared her. Something caused her to run away from me, and I wished I knew how to find her.

FONIA

I'd had a productive morning. I picked up groceries, bought cookware and other badly needed household items. I needed a lot more before I'd be comfortable in my new place, but at least I could finally prepare the kinds of meals I was accustomed to eating. After gorging on pizzas, hoagies, cheesesteaks, burgers, and fries for the past week, I had fulfilled my desire for greasy food. I'd probably gag if I tried to eat any more of that garbage.

One of the many things I'd left back at the townhouse that I really missed was my treadmill. Though my new apartment complex had a fitness center, I hadn't gotten around to checking it out. There was also a hospitality room where residents got together for meet and greets. I'd been receiving flyers in my mailbox, announcing the Thursday night mixers, but I had no desire to get familiar with my neighbors. Keeping to myself and not socializing with neighbors was something that had been instilled in me by Mr. Lord, and old habits were hard to break.

My body was screaming for a workout and so I changed

into a pair of shorts and a tank top. The fitness center was in Building G, which was quite a hike from my building, but I walked in the hot summer sun instead of driving, trying to make up for all the overeating and the sedentary lifestyle I'd adopted. With my favorite music queued up on my iPod and toting a chilled container of Fiji water, I was mentally prepared to work out for at least two hours.

The extremely small and modest fitness center was a disappointment. There were only two outdated treadmills and both were occupied. At the townhouse, I had a high-end treadmill with a personal screen and a virtual trainer that talked me through the workout. Or I could watch movies or play a game of solitaire while listening to my playlist.

I glimpsed at the two women using the treadmills, trying to determine if they were nearing the end of their workouts. One woman was grimacing with her eyes closed as she trotted along, gripping the handrails. I was inclined to ask her if she'd be at it for much longer, but that seemed rude. The other woman had a yellow towel draped around her neck and was moving at a leisurely pace. With headphones hugging her ears, she had a look of contentment on her face, and I doubted if she'd be getting off the treadmill any time soon.

I glanced around to see if there were any other cardio machines— a spin bike perhaps—or some other tech-savvy equipment. But there were only odd-looking, rusty pieces of equipment crammed into the sad, little room. I also noticed a paltry set of free weights, exercise balls, and a few mats for yoga or Pilates, none of which interested me in the least.

Obviously, I'd have to dip into my savings and invest in a new treadmill. I opened the door to leave and bumped into a slim, brown-skinned guy who was entering. He was wearing oversized glasses, a beige tee with the dark brown logo of the apartment complex, and a pair of khakis.

"Hi, are you a new resident?"

"Yes."

"Welcome, my name is Wyatt, and I sort of oversee the fitness center."

"My name is Fonia," I replied.

"Did you sign in?" he asked, glancing toward a clip-board that dangled from a hook on the wall.

"No, I'm not staying. I wanted to use the treadmill, but…" Nodding toward the two women that were using the treadmills, I allowed my voice to trail off.

"If you can wait about ten minutes, one of the machines will be free." He pointed to the woman with the towel draped around her neck. "Janice always leaves at around one-thirty."

"Hmm," I uttered as I thought about it.

"You can kill time with the exercise ball."

I frowned. "I don't even know what to do with an exercise ball."

"I can show you some exercises."

"No, thanks," I said with a frown.

"How about the glute machine?" He gestured toward a complicated apparatus. "It strengthens your butt muscles," Wyatt said with a little laugh. "If you'd like, I can show how to use it."

"That's okay. I'll come back some other time," I lied. I had no intention of ever returning to the dreary fitness center.

"I'm trying to keep you here, but I'm running out of ideas." He smiled at me and I realized he was flirting with me. I looked beyond those big, geek-chic glasses he wore, and noticed that he wasn't bad-looking. And he had an appealing sense of confidence.

It seemed that the moment I decided that he was somewhat attractive, I also became aware of my vagina. It hadn't gotten overly moist nor was it throbbing, but there was this dull, persistent ache that required attention. I don't know if I gave off a sudden whiff of pheromones that indicated my desire for sex or if the hunger between my legs was apparent in my eyes, but somehow Wyatt knew that I wanted to fuck.

"There's, uh, like a utility room we could use," he said, nodding toward a door behind the rack of weights.

As if in a dream state, I followed Wyatt to the utility room and slipped in behind him. I didn't care if the two women on the treadmills were watching us or not. The utility room was actually the size of a broom closet. Very claustrophobic. But I was too horny to care about the tight fit.

Wyatt took off his glasses and perched them on an overhead shelf. As he began to undo his pants, I pulled down my shorts.

"Can I get some head?" he asked, holding his dick in his hand.

I'd never done it, but I had the desire to learn. If it was as good as sucking Mr. Lord's finger had been, I was sure I'd like doing it. Agreeing to suck his dick, I nodded. He urged me to stoop down by pressing down on my shoulders.

Kneeling on the grimy floor, I felt like a dirty slut. With a sense of wanton, whorishness, that was completely liberating, I took his dick inside my mouth and sucked it. Enjoying the smooth flesh, and completely captivated by the hardness that filled my mouth, I moaned with pleasure. I was astonished at how good it was to have a stiff dick gliding back and forth over my tongue. Sucking a finger could not compare to this euphoria.

"Aw, yeah, you're a good, dick-sucking bitch," he groaned, one hand gripping my shoulder and the other tugging on my ponytail. Aroused by his coarse words, and the mild pain he inflicted with the hair pulling, I pulled him in deeper. So deep, I could feel myself beginning to gag, but I kept going, tightening my lips around his length, licking the salty moisture that trickled from the head of his dick.

"I'm about to cum," he warned, pulling out. I would have felt deprived had he not instantly yanked me off my knees, filling my pussy with the hardness that had been in my mouth. Standing upright, I was backed into a wall inside the tight confines of the closet. My shorts were wrapped around my ankles, but I was able to kick them off when he lifted one of my legs and plunged deeply inside me, giving my pussy hard thrusts that soothed the ache.

A large, smelly industrial mop stood upright, next to my head. As Wyatt plowed into me, the filthy mop strands brushed against my face. For some strange reason, this added to my arousal, and my pussy clutched his dick possessively as I climaxed. I came hard, letting out a long moan while my body shuddered.

"You get yours, baby?" he questioned in a gruff whisper.

The orgasm was so intense, I couldn't articulate with words. I nodded my head and murmured a barely audible, "Mmm-hmm."

After a few more thrusts, I felt the wet heat of his ejaculation, which stimulated my pussy into yet another orgasm. Even though I still hadn't experienced getting my pussy eaten, getting two strong orgasms back to back was completely satisfying.

Without a doubt, dirty sex was the best!

FONIA

I ordered a state-of-the-art treadmill with a fifteen-inch personal viewing screen and entertainment controls integrated into the display. Trouble was, I needed someone to assemble it. I figured Wyatt could help me out.

Since our tryst in the closet, we hadn't gotten together again. I wanted to, but he kept giving me excuses. He finally admitted to being in a relationship. He said his girl picked him up from work and the only free time he had for sex-on-the-side was while he was at work.

"Do we have to use the closet again?" I had asked.

"That's the only private place."

"But it's not all that private."

I would have agreed to meeting back up at the fitness center and even going back into the utility closet if he could have assured me that we'd have the place to ourselves, but he couldn't. I dreaded seeing those same two women that had been on the treadmills.

That day at the fitness center, Wyatt and I had emerged from the closet, adjusting our clothes. Shame washed over me when the two women looked at me scornfully, shaking their heads in disgust. The one with the towel wrapped around her neck hadn't left at one-thirty after all. She glared at me and turned up her nose as if something stank. I'd had urgent, steamy sex in a broom closet and I deserved every bit of their disdain.

As badly as I wanted to get together with Wyatt, I couldn't deal with the scornful looks from the residents using the gym.

"I can't put together a treadmill," Wyatt said. "I'm a cerebral-type guy; I'm not good with my hands."

"Don't you maintain the equipment at the fitness center?"

"I disinfect and wipe the equipment down, but if something breaks, I call the manufacturer."

"Darn."

"But I have a friend who's pretty handy; I'll give him a call and get back to you."

"Okay, thanks. Let your friend know that I'll be happy to pay him for the labor," I said.

Wyatt and I hung up and I absently watched TV while waiting to hear from him. Call it a sixth sense or instinct, but something made me rise from the sofa and peer out my kitchen window. A black Town Car was parked across the street, and though I couldn't see the driver through the tinted windows, I had the distinct feeling that Mr. Lord was in the back seat, staring at my apartment.

Panicked, I shut the blinds tightly and backed away from the window. Although his honeymoon was over, he should have been busy getting into a comfortable routine with his new bride. My imagination was running wild, I told myself. Between running a business and dealing with a new marriage, how would he have the time to hunt me down and spy on me?

My cell phone rang. Jolted by the sudden sound, I nearly jumped out of my skin. Even though I had a new number, I wouldn't have been surprised if Mr. Lord had found a way to get the information. I breathed a sigh of relief when I saw Wyatt's name on the screen.

"I gave my friend, Aaron, your phone number. He says he can put the treadmill together for you, and you can pay him with a six-pack of Guinness."

"Really?"

"Yeah, I told him you were a special friend of mine. So, he's doing it as a favor to me."

"That's so sweet of you, Wyatt." Another call came through…a private number. I instantly became worried, thinking Mr. Lord was calling me with a blocked number. "Hold on, I have another call."

"It's probably Aaron," Wyatt said. "Go ahead and set it up; I'll talk to you later."

"Wait," I said suddenly. "Can you get away from your girlfriend…like…tomorrow night, maybe?" The feeling that Mr. Lord was watching me had me nervous and tense. I could use some company and a firm dick to calm my nerves.

"I'll have to get back to you on that," Wyatt said. After we disconnected, I switched over to his friend, Aaron.

Aaron had a nice voice. Deep and masculine. He asked for my address and as I rattled it off, I held the hope that Aaron appealed to me in a way that would inspire me to give him a lot more than a six-pack of beer.

Since losing my virginity, my sex drive seemed to be out of control. And the desire for sex wasn't only in my mind. I had physical reactions to the oddest stimuli. Earlier today when my treadmill was delivered, my hand accidentally touched the delivery guy's fingers and my nipples instantly stiffened. It took all my willpower not to drag him into my bedroom and rip his uniform off. Oddly, I barely looked at his face, and can't even recall what he looked like.

Another strange moment happened when I thought Mr. Lord was watching me from the parked Town Car. The fear of being discovered by him made my heart race erratically, but that same fear also caused my pussy to pulsate with desire.

There seems to be a constant flame between my legs that needs to be extinguished. I've become obsessed with sex, and I fear that I'm a nympho. If I keep having sex with strangers, I may need to talk to a shrink.

The doorbell rang and all my worries of being a nympho went out the window. *This will be my last random sex act*, I told myself, deciding that I would fuck Aaron whether I was attracted to him or not. I had to; my pussy was on fire. And while I was in this severe state of heat, no one with a dick was leaving my apartment without sharing it with me.

I took a deep breath before opening the door, hoping that Aaron didn't turn out to be gay. A gay friend would be okay after I got my desperate, sexual situation under control, but right now, I only wanted to deal with men that enjoyed having sex with a woman.

I opened the door and to my surprise, Wyatt was in my doorway with his friend, Aaron. I was thrilled to see him. Imagining the sex session that was going to transpire between Wyatt and me, I nearly cried with joy.

Wyatt looked me over and smiled appreciatively. I was wearing a ruffled skirt and clingy pink top that gave me a more girly look than I'd had when we first met at the fitness center.

Wyatt introduced Aaron and me and I noticed that Aaron seemed timid; he kept his eyes down and was very quiet. Wyatt did all the talking as he and Aaron carried the large box that contained the treadmill into my bedroom.

Aaron wasn't ugly and he wasn't cute. He was nondescript, and luckily, I didn't have to rely on him to fulfill my needs. He was really quiet and a little creepy. My plan was to leave Aaron in the bedroom working on the treadmill while Wyatt took care of me in the living room.

"Did you get the beer?" Wyatt called from the bedroom.

"Yes, do you want it now?"

"Yeah, bring us a couple of beers. Aaron works better when he has a buzz."

"Okay," I replied. But instead of grabbing two beers, I only grabbed one. In the bedroom, I handed Aaron a bottle of beer.

"Where's mine?" Wyatt asked.

My whole body was thrumming in anticipation of the delicious sensations that would take the place of the perpetual yearning that burned between my thighs. Wearing a sneaky smile, I crooked my finger.

He knew what I wanted. He could see the look in my eyes. "I'll be right back, man," he told Aaron.

As soon as he came out into the hallway, I entwined my arms around his neck and kissed him—a slow deep kiss that told him exactly what I needed. He worked his hands beneath my top, fondling my sensitive breasts. His mouth and his heated touch stole my breath, making me nearly delirious with desire as he guided me back to the living room without breaking the sensual kiss.

In my small apartment, his friend could probably hear our breathy moans and gasps, and though I'd probably be embarrassed later, I was too caught up in the moment to care.

I shed my top and collapsed onto the couch. Wyatt fell on top me. "I missed you so much," he said in a rough voice, his hands brushing over my face, my neck, my shoulders, and then resting on my breasts. "Pretty titties," he murmured with his lips puckered around my one nipple and then the other, his tongue stroking the pebbled flesh, making me gasp and ache for him.

I wanted to feel his hard dick pushing past my lips again, while at the same time, I wanted my pussy to be filled with the heat of his erection.

I ran my hand between our bodies, grasping the bulge inside his pants, and I moaned with yearning. With shaking hands, I quickly unzipped his pants and squeezed his dick; which had grown hot and hard inside my palm. Wyatt didn't have to ask me to go down on him. I knew what he wanted and was more than willing to give.

I scooted down to the floor and guided his dick to my open lips. A harsh moan escaped him the moment my tongue swiped against his stiffened dick. I took him inside my mouth, in small increments, first the head and then an inch of throbbing shaft. With the tip of my tongue, I teased along the seam of his dick, and then licked him up and down with the full width of my tongue.

"Damn, girl. You trying to drive me crazy?"

I sucked him in deeper and I became lost in the thrill of giving, and his throaty moans told me he was enjoying every moment of the thorough tongue lashing he was receiving.

The sound of the fridge opening startled me and I went still, my jaws slackening.

"Don't stop, baby. That's only Aaron getting another beer. Keep sucking, baby. Don't stop," Wyatt urged, stroking my hair.

But I felt self-conscious. "Wait until he goes back in the bedroom," I whispered, hiding my embarrassment at being caught by burying my face in Wyatt's crotch.

I heard the fridge door close and waited to hear Aaron's retreating footsteps. But I didn't hear a sound. The kitchen was only a few feet from the living room and Aaron had a bird's eye view of me crouched between his friend's legs.

"Let him watch," Wyatt whispered. "Let him see how much you love sucking dick." Wyatt gripped his dick and stroked it. He lifted my chin that was resting on his thigh. "Here, baby. Open your mouth and suck this," he murmured, brushing the smooth crown against my lips.

The shame of knowing Aaron was watching sent that familiar heat of arousal coursing through me and I obediently parted my lips.

"You want this good dick, don't you?" Wyatt asked with his hands clamped against the sides of my head.

"Mmm-hmm," I responded, humiliated that his friend could hear and observe.

"Suck it the way you did the other day."

The gruffness of his voice, the crude way he spoke to me reminded me of Mr. Lord, and my vagina clenched tight with need. I wanted to suck his dick until his ejaculation splashed inside my mouth. I wanted to go wild and act like a whore.

I tried to participate fully, tried to bob my head up and down, but he held my head between his vise-like grip, and said, "Stop sucking. All you need to do is open up and let me do the fucking."

Obediently, I opened my mouth for him. He proceeded to ram my mouth with his dick. Plunging so deeply, I gagged painfully, and my eyes watered as he determinedly shoved hard dick down my throat. Finally, he withdrew his shaft that was slick with my saliva.

Breathing harshly, his chest heaving up and down, Wyatt said, "Time out; I gotta catch my breath."

"Nooo," I moaned, trying to retrieve his dick. I wanted more lust, more painful thrusts, and more humiliation.

An empty beer bottle rattled as it was tossed inside the recycle bin and I jerked my head toward the sound. Aaron began to slowly advance toward the living room and the look in his eyes frightened me. "Why is he coming in here? Tell him to go back in the kitchen!" I said, wrapping my arms around Wyatt's waist, trying to hold onto him in case his friend intended to throw me down on the floor and have his way with me.

"Aaron's cool; it's all good," Wyatt said, smoothing my hair.

I was crouched on the floor with my back to Aaron, but I could feel his creepy presence; I could hear his lustful breathing. "Oh, my God!" I shouted. "What's he doing; make him get out of here!"

"It's cool, baby. Take your skirt off for Aaron. He just wants to see your pussy. Right, man?" Wyatt said, looking at Aaron.

I was mortified but my body was on fire. A prisoner of my own desire, I rose to my feet and allowed Wyatt to pull my skirt down.

"Take off your panties."

I shuddered as I rolled pink silk over my thighs.

"She's got a pretty ass," Aaron said, still standing behind.

"She has a pretty pussy, too," Wyatt added. "Turn around, Fonia. Show Aaron your pussy."

My skirt and panties were on the floor, and I was standing naked in front of two men. My face was hot with humiliation, and my vagina enflamed. I turned slowly and when I faced Aaron, he dropped to his knees so suddenly, I flinched.

"Give it to him," Wyatt ordered.

"Give him what?" I asked, looking over my shoulder at Wyatt. He bent down and from behind, he reached around and separated my pussy lips, spreading me open and exposing my throbbing clit to Aaron.

While Wyatt held my pussy open, Aaron scooted forward and circled my clit with his tongue. I gave a sharp intake of breath at the first touch of his tongue.

Electrical jolts seemed to hit me from every angle as Aaron took my hardened nub between his soft lips. He alternated between licking and sucking my clit, and audibly lapped at my juices that ran down Wyatt's fingers. The pleasure was so intense, my knees began to buckle. I became so far gone with need, I pushed Wyatt's hands away, and spread my thighs wide for Aaron.

"She wants you to get inside that pussy hole," Wyatt said, expressing my desires precisely.

Giving me what I wanted, Aaron's tongue traveled from

my engorged clit to the slippery entrance of my pussy, and then thrust inside me. Feeling a warm, thick tongue burrowing into that sensitized area was beyond anything I had imagined. He lapped at me, licking with slow, torturous strokes, making me writhe and cry out in passion.

"It's my turn, man," Wyatt said, possessively pulling me away from Aaron. I didn't want to be separated from Aaron's tender tongue, but the moment Wyatt inserted his rock-hard dick, I released a blissful sigh.

Wyatt had me on the floor, lying on my back while he fucked me. My eyes fluttered opened and I caught a glimpse of Aaron, eyeing Wyatt and me as he unzipped his pants and fondled his dick.

"Mmm," I moaned loudly as I observed Aaron stroking himself. His dick was incredibly long and thick. My hips rose off the floor and wound in frantic circles. While Wyatt fucked me, I couldn't help wondering how it would feel to have Aaron embedded inside me.

I got the answer a few minutes later when Wyatt came with a howl and rolled off me.

Aaron didn't waste any time, pulling me to my knees and taking me from behind. I could feel Wyatt's hot cum spilling down my thighs as Aaron eased in and out of me, slowly and deeply, hitting a spot that I didn't know existed. A spot so sensitive, my legs shook uncontrollably. I shouted, shed tears, and then collapsed in ecstasy.

JAGUAR

The money I earned at the S&M party increased my savings to seventy-five hundred—money I should have put toward paying down my debt, but in desperate need of transportation, I went to the auction and bought a Jeep Grand Cherokee. And I spent even more money getting the truck detailed. I got it waxed to a high-shine that made it look brand-new.

Down to my last two hundred dollars, I went to work realizing that I needed all the tips I could get in order to pay my weekly rent at the hotel. I hustled hard all night at The Dive. Hustled so hard, my face hurt from smiling and laughing, and busting it up with the customers. Toward the end of the night, a glance at my tip jar, which was practically overflowing, told me that all the extra effort had paid off.

After work, when I left the bar and walked over to my shiny truck, I felt good...felt like the money had been well-spent. Then, fifteen minutes into my drive to the hotel, the joy of having reliable transportation disappeared as I was hit with an onslaught of bad memories. First, I thought about my man, Curt, who was holding on to life in a nursing home. Guilt hit me hard.

Survivor's guilt. It could have easily been me laying up in that nursing home. Curt had gotten sprayed with bullets because he'd been going faster than me and our enemies set eyes on him first.

Morose thoughts shifted from Curt to the S&M party. Since that night, I'd been haunted by the image of that poor girl getting whacked repeatedly by the sadist. Though both Sharif and the butler had told me that the party guests were living out their fantasies, I couldn't shake the feeling that something wasn't right with the scenario I had witnessed. The girl had been crying and pleading for mercy. I don't know much about masochists, but from my understanding, they relished pain. If that girl was enjoying the beat down, wouldn't she have had a crazed smile plastered on her face instead of tears? Since I had no intention of bartending another S&M event, I supposed I'd never find out.

The next morning, I got up early and drove to the nursing home. I showed my identification and signed in on the visitor's sheet. Seven years was a long time and no one seemed to remember that I'd been banned from visiting Curtis Brown. As I exited the elevator, that sickening nursing home odor started getting to me, reminding me of what a dead-end place Curt was in. This nursing home was the final stop, and I felt a strong urge to turn around and run for my life, but I pushed onward.

I made slow reluctant steps toward his room, and it dawned on me that being banned from the nursing home had been a handy excuse. I could have gone to legal aid for assistance, but I'd readily accepted being banned. Seeing my boy in that messed up condition had been hard on me. Unbearable. Getting banned had spared me from having to witness him slowly deteriorate.

I paused outside his room. Taking a deep breath, I braced myself for how badly he might have declined over the years. I stepped inside the room and covered my mouth in shock. Curt had dwindled down to skin and bones. My twenty-six-year-old friend had taken on the appearance of a wizened old man. Merely a shell of his former self; he looked barely alive.

Fun-loving and free-spirited, Curt didn't deserve to go out this way. I uncovered my mouth and ran a shaky hand over my face. It was heart-wrenching to see my boy balled up in a fetal position, with tubes running everywhere. "Hey, Curt, it's me, Jaguar," I greeted as I pulled a chair up to his bedside.

I looked around his quiet, dreary room. There was no TV, no radio. The curtains were drawn tight, making it look like early evening instead of a bright, sunny morning. It was the middle of June, yet childish Easter decorations still covered one of the walls in room. Clearly, whoever had hung those decorations had forgotten to take them down.

Sighing, I leaned toward my friend. "How you been, man?" It was a stupid question, and I was relieved that he couldn't answer. In a fake, cheerful voice, I carried on a one-sided conversation, reminiscing about the good old days, reminding him of the fun times we'd shared together. Realizing that most of our "fun" times had been spent doing something illegal or immoral, I changed the subject and told him what I'd done with my life since leaving Philly. "I'm an educated Negro. Can you believe that? Anyway, man, now that I'm back, I'll be visiting regularly."

He looked straight ahead, giving no indication that he was even aware of my presence.

The nurse came in to give him care and that was my cue to exit. I'd done my duty. Sitting in that dismal room with Curt wasn't enjoyable. In fact, it felt like some sort of punishment.

"I'll see you next week, man," I said, giving his hand a squeeze. "Stay strong," I added, not knowing what else to say to an incommunicative person.

"It was real nice of you to come see him. He never has visitors," the nurse said. "I can tell he appreciated the time you spent with him."

I peeked at Curt to see what the nurse saw, but I didn't see any changes in his expression. Bewildered, I gazed at the nurse.

"Oh, Curtis and I have a special way of communicating. It may appear that he doesn't know what's going on around him but he does."

Seven years ago, I'd felt the same way as the nurse did. But not now. It was hard to believe that my friend was inside that withered body.

"Doesn't his mom visit?" I asked the nurse.

"I've never met her. I heard that she stopped coming to visit years ago; she said seeing him in this condition made her blood pressure rise."

I shook my head. His own mother had bailed on him. "I'll be back next week," I assured the nurse. I moved toward the door and stopped. "By the way, why are those Easter decorations still up?" It bothered me that no one had bothered to put up current decorations in his gloomy room.

"Most residents have family members that decorate and brighten up their environment, but when the family isn't involved, the recreational therapy department does the decorating." The nurse nodded toward the large, colorful Easter egg that was surrounded by pictures of baby chicks. "I guess rec therapy will get around to removing those decorations when they put up Fourth of July adornments."

A rush of guilt flooded my system. My boy had been deserted by the whole world, including me. I had to do better. The least I could do was make his environment a little more cheerful.

"If you tell his social worker that you're a relative, you can request that he gets a TV and a radio for his room. There's a fee, but it's affordable. To be honest, I think part of the reason he's been declining is that he's sensory deprived."

Damn with all he'd lost, it was fucked up that he was being sensory-deprived. "What's the social worker's name?"

"Ms. Beckwith."

"Okay, I'll give her a call."

On my way to the elevator, I peered in the patients' rooms as I passed by. There were cheerful wreaths on the doors, flowers and plants on dressers. Curtains pulled back to admit sunshine. Signs that the other patients were loved and cared for.

After I left the nursing home, I sat in my truck for a moment as my eyes swam with helpless tears. I had to do better by Curt. He'd been my best friend and he should have been able to count on me. With the back of my hand, I wiped my eyes and started the engine.

I slipped up—had a sexual relapse.

I had planned to check out a new action flick that was playing on Delaware Avenue, but after visiting Curt, I was too depressed to do anything. In a somber mood, I went back to my hotel, deciding to lie around and contemplate the meaning of life before starting my shift at six.

As I approached my room, I noticed that the door was open. Rayna was inside, cleaning. "How long are you going to be?" I asked as politely as I could. I didn't want to say anything that was liable to set her off. She'd finally stopped sucking her teeth and rolling her eyes whenever she saw me, and I didn't want her to revert back to that behavior.

"I'm almost finished," she said. Surprisingly, Rayna had a pleasant tone in her voice, which I appreciated. I was too emotionally fragile after my visit with Curt to deal with her sulking and murmuring under her breath.

"What's wrong, papi? You seem a little down. Like you lost your best friend in the world."

I gave a wry laugh. "I did lose a friend."

"Wanna talk about it?" Rayna asked, closing the door.

I shook my head. The pain was too raw. Shedding a few tears alone in my car had been bad enough, but to spill my guts and expose my sensitive side in front of Rayna was out of the question.

"Do you mind if I have a drink?" Rayna pointed to the bottle of scotch on my nightstand. Hard liquor helped calm my nerves after work whenever I was too wired to sleep.

"Help yourself," I said.

"I hate drinking alone; why don't you have one with me."

I nodded and she poured liquor into two tumblers, and handed me one.

Rayna sipped slowly, but I downed my mine in a few seconds, welcoming the burn as the alcohol traveled down my throat.

She lifted the bottle. "More?"

"No, I'm good."

"Is your friend a female...did you two get into an argument?" Rayna pressed.

"No, my best friend was a dude I grew up with. He's in a bad state. Totally paralyzed and brain dead from a shooting incident."

"That's too bad," she said, taking a seat next to me on the bed and patting my thigh comfortingly.

Like they say, one thing led to another, and before I knew it, Rayna offered her lips and my lips opened over hers. Welcoming the intimate contact, which was long overdue, my hands shook with urgency as I unbuttoned the front of her uniform, running my hands over the soft skin of her shoulders and liberating her breasts from her bra.

Hungered lips sought her bare breasts. The feel of a firm nipple inside my mouth was pacifying. The longer I sucked, the harder my dick got. My body ached for a woman; I'd denied myself for too long. In that moment of heat, I convinced myself that being celibate was torturous and served no purpose whatsoever. The moist sex between Rayna's legs was the only thing that could heal me. Yes, a sexual healing was exactly what I needed.

Rayna fondled my erection. "Missed you," she murmured hoarsely, and my dick responded with visible quivers and jerks.

She came out of her uniform swiftly, and I untied my sneakers and yanked off my pants. As I pulled my shirt over my head, she stretched out on the bed and spread her ample thighs for me. Rayna was so far gone with need, she began fingering herself as she waited for me to join her.

I inhaled sharply as I watched her play in her pussy, and then suck the moisture from her finger. Wanting a taste of her flavor, I pulled her to the side of the bed and knelt before her, spreading her legs further apart.

At the first flick of my tongue against her pussy lips, she gasped in appreciation. "You got a fat pussy," I murmured lustfully as I spread her petals apart with my fingers. I lapped between those satiny lips in slow strokes that made her squeeze her eyes tight and shake her head back and forth as if the pleasure was unbearable. With my tongue embedded inside her pussy, I began thrusting it deeper, causing her hips to rise off the bed and her thighs to tremble.

"Good pussy, baby. So sweet!" I murmured between laps.

"Jag. Oh, my God, you're driving me crazy. I've been waiting so long for you to give me some more dick; I'm ready for you to fuck me," she cried in desperation as she pulled me on top of her.

Entering her slowly, I fed her dick in increments until

her pussy was filled so exquisitely, she threw her legs around me, tightly, locking my body against hers until we were sealed together, skin against skin.

"Deeper," Rayna whimpered as she thrashed, nearly delirious from desire. Each thrust seemed to send her deeper into the depths of sexual madness.

Steady and slow, I set the pace, forcing Rayna to slow down. I enjoyed watching as my dick eased in and out of her pussy. The sight heightened my arousal, prompting me to increase the speed of my stroke.

Rayna cried out, thrusting as she tightened her legs around my back. Spasms wracked her and she writhed and bucked beneath me. She clenched the sheets as she came. Moving in tandem with her, I groaned as I gave into the sensations that had been bottled up inside me.

FONIA

After that first night with Wyatt and Aaron together, we got together as a threesome twice more. Wyatt couldn't get away very often, but Aaron was single and available. The first and only time Aaron spent the entire night with me, we had sex nine times in a row. I had tried to get him aroused for the tenth time that night but my pussy lips were swollen and Aaron's dick was so raw and chafed, we had to take a break.

An ice pack brought the swelling down for me and I was eager to get started again. Trying to get him in the mood, I ran my hands over his chest, trailing lightly down to his groin. He moved my hand away. "I'm tired," he'd told me. "I have to work in the morning—gotta get some sleep."

I slept fitfully next to him. Every few hours I'd wake up and try different methods to arouse him again. Nothing worked; he slept like a rock.

The next morning, I was more than ready for a quickie before he went to work, but he rebuffed me. He covered his dick with his hands when I had attempted to give him a blowjob, claiming his sore dick needed a rest.

A sense of deep sorrow engulfed me as a watched him dressing for work. Although I didn't have genuine feelings for Aaron, I was very much attached to the pleasure-giving appendage that dangled between his legs.

"Please, Aaron, can't we do it once more?" I begged, feeling hornier than ever.

"No! I told you my dick is sore; what's wrong with you?" Muttering under his breath, Aaron dressed quickly.

"What about tonight? Can you come back tonight?" I said in a pleading voice. I didn't mind begging at all.

Annoyance flared in Aaron's eyes. "I'm not sure about tonight. I fucked you nine times last night—how much dick does it take to satisfy you?"

I didn't have an answer; all I could do was shrug.

"Wyatt told me you were a nympho; and it's true. You might want to get some help."

"You're right, and I will get help eventually, but can't you give me what I need? If not tonight, can you stop by tomorrow?"

"No, I'll get back to you. Maybe in a few weeks."

"A few weeks!" I shrieked, horrified at the thought of not having a regular sex partner for that length of time.

"Yeah, a few weeks—maybe. I'm not sure if I want a sexual relationship with you, anymore."

"Why not?" I thought we had great sexual chemistry, and I was stunned.

"The more dick I give you, the more you want. I don't know what it takes to satisfy you."

"You *do* satisfy me!"

"It doesn't seem like it. Most women want to sleep or at least take a rest after busting one or two nuts, but not you. You don't ever want to stop."

"I can't help it," I said unhappily.

"Why don't you buy yourself a sex toy?" Aaron said on his way out the door.

Usually a man of few words, Aaron had spoken more that morning than ever before. It saddened me that he chose to open up and express himself on the day that he was walking out on me.

After Aaron had deserted me, the mounting pressure between my legs was so strong, it was practically debilitating. Someone had to help me. I picked up my phone and sighed. I didn't have a long list of men to choose from; there were only a few names in my contact list. Feeling as if I had no choice, I humbled myself and called Habib. "Could you stop by while you're making your deliveries?" I had asked.

"I'm surprised to hear from you; I didn't think you wanted to see me again."

"I changed my mind."

"I like you a lot, Fonia, and I'd love to spend time with you, but please don't try to coerce me into doing filthy things that are against my religion."

"I won't," I agreed and anxiously waited for Habib to

ring the bell. He took a lot longer than I'd anticipated, but when he finally arrived, I greeted him at the door, naked beneath a silk robe.

"I'm ready for you," I said, giving him a sensual smile. Habib seemed surprised by my boldness. A lot had happened in the short time since I'd lost my virginity to him. I was no longer an innocent young woman. I had been fucked by three different men, and something had been awakened inside me—a deep hunger that couldn't be satisfied.

Habib had seduced me the first time, but this time, I seduced him. Hastily, I undressed him, and climbed on top of him. Straddling him, I rode him fast and furiously. Unfortunately, Habib didn't last as long as he had the last time we were together.

"I'm sorry," he said. "Maybe it was the position we were in. I last much longer in the missionary position. It's not natural for a woman to be on top of man."

"Let's switch positions; I don't mind being on the bottom. Or we can do it doggy-style," I suggested.

Habib looked at his watch. "I have to get back to work," he said, reaching for his underwear. My heart sank as I watched him dressing hurriedly. Moments later, he walked out the door.

Naked, frustrated, and unfulfilled, I sat on my bed, trying to figure out a way to resolve my problem. *I should get help. Look on-line for the number of Sex Addicts Anonymous. Or find a chat room online with professionals that can help me through this crisis.*

But after giving it more thought, I decided that having sex with only four men didn't make me a sex addict. Still wanting to get laid, I thought of the older man I'd slept with. What was his name? Oh, yeah, Eddie. Trying to get in touch with him was pointless. His fiancée was guarding him like a watchdog. I knew this because I'd driven past his place several times, and each time I cruised by—night or day—her car was always parked in the driveway.

Desperate for a good fuck, I called Wyatt at the fitness center and asked if it was okay for me to drop by.

"It's not a good time; there's a Pilates class going on," Wyatt said.

"How about later?"

"I don't know, Fonia. Messing around on my job isn't a good idea. People might start talking, and you know, if word gets back to my supervisor, I could get fired."

I sighed audibly.

"If you want, I can come by your place on my lunch break. How about tomorrow?"

"But I need to see you on your lunch break, today!" My voice was frantic.

"I can't. I already had lunch."

"After work?"

"My girl picks me up after work."

I scratched my head, trying to think of a solution. "Do you have any more friends? You know…besides Aaron?"

"Yeah, but they're not into freaky stuff like Aaron and me. And they run their mouths. I wouldn't want any of this information to get back to my girl." Wyatt went quiet for a few moments. "Maybe we should break things off, Fonia. I mean…we both had our fun, right?"

"I guess…" Realizing that Wyatt wasn't going to help me, I told him goodbye. I moped around my apartment for a few minutes, and then masturbated for the next hour.

JAGUAR

I'd failed miserably at being celibate. To my credit, I wasn't man-whoring around with multiple women; I was only sexually involved with Rayna. Although I'd made it clear that our relationship was strictly sexual, she insisted on bringing me home-cooked meals. And the girl knew how to serve me. She came over with piles of beef stew with yellow rice and peas. Her Puerto Rican cuisine was banging; she had the ability to make something as simple as rice and beans and chicken gizzards taste like a gourmet treat.

Not wanting to take advantage of Rayna's kindness, I decided to reciprocate, and invited her to go see a movie on my day off. I let her pick the flick and we ended up seeing a sappy, romantic comedy. After the movie, we stopped to have drinks at Tex-Mex, a little spot with good Margaritas and Mexican food.

We were nothing more than "friends-with-benefits" sharing a drink and having a conversation, but the candle on the table and the dimly lit restaurant gave a romantic touch to the evening, sending out the wrong message.

Smiling, Rayna leaned forward and placed her hands over mine. "I usually don't bring men home to meet my kids, but you're such a nice person, I'd love to introduce you to my boys," she said, gazing at me hopefully.

"Uh…yeah, one of these days." I squirmed in my seat, and took a swig of beer.

"If you don't have any plans, I was wondering if you'd like to come over for dinner on your next day off…you know…so you can get to know them."

"I thought we had an understanding," I said, struggling to keep the irritation out of my voice.

"We do—we're friends."

Rayna was trying to put me in an uncomfortable situation. I couldn't look her kids in the eyes, knowing that I didn't have honorable intentions toward their mother. "Do you think it's wise for me to meet your children? I mean, I don't want to give them the wrong impression."

"They know all about you, Jag. I talk about you all the time; they know we're involved."

"Involved! We're not *involved*. We're just friends— two people who enjoy being around each other. I was up front with you, and we agreed that we wouldn't attach any labels to our relationship. I don't think you need to bring your kids into something that's not going anywhere."

My words hurt her, I could tell by the wounded look in her eyes.

"But…our friendship is growing. It's changed into something more intimate—hasn't it?" she asked with a nervous tremor in her voice.

I shook my head. "Not really."

Her eyes became dark with anger. "Do you have fun playing with my heart and hurting me?"

"That wasn't my intention."

"You take me out for a romantic evening," she said, gesturing toward the candle in the center of the table. "Then you tell me I'm never going to be more than an extended booty call."

"That's not how I put it."

"But that's what you meant."

Taking her out was clearly a bad idea, I thought with a sigh. "I told you that I'm not ready for a serious relationship. I thought we agreed on how this situation was going to work."

"We did. But then we started having sex damn near every day. That seems pretty fucking serious to me," she said in a voice that was louder than necessary. "And if there's nothing serious between us, why'd you take me out on a romantic date?"

"I was holding up my end of the friendship," I said weakly.

She glared at me. "That's cruel, Jaguar. Why would you make me think this was going somewhere? Why do you call me, text me, and check in on me all the time? Huh? If we're only having sex, then you should fuck me and leave me. You shouldn't call me again until you're ready for another go-'round."

"I'm sorry, Rayna. I didn't mean to give you mixed-messages. I was only trying to be nice."

"I'm not a charity case," she blurted and stood abruptly. "I'm ready to go. Take me home."

I waived over the waitress, and Rayna stalked away from the table while I paid the bill.

She gave me the silent treatment for the first half of the drive to her house, but as we grew closer, she began to mutter to herself. "I'm so tired of no-good mother-fuckers."

I pretended not to hear her.

"Niggas ain't shit," she complained, punching her open palm. "If this bitch thinks he can treat me any ol' kind of way, he must be crazy." She punched her palm extra hard, creating a loud and intimidating sound effect.

Having had enough, and not knowing if I would get sucker punched at any given moment, I slammed on the brakes. "You're not going to sit in my ride and threaten me. Get the fuck out!"

"Fuck you! *You* get the fuck out; I'm not going any-where!"

The girl sounded deranged and I only had myself to blame for messing around with her again. She'd already shown signs that she was a psycho chick, yet I'd chosen to play with fire again.

I got out of the truck, walked around to her side and opened the door.

"Don't touch me, motherfucker. Don't you put your hands on me!" she shouted, opening up her purse like she was going to retrieve a can of mace...or a gun.

Believing that she was crazy enough to shoot me, I grabbed her by the arm, and pulled her out of the passenger's seat. I yanked her so hard, she lost her balance and landed on her ass on the ground. Her purse skidded out of her reach. Relieved that she couldn't get to her purse and pull out a pistol, I rushed back to the driver's side, and hopped behind the wheel. I sped away, leaving a trail of dust and exhaust smoke.

In the rearview mirror, I could see Rayna sitting on the ground, holding her face in her hands. She looked pitiful, and I felt so bad for her, I had to fight the urge to turn around and offer her a ride home. But the knowledge that she was prone to violence motivated me to keep going.

FONIA

I was out of control. Trying to satisfy my cravings, I had begun picking up men wherever I could. Parking lots, the bank, construction sites. I'd even lured one of the gardeners that maintained the grounds at my complex into my apartment. His name was Emilio and he had a small dick, but was extremely skilled with his tongue. Emilio had licked my pussy and my ass, and the feeling had been electrifying. I wanted more, but the next time I saw him, he seemed embarrassed. Pretending to be engrossed in trimming hedges, he wouldn't make eye contact with me.

Today, I went into a mini mart to buy gas and the guy making sandwiches behind the deli counter caught my eye. I stepped out of line to pay for gas and moseyed over to the deli department. I browsed the menu, but it wasn't deli meat that I was interested in.

While people were staring at the menu, I approached the counter and mouthed the words, *I want you.* He quickly wrote his number on a piece of scrap paper, and discreetly handed it to me.

I returned to the counter up front and paid for gas. After I filled my tank, I stood outside the store and called the cute deli worker. "I'm not kidding; I really want you," I said with a smile in my voice. "Can you get away for a few minutes?"

"Like when?"

"Like right now."

"Right now?" he asked, surprised.

"Uh-huh. Can't you take a smoke break or something?"

"I don't smoke, but I can probably get someone to cover for me for a few minutes."

"Okay, good. I'm going to go back inside the store and get the key to the restroom."

"The public restroom—outside?" He sounded incredulous.

"Sure, why not?"

"Sounds freaky, but okay. Uh, my name is Ron, by the way."

"See you soon, Ron." I didn't bother to give him my name. I hung up and went back inside to get the key to the restroom.

With the key in hand, I gazed over my shoulder, giving Ron a suggestive look before exiting the store.

I stood inside the unisex restroom that was disgustingly filthy, anxiously waiting for Ron. A normal person would have turned around and walked out, the moment they smelled the stench, but I ignored the smell and the deplorable conditions. Having my sexual needs met was all that mattered. Eager to get started, I removed my panties and stuffed them in my handbag, and began patting my impatient pussy, trying to calm it down.

A few minutes later, Ron stepped inside the restroom, grimacing. "Jesus, it stinks in here. How can you stand the foul odor?"

I shrugged. Taking his mind off the stench, I suggested, "Why don't you take your dick out and let me suck it?"

"Oh. Okay." In less than five seconds, his fly was open and his raging hard-on was in his hand.

Having gone my entire life without seeing or touching a penis, I had developed an almost worshipful appreciation for the shape and attractiveness of the male appendage. Gazing at his dick sent tingles up my spine. I caressed Ron's dick, enjoying the smooth glide as the pad of my finger slid up and down his length. Gently, I cupped his scrotum and let out a tiny moan. I had to get a taste of him. I sank down to my knees, becoming eye-level with his groin. My mouth watered at the sight of his rigid dick, which was pointed directly in my face.

He began stroking himself and each time the head of his dick peeked through the opening of his hand, I licked at it, polishing it with my moist tip of my tongue.

"This must be my lucky day; I've dreamed about meeting up with a freaky chick like you," he said excitedly.

Grasping his erection, and ready to suck the cum out of him, I smiled politely, though I wished he'd stop chattering so much.

"Seriously, I can't believe this is really happening. What made you—"

I silenced him with a tongue stroke that began at the smooth crown and ran the length of his shaft, all the way to the hilt. My mouth watered for the taste of his dick, but my pussy was also tense and hungry with desire. I began breathing heavily as dual needs twisted through me.

Deciding to satisfy my oral fixation first, I pressed my closed lips against the head of his dick. I didn't part my lips, I didn't move. I wanted Ron to force his dick inside my mouth. I wanted him to curse at me, to slap me, and pull my hair. But I didn't know how to express those unusual desires. Catching on somewhat, Ron thrust between my lips, and roughly pushed inside the warm wetness of my mouth.

"This is too good; I can't take anymore," Ron admitted, tugging on my short skirt until it had gathered around my waist. Providing him with more access to my pussy, I threw a leg up on the trash bin that was filled with unimaginable crap.

Realizing that he didn't have to struggle with the task of getting my panties off in the tight confines of the restroom, Ron remarked, "Wow! I can't believe you were walking around in the store in that short skirt, without any panties on?"

"Panties get in the way."

"So you never wear them?"

"Not when I'm in the mood to be a nasty bitch," I

said, hoping to encourage him to call me names and to treat me like a whore. I yearned for humiliation and pain, but had yet to find the man that was willing to indulge my dark cravings. "I'm ready to act like a whore," I finally told him, mimicking the perverted expression that Mr. Lord used to make me say.

"Damn, you're so pretty and classy looking; I can't believe you're talking like this."

"I'm not classy; I'm a filthy whore. You can do whatever you want to me."

"Talking like that is getting my dick extra hard," he groaned as he fitted the head inside my overly moist entry.

As he pounded into my pussy, electrical currents zipped through me, but I wanted more. "Slap me," I demanded.

"Huh?"

"Call me names and slap me!"

"Bitch," he said meekly.

"Call me a whore and slap me!" I shouted as I fucked him back as hard and as fast as he was fucking me.

A sudden slap across my face momentarily stunned me. And then he slapped me on the other side of my face. I groaned as a hot sensation began mounting between my legs. The orgasm was huge. A powerful explosion that had me slumped over, barely able to stand up. Ron kept humping as he held my shuddering body upright.

He let out a groan and his body shuddered as he ejaculated. At that point, my foot that had been propped up on the trash bin slipped inside. My ankle and calf were immersed in trash that contained used tampons, discarded tissues, and other unspeakably vile items.

Back in my apartment, I enjoyed the afterglow of raunchy sex with a stranger for a few moments. Ron had been the eighth man I'd picked up in the past few days. All total, since moving into my apartment, I'd had sex with twelve different people. And I still wasn't satisfied.

I wished I could relax and enjoy the aftereffects of good sex, but I had already begun to grow concerned about my next fix. Though I tried to get the phone numbers of my sex partners, many were only interested in sex in the moment. They were either married or in serious relationships and didn't want to be reminded of their perverted indiscretions with me.

Though my pussy was in a state of satisfaction, it was only a matter of time before it would begin to twitch and clench, demanding to be given what it needed. Figuring that I had at least an hour or two, I began calling the numbers I'd accumulated, hoping to find a willing partner. I kept getting voicemail. No one would take my call.

My anxiety intensified, and I felt a small lump in my throat, getting close to tears as the realization hit me that I would have to go out and find another willing participant. Prowling around both day and night looking for sex was beginning to wear me down. Almost everyone I encountered remarked on my looks. "You're such a pretty girl," they all said, sounding surprised that someone with my looks would stoop so low as to pick up strangers for sex.

But I didn't feel very pretty. I felt like scum. And I simply couldn't stop my wanton behavior.

With nowhere else to turn, I called Habib's cell and left a message, letting him know that I was available if he wanted to drop by while making his deliveries. Habib was less than desirable in bed, but he could cool down my fire until I found someone more virile.

Even the most long-lasting and kinky lover still lacked an important trait. I needed a man to take control of me. To indulge my submissive nature. So far, I hadn't found anyone who was willing to humiliate, discipline, and completely dominate me the way I'd grown accustomed.

My doorbell rang, and a slight smile fell on my lips. Habib to the rescue! I wondered if Habib would be willing to dole out physical punishment if I explained my needs to him.

A peek through the eyehole nearly sent me into cardiac arrest. It wasn't Habib standing outside my door. It was a familiar face that filled me with terror and dread, and had me gasping for breath. Carrying a briefcase and wearing a luxurious suit and tie, was…oh, my God…Mr. Lord!

FONIA

F rozen with dread, I stood with my back against the
door. The bell rang again and I nearly jumped out
of my skin.

"Open the door, Fonia." The tone of his voice was
impassive, betraying neither anger nor impatience.

Against my will, I turned the lock and slowly opened
the door. Years of obedience training left me feeling that
I didn't have a choice. Shame-faced, I stood with my eyes
downcast.

"Fonia," he whispered softly as he set the briefcase
down. "Come here, Princess."

I glanced up and saw his arms outstretched, and there
was warmth and love in his eyes. A sob tore from my
throat and I rushed into his arms and it felt like home.
"Mr. Lord! Oh, Mr. Lord. I'm so sorry," I said with my
face buried in his chest, inhaling his magnificent fragrance.
Rebelliousness had caused me to search for love in all
the wrong places…and here it was. Everything I needed,
this man possessed.

"I'm so sorry I disobeyed you," I whimpered in a child-like voice. "Can you forgive me? Please forgive me," I said, meaning it with all my heart.

He patted me on the head. "I don't understand why you ran away from me, but of course, I forgive you. You're my princess—you belong to me."

He was so handsome and powerful, my heart swelled with love. The gleaming platinum wedding band that graced his ring finger was a reminder that I would never be his wife...only his concubine. But it didn't matter anymore. His marriage of convenience seemed unimportant—a piece of paper that I had foolishly allowed to interfere with my devotion to the only man who had ever loved me. That he could find it in his heart to forgive me meant the world to me. Overcome with emotion, I cried tears of joy.

When I finally stopped sniffling, Mr. Lord told me to go wash my face. He followed me into the bathroom, watching me intently—inspecting me. "Your appearance is startling. Why are you dressed like that?" he asked, referring to my very casual denim skirt and rumpled top. "And your hair is a mess."

"Lately, I haven't had any reason to dress up."

"You don't need a reason. I trained you to maintain your appearance at all times, didn't I?"

"Yes, Mr. Lord. You did."

I pulled the elastic band from around my messy ponytail and diligently began brushing my hair. Mr. Lord walked out of the bathroom and walked around my apartment, quietly inspecting each tiny room, and then returned to the bathroom.

"Pack your things. No wonder you look like a vagrant; this place is a dump. It's utterly depressing."

Dutifully, I went to my bedroom and emptied my closet and the contents of my drawers into my luggage. Mr. Lord glanced at the treadmill disdainfully. "You have high-end equipment at home. This cheap piece of trash stays here."

"Of course," I murmured.

After I finished packing, I stepped into the kitchen, but one glance from Mr. Lord and I knew I was forbidden from bringing any of the items I'd purchased for the apartment back to the townhouse.

We arrived home and I was instructed to take a shower and to make myself presentable. When I stepped out of the shower, I saw that Mr. Lord had laid out the outfit he wanted me to wear: a pair of yellow panties and a matching bra, a bright-colored, ankle-length dress that I'd never seen. The island flair of the dress gave me the impression that it had been purchased during his honeymoon in Bermuda.

I put on the underwear and then looked in my closet and examined my vast shoe collection, looking for the perfect sandals to complement the dress.

Mr. Lord walked up behind me, startling me. "No shoes," he implored. "That dress was meant to be worn barefoot during our honeymoon. The honeymoon you denied me," he reminded with an edge to his voice.

"I was jealous and I acted impulsively."

"I forgive you. But I need to know something? Have you been a good girl?" he asked, standing behind me and stroking my neck.

I swallowed, took a deep breath, and shook my head.

His caressing fingers went still. "What are you saying?"

"I've been bad," I whispered fearfully.

He grabbed me by the shoulders and forcibly turned me, compelling me to look him in the eye. "How bad?" he said through clenched teeth, the volume of his voice making me flinch.

"Very," I reluctantly admitted.

"You're still pure, aren't you? Please tell me you haven't allowed someone to defile you," he said, his words coated in anguish.

The grief in his voice caused my stomach to knot painfully; he wasn't going to like my response at all. I forced myself to look him in the eye. "I'm impure, Mr. Lord. I've lost my virginity."

He emitted an agonized sound and covered his face with his hand. When he looked up at me, his eyes had turned to ice. His face was hard and grim as he sought to control his anger. "Lost it?" He uttered a scoffing sound. "You didn't lose it; you spitefully and willfully gave it away, didn't you? You gave away something that belonged to me, and you did it to hurt me!"

Ashamed, I looked down and nodded my head. "I regret my actions…I'm so sorry, Mr. Lord."

"How could you? After all the training…all the time

I've put into you. How could you do something as despicable as that? I could have taken your virginity years ago, but I considered it a sacred treasure. Do you realize that I had a commitment ceremony lined up for us in Bermuda? A ceremony that would have made you the wife of my heart. I wanted to prove that I cherished you, Fonia. I absolutely cherished you." He clenched his teeth and then shook his head woefully. "But not anymore. You betrayed me…and that's unforgiveable."

He stalked out of my bedroom and returned a few minutes later, holding a paddle—one that I'd never seen before. "I had this made especially for you." He held the shiny wood handle of the instrument, showing me that the word "Princess" had been embroidered on the soft fabric that covered the front of the paddle. Glaring at me, he turned it over, revealing the word, "whore" that was crudely etched into the wood on the back of the paddle. No soft fabric cushioned the "whore" side.

"Which side should I use?" he asked.

"The 'whore' side," I muttered shamefully.

"You're right. It's going to be a long time before I use the other side of this paddle." Giving me a harsh shove, he said, "Get up against the wall, you filthy slut!"

Feeling him behind me, his eyes scorching my body as he appraised me, filled me with desire.

"How could someone so beautiful be such a vile and disgusting person?" he said contemptuously.

"I don't know," I said with my face pressed against the wall.

Irritated by my response, he let out an unsatisfied grunt.

I shuddered in fear and desire when I felt his hands unclasping my bra. He roughly yanked the straps from my shoulders, and discarded the article, allowing it to drop to the floor. As if testing my state of arousal, he pressed close to me. With his arms closed around me from behind, he cupped my breasts. His thumbs harshly massaged my nipples, and then he twisted and pinched them. I bit my lip to keep from crying out as he coerced my nipples to form into stiff peaks.

"How many men have you been with?"

My immediate impulse was to lie, to tell him that I'd only been with one man. But my instincts told me that his driver had been watching my every move, reporting my despicable actions to Mr. Lord.

"I've been with numerous men," I admitted.

"A dozen," he informed. "I treated you like a princess, but you're lower than scum," he whispered gruffly in my ear, his voice vibrating with tension.

"I'm sorry." I didn't know what else to say.

"You're worse than a prostitute…giving yourself away to strangers on the street," he said sneeringly. "Nothing but a dirty whore."

Responding to the coarse insults, my body began to pulse with desire. I was hot all over and I desperately wanted to feel the sting of that paddle.

He gripped the elastic band of my panties, and the touch of his fingers grazing against my skin gave me hot sensations that caused me to flinch. He pulled my panties down, exposing my ass, and for the first time in my life, I could feel Mr. Lord's erection jutting out as he rubbed his groin against my bare ass.

"Mr. Lord!" I cried out in passion, uncontrollably rubbing my hot ass against the bulge in his pants. "Oh, Mr. Lord!" My body and mind were aflame with desire. I wanted pain. I wanted pleasure. I wanted to hear him curse me with vile names.

He stepped away from me, denying me the feel of his hard masculinity. "You don't get that," he said tauntingly. I dropped my head, and uttered a cry of remorse.

For a long, agonizing moment, I waited to feel the sting of the paddle, but there was nothing. Not a word from Mr. Lord and not a touch from his hand. He stood behind me silently seething, and the long silence was incredibly ominous.

Had his heart softened toward me? Was I forgiven? Though I was deeply curious, and wanted to see his expression, I didn't dare lift my head or turn around.

A sudden hard thwack across my ass sent fiery bolts of passion to my core. He hit me so forcefully, my head bumped into the wall and I was stunned silent, too shocked to make a sound. He hit me over and over until my legs gave out and I toppled down to the floor.

His eyes cold and hard, he looked down at me. "If you ever run away from me again, you're going to wish you were dead. Understand?"

"Yes."

Then his expression softened. He scooped me up from the floor. Cradling me as if I were a fragile babe in arms, he carried me to the bed. "Your punishment is over...for now. Are you ready for pleasure, Princess?"

Smiling dreamily, I nodded my head.

JAGUAR

The bikers were back for their monthly pool tournament. The place was packed and I couldn't get a rhythm going. Everyone wanted a drink at the same time. Customers kept yelling my name; an obnoxious biker chick actually put her fingers in her mouth and emitted a high pitch whistle in order to get my attention. And a college kid frowned at me and agitatedly waved his money in the air.

In addition to all that madness, Bee-Sting, the hot black chick with the yellow bee tattoo on her left breast, was back. While her biker boyfriend shot pool, she sat at the bar drinking a Spunky Monkey, her favorite cocktail.

Bee-Sting was real easy on the eyes with her cute face, trendy hairdo, and extraordinary boobs that she liked to put on display. She was keeping me busy, though. Every twenty minutes, I was back at the dreaded blender, whirring up another Spunky Monkey.

Every time I finished waiting on a customer, I seemed to find my way back to Bee-Sting. She was a little nutty, but her conversation was thoroughly entertaining. And she had that bad girl kind of sex appeal that a reformed bad boy like myself was drawn to. She reminded me of the girls I'd grown up with in the 'hood. She laughed loud, talked slick, and walked like she knew how to ride a big dick. I wouldn't have expected a girl like her to be hooked up with a white boy. Especially a biker. They were from two different worlds, but I suppose opposites attract.

The more Bee-Sting drank, the more openly she flirted. But I wasn't hitting on her; I was merely enjoying the company of a pretty girl. Knowing she had a man who was only a stone's throw away kept me from misbehaving. I made sure not to say anything that could be misconstrued or misinterpreted.

After the relationship drama that had occurred between Rayna and me, it was refreshing to enjoy the company of a confident woman, who was stroking my ego with flattery and flirtatiousness.

"What high school did you go to, Jag?" she asked, licking froth from around the rim of her glass.

"I went to Bartram."

"Hmm. I would have expected you to say Central High or one of the other top schools in the city."

"Nah, back then my grades were below average."

"Below?"

"Yeah, I barely graduated."

"But I heard you were a lawyer. Humph! Remind me not to use your services the next time I get in trouble."

I laughed heartily. "I haven't taken the bar exam yet, and I won't be practicing criminal law."

"Oh, no? What kind of lawyer are you gonna be?"

"Corporate."

She dropped her head and made snoring sounds. I laughed again. When she lifted her head, she said, "Corporate law sounds boring as hell. Good luck with that."

I made Bee-Sting another drink and when I set it in front of her, she allowed her fingers to graze the top of my hand. Her eyes were filled with mischief and sensuality as she teased me by trailing a long, pointed nail along my hand and up to my wrist.

"Behave," I cautioned. "Your boyfriend might get jealous."

"No, he won't."

I raised a brow.

"He likes for me to enjoy myself. As long as I'm happy, he's happy."

I cut an eye at her biker boyfriend and the moment we made eye contact, his eyes darted away.

"What are you saying? You two are in an open relationship?"

"Sort of."

"Sort of?"

"I'm open. He's not. He only has eyes for me, but I get to experiment with other partners. He lets me do my thing."

"Interesting. Are you in love with him?"

"With all my heart."

"So why do you need to fuck around?" I was really curious and wanted to know what she had to say from a woman's perspective.

"Put it like this…I would never fuck around with another white dude, but I get lonely for the company of a black man. Listen, I'm keeping it real, can't nobody fuck me as good as a brother can."

"So why are you in a relationship with a white man?" My tone was somewhat hostile and it occurred to me that I didn't like the idea of a black woman crossing over to the other side.

"Spike—my husband—he treats me like the queen bee that I am."

"You two are married?" I looked at her ring finger pointedly and noticed the tattoo of a black snake coiled around her finger.

"We don't wear traditional wedding rings. Been married for three wonderful years, and I'd be crazy to leave him for a dude that has three baby mommas and a couple of chicks on the side. When I get to yearning for black dick, I go out and get me some." She touched my hand again and smiled provocatively.

I gazed at her hand as it stroked mine. "Is that what you're doing now…trying to get some of this black dick?"

"I sure am. But don't get it twisted, I love my husband. Spike isn't threatened by black men; he knows that all I want from a brother is a good, hard fuck, but my heart belongs to him."

"Wow," I said and involuntarily moistened my lips. Bee-Sting was in luck because I was in the mood to give her exactly what she wanted. Hell, I'd failed at celibacy and I'd failed at trying to have a no-strings-attached relationship with Rayna. A girl like Bee-Sting was the perfect chick for me at this phase of my life. She was in love with her husband and only wanted to use me for sex, which was fine with me. I wouldn't have to worry about her being clingy or trying to take things to the next level.

"So you just want a sex partner—nothing else?" I clarified.

"I'm very happily married…what else would I want besides a hard fuck?"

"Okay. I guess I can help you out with that," I said and winced as my dick began to stiffen inside my pants.

"So…" She leaned forward and looked at my crotch. "Can I get a preview?" she asked.

I scowled in bewilderment.

"I wanna get a look at that thick, Nubian chocolate that you're gonna stuff in my mouth and down my throat…"

Bee-Sting paused, watching me and waiting for a reaction. But she was talking so damn dirty, and looked so hot while she verbally seduced me, I was rendered speechless. My dick had uncoiled and was sticking out, forming a tent in the front of my pants. It was painful as fuck, and I wanted to stick my hand inside my fly and readjust my shit to a more comfortable position. If the bar hadn't been so crowded, I would have escorted her to the sex-corner behind the restrooms and given her a look and a quick sample of the goods. But I had to control myself. Taking risks could cost me my job. And my pockets were too light to be playing around with my livelihood.

"I'd love to show you what I'm working with, but unfortunately you're going to have to take my word for it…you won't be disappointed. I don't get out of here until around three. Will that be a problem?" I asked in a lustful voice.

"No, it's cool. I'll give you our address and you can swing by when you get off."

I had assumed we'd go back to my place, and I was taken aback. "You want me to come to you and your husband's crib?"

She nodded. "Don't worry about Spike; he knows that I have the hots for you. He's down with whatever makes me happy…as long as he can watch." She gave me a conspiratorial wink and continued caressing my hand.

"Hold up. Your man wants to watch me banging you?" Appalled, I glanced in the direction of the pool area, and Spike was watching Bee-Sting and me closely. His stare was creepy as hell and my hard-on instantly deflated. Having a complete change of heart, I slid my hand away from Bee-Sting. "No offense, but I've changed my mind," I said as I edged away and began serving customers at the other end of the bar.

An hour or so later, I noticed Bee-Sting cozying up to my buddy, Buddha. Working her charm, she had Buddha laughing and blushing as she talked shit and sneakily caressed his inner thigh. All the while, her husband was watching from the sideline. Even licking his lips as if he couldn't wait for Bee-Sting to get Buddha into their marital bed.

Once again, I'd almost allowed my dick to get me into trouble. I would have had to whoop Spike's biker-ass if he tried some funny business while I was busy smashing his wife.

I glanced at Buddha. Bee-Sting had him in the palm of her hand. He was grinning from ear to ear, probably planning on putting to use some of his legendary tongue tricks and oral skills.

I wanted to holla at Buddha—pull my man's coat. But sometimes a horny, knucklehead has to learn the hard way that all that glitters is not gold.

The night finally ended and I was dog-tired. As crowded as the bar was, I only made half the tips I usually earned on a Monday night. After buying the truck, my savings were depleted and my cash on hand was perilously low. Making matters worse, Rayna had been unforgiving about being thrown out of my ride. In super bitch-mode, she'd been lurking around the hotel, giving me the evil eye and muttering under her breath whenever we crossed paths.

And I suspected that Rayna had been rifling through my personal things. It made me uneasy that a woman that felt scorned by me had complete access to my room and personal possessions. Of course, I should have thought about that before I slept with her five times in a row. I know, I know…I'm a dumb ass for allowing my little head to do the thinking instead of using my brain.

I seriously had to get out of that hotel and find an apartment. As distasteful as the thought was, I was so strapped for cash, I was considering working another freak party. Convincing myself that I could handle it, I decided that all I had to do at the next event was mind my business and not get emotionally involved when I saw someone getting their ass walloped with a paddle. Like the butler had said, they were all consenting adults. Grown people living out their freakish fantasies.

Deciding that I could handle a few more parties until I got my money up, I made a mental note to give Sharif a call in the morning—find out if he could hook me up with some more work.

FONIA

Cradled in Mr. Lord's arms, I smiled when he whispered, "I love you, Princess," in my ear.

Happiness doesn't begin to describe my emotions as I sucked his finger while he stroked my hair. I was naked and he was fully clothed, yet in this moment, I felt so sheltered, so protected, and so loved, it was hard for me to make sense of why I had run away from this kind of intense love. I deeply regretted not going to Bermuda with him. My rebelliousness had caused me to miss out on a ceremony that would have made me the wife of his heart.

He eased his finger from my suckling lips. "Does my finger still satisfy you?" he asked in a tender voice.

"Yes."

"Be honest with me, Princess."

I shook my head. "I still like it, but I want more."

"What do you want?"

I felt shy and awkward. Ashamed to express my desires. "I don't want you to get upset with me."

"No secrets between us, Fonia. Now, tell me what you want," he said sternly.

I lowered my eyes. "I want to suck you down there," I murmured in a soft, embarrassed tone.

"If I give you what you want, will you promise to stop roaming the streets like a whore?"

"Yes, Mr. Lord. I promise." My eyes latched on to his manicured fingers as they worked to undo his belt and his fly. My heart rate sped up and began to thunder in my chest. What he unleashed was a glorious sight. His dick was larger than any of my random sex partners. It was more beautiful and magnificent than I had ever imagined it to be.

I wanted to fall on my knees and utter worshipful prayers, while at the same time, I wanted to pounce on him and swallow it whole. But Mr. Lord would have frowned on such aggressive and unladylike behavior, and so instead of urging him to ravish my mouth, I politely waited for him to give me permission to perform fellatio.

Without a word, he pointed to the floor and I scrambled off the bed, assuming a kneeling position before him. He rose and stepped out of his pants, shirt, and underwear. I'd never seen Mr. Lord without clothes on and I couldn't pull my eyes away from the thick, roped muscles of his arms or his strong, dark velvet thighs.

I was entranced by the length of his manhood. Semi-soft, he held it in his large hand, and I watched in adoration and amazement as it grew longer and larger. He beckoned me closer, and I immediately scooted forward. As he caressed the side of my face with the head of his dick, I licked my lips and a faint sigh escaped my parted lips.

I wanted to taste him, wanted so badly to have my mouth filled with his hardness, I could have cried.

He finally stopped teasing me and let me suck his dick. I was slobbering and moaning with excitement as he stroked in and out of my mouth. He made a sound of pleasure that informed me that I was meeting his expectation. Wanting to make him proud of me, my puckered lips grew more urgent and I sucked harder, all the while licking at the smooth, hardened flesh.

He gave a deep groan, and a part of me feared that he might pull out. "Please," I pleaded, holding him captive inside my warm mouth.

"That's enough, Fonia." He eased his steely length from between my lips and told me to lie down on the bed with my arms pressed against my sides. I complied. With my pussy throbbing with need, I waited in hot anticipation for whatever he had in store for me next.

"Close your eyes and don't move," he warned, and then astonishingly, he picked up his clothes from the bed and left my bedroom. I didn't know if he was coming right back or if he was going home to his new wife.

Obeying Mr. Lord, I kept my eyes closed and didn't dare turn my head or move a muscle. I lay in sexual agony, trying not to squirm as I listened for any sound that would give me a clue to where he was.

But there was only silence.

After an eternity, he returned to my bedroom. A relieved smile spread across my face.

"Turn over," he told me, and I didn't hesitate to follow

his command. On my stomach with my face buried into the pillow, I felt his finger trail from my neck, down my back, and then linger at the crack of my ass.

The mere touch of his finger sent lightning bolts of pleasure racing through my body. My mouth formed into a grateful smile. The pleasure of Mr. Lord's single touch was more delicious than every dick I'd fucked and every tongue that had licked its way into my whoring hole. It felt so good to be home! Back with the man whom I was devoted to. I'd never stray again...never! I'd be perfectly obedient—a good girl for the rest of my life.

He squeezed my buttocks and then parted the round orbs, exposing my anus. "Is this virgin territory?"

I lifted my head from the pillow. "Of course, Mr. Lord."

"That's a relief," he said as he slathered a warm, lubricating substance between my butt cheeks.

Engulfed by fear, my anus clenched. I'd experienced a finger in my ass, but never a big dick.

"Relax, Princess," he said in a soft tone intended to put me at ease.

But I was terrified. "I'm trying to relax, but I can't," I squeaked.

"Do you want me to forgive you?"

"Yes."

"Then relax. I can't have sex with you in the traditional manner. As far as I'm concerned, your vagina is contaminated. I can't go anywhere near it; not even with a condom. You understand how I feel, don't you?"

Shamefully, I muttered, "Yes, Mr. Lord." But I ached to feel him inside my pussy, not my ass. My thoughts raced, wondering if somehow I could persuade him to fuck my pussy. I felt him straddle me. Felt him ease a portion of his dick into my tight, back passage. Then I felt the heat of what felt like fire. It seemed that a red, hot poker was being forced inside my ass. I screamed and writhed in pain, but he didn't relent. With sadistic pleasure, he drove himself deeply, tormenting me with a fiery pain that was unlike anything I'd ever experienced.

Eventually the pain turned into pleasure and it seemed as if my asshole had transformed into a throbbing clit.

I bucked upward, eager for him to plunge deeper. Pleasurable sensations flooded the underside of my clit as he fucked my ass with long, strong thrusts.

Finally, we exploded together; his body bucked and he gasped as he filled my ass with sweet cum. Overcome with emotion, I cried into the pillow, thanking him over and over for giving me such a sweet orgasm.

He smacked my ass. "Clean yourself up and get ready for bed. I'll have groceries delivered tomorrow."

I gazed at him quizzically. I'd always shopped for groceries myself; I was surprised that he was having them delivered.

"You no longer have transportation. I've had your car towed and returned to the dealership. I can't allow you to escape from me again."

"But…I won't try to escape, Mr. Lord. I made a mistake."

"It's going to take a long time before you regain my trust."

"I understand," I said sadly.

"Your bank account has been closed," he added with a cruel smile. "You can't be trusted to manage funds. I've also retrieved your cell phone. I don't want you communicating with those men that violated you. Is that clear?"

I nodded.

"The landline phone is for me to contact you. And you're not…under any circumstances…allowed to leave this house unless you're accompanied by me." He lifted my chin with his finger and looked into my eyes. "You're my possession, Fonia. You realize that, right?"

"I do."

"No one understands you better than I do. I know what's best for you."

He put on his suit jacket and straightened his tie and began to head toward the door. "I left your daily schedule on the fridge…the time of your meals, your workout schedule, housekeeping, et cetera. Oh, it almost slipped my mind."

I gave him my rapt attention.

"I have a bit of good news for you," he said and I gazed at him eagerly. "You and I will be attending special dinner parties twice a month. Private and very special dinner parties where you'll be able to demonstrate your good training and your devotion." He brushed a hand against my face. "I think you're going to like the parties, Princess."

I hope so. I thought of the parties my mother had described. Parties where men urinated on her. I was terrified, but knew that I had to do whatever Mr. Lord thought was best.

I was a prisoner again. And with no car, no bank account, no freedom to come and go at will, I was more of a prisoner than ever before.

I hugged myself. Took a deep breath, trying to embrace my predicament.

JAGUAR

I had just started my shift when Sharif popped his head inside the bar. "Step outside for a second, bro; I wanna show you something."

I followed him outside and actually had to shield my eyes from the gleam of the rims on his Mercedes—a G-Class SUV, a hundred-thousand-dollar vehicle. "You getting it like that?" I asked, incredulously.

"Yeah, man. I'm living the sweet life," he responded in a taunting tone.

"Did you get the message I left you? I'm ready for some work," I said, not caring that I probably sounded thirsty as hell.

"I got the message, but I'm not sure."

I gave him a look. "Not sure about what?"

"This ain't no game, Jag. You can't keep changing your mind. Either you're in or you're not. My people are hosting more parties than usual, and they need someone who's dependable. You can't be taking on a holier than thou attitude. Those people are paying too much damn money for your services for you to be turning up your nose like you're better than them."

"I know, man," I said, contrite.

"And from what I remember, you ain't no saint your damn self. You were in on that train that all of us pulled on LaShondra back in '06."

I grimaced at the memory. I didn't like being reminded of my young, wild, and grimy days. That chick LaShondra had been madly in love with Sharif, and he talked her into letting all of his crew get a piece of ass, just to prove that he had her nose wide open. Like many episodes of my past, that wasn't something I was proud of.

"You're in luck," Sharif said. "But if you quit again… that's it. I don't care how close we were back in the day. Business is business and your indecision reflects badly on me."

"How's that?"

"The hostess asked for you specifically and I had to make up some bullshit story. Couldn't tell her that my friend didn't have the stomach for how real her parties get."

"I'm past that. I can do it."

"All right," he said doubtfully. "We'll see."

Reluctantly, he hooked me up with another bartending gig. This time it was a dinner party, being held at another remote location—an isolated, former horse farm near Chadds Ford, Pennsylvania. I was glad I had my own set of wheels. I didn't think cabs drove that far out into the boonies.

Sharif came inside the bar and had a drink. I mentioned that I'd visited Curt, told him how our boy had withered down to skin and bones.

"I heard his mom stopped going to see him. The nurse said I was his first visitor in years. What happened, man? Curt was our boy; why'd everybody turn their back on him?"

"Here you go, always acting like you're better than everybody else."

"I'm asking a simple question. How is that acting like I'm better than anybody?"

"Did you visit him in the past seven years?" Sharif asked with a sneer.

"No, but…"

"But, my ass. New York isn't that far away. You could have visited. But you couldn't stand to see him like that. Nor could anyone else."

"Nah, man. It wasn't like that. I was banned from the place."

"You got legal skills, don't you? You could have worked around that." Sharif gave me a scathing look. "Look, Curt's brain is fried. He don't know who's there and who's not… so what's the point of sitting up in his room and feeling bad?"

"I know visiting him is unpleasant, but it just seems like it's the least we could have done—myself included."

"Then, knock yourself out! Keep on visiting that nursing home; ain't nobody stopping you. But sitting around making small talk with a dude that can't understand a word you're saying is nothing but a waste of time."

Wearing an irritated expression, Sharif finished his drink and stood up. "I'll talk to you later, man."

My mood was pretty gloomy until Buddha strolled through the door. "What's up, my man?" I greeted. "How did things go with, uh…the chick you were talking with the other night?" I couldn't think of Bee-Sting's real name. Wasn't sure if she'd ever told me.

"Who? Vanessa?"

"The girl with the bee tattoo."

"Yeah, Vanessa," Buddha confirmed. "Man, that chick is wild. A natural born freak. But I calmed her hot ass down." He wriggled his unnaturally long tongue. "You won't believe what happened?"

"What?"

"Her man, that biker dude, Spike, went into the living room and turned on the TV. He told me and Vanessa to enjoy ourselves when we went into the bedroom. He acted like there wasn't anything really going on between them, so I took him up on the offer. So I'm deep into my tongue strokes, holding up one of Vanessa's legs with my face buried in the pussy, and I hear something behind me. I stop what I'm doing and look over my shoulder, and I'll be goddamn if Spike ain't in the bedroom with us, jerking his dick."

"What did you do?"

"What could I do? I couldn't put the man out of his own house. I kept on doing what I was doing and then I laid some pipe."

"You pulled your dick out in front of another man?"

"Man, I was butt-ass naked when he came in the room.

I ignored him and took care of business. The whole time I'm fucking his wife, he's moaning and groaning like he's the one up in the pussy. All three of us came at the same time. That was the freakiest shit I've ever been involved in."

"You dealt with that better than I would have. That freak invited you to fuck his wife; he didn't get your permission to turn it into a threesome."

"True dat. But I had my fun, so I can't complain," Buddha said as I set a glass of Tanqueray on the rocks in front of him.

"So whatever happened to that girl you was so crazy about?"

"Who? Myeesha?"

"Yeah, the chick that wanted to turn you into a porn star."

To me she would always be Rat-Face. I had nicknames for many of my customers. Hell, I couldn't even remember Buddha's real name. If he ever lost his big belly, I'd have to give him a new moniker.

"Man, I don't mess with her anymore. That chick wouldn't stop pestering me about being a porn star. I tried to get her to understand that I have an image to uphold. I'm a family man, a church member, and a pillar of my community. See, some people don't have any scruples, but I have family values, man. I'm not getting all up in front of the camera…putting myself on Front Street like that." Buddha took a big gulp of liquor and grimaced as it went down.

Everything about Buddha's activities was unscrupulous, but I suppose most people, including myself, had figured out reasons to justify their misconduct and hedonistic behavior.

I'd called the nursing home and made arrangements with the social worker to have a TV delivered to Curt's room. On my next visit, I gathered up all the pictures I had of Curt that spanned his childhood and teens. And I enlarged a photo of the two of us sitting on our dirt bikes, posing. In addition to the photos, I also bought two poster-size photos of dirt bikes—something that Curt loved.

I replaced those Easter decorations with pictures that were familiar to Curt. I also enlivened his room with cacti and other plants that were easy to care for.

"Good morning," the nurse said when she came in, casting a sweeping gaze over the pictures and plants. I stood up to leave, intending to give her some privacy to do whatever it was she did. "You don't have to leave; his care nurse washed him up and changed him early this morning. I came to check his bandages," she said, lifting up the blanket that covered him.

"Why does he have bandages?"

"Decubitus wounds."

I frowned. "Bed sores?"

"It's very common for people that lie in bed twenty-four hours a day."

"Do they hurt?"

"They would hurt if he had any feeling in his legs."

"I guess that's good, then."

She pointed to the dirt bike posters. "Are you sure that's in good taste? Wasn't he riding one of those things when he got hurt?"

"He loved dirt bikes. It wasn't the dirt bike that did this to him; the people that opened fire on him put him in this situation."

"He was only twenty or twenty-one back, then…right?" the nurse asked.

"Yeah, he was twenty. I was a year older." I looked down briefly. "I was riding with him when it happened."

She nodded, and continued checking his legs and feet. "His wounds are healing," she said with a smile and then walked over to the pictures that I'd framed and placed on the wall.

"Is that Curtis?" she asked, staring at one of the pictures of him and me posing on our bikes at the plateau in Fairmount Park.

"Yeah, that's us."

"Look at you two handsome boys…I know you were driving the girls crazy," she said with laughter. Then she gave me a certain look. "And I bet you still are."

I laughed along with her and cut an eye at Curt, and I could have sworn that he wore a faint smile.

FONIA

I hadn't been to many dinner parties, but this particular soiree was fancier than any that I'd ever attended. Mother's warning no longer seemed believable. Merely drunk talk. Nothing as bad as she'd mentioned could possibly occur at such an elegant party. The next time she contacted me, I'd be sure to tell her that she was a liar.

I was very proud to enter the party holding Mr. Lord's arm. I felt like a princess, dripping in jewels and swathed in a body-fitting, black Giorgio Armani gown with a slit in the front and a plunging neckline. Of course, I didn't select the dress. Mr. Lord has excellent taste, and he knows better than me what looks good on me. I felt truly beautiful in the revealing black dress.

The guests were dressed in formal attire; the men in tuxedos and the women wore evening gowns.

The party was held at a large estate that was situated on a horse farm with many acres and miles away from civilization. There were eight guests at the elegant dinner: Madam Midnight and her date, a much younger and gorgeous man named Theodore; a handsome bald man named Colden and his date, Melanee, an old, grey-haired, married couple named Lane and Prudence Meyers. And of course, Mr. Lord and me.

The serving girls were young and beautiful. They all wore thin, linked chains that revealed their shaven pubis, the mounds of their asses, and their high, pert breasts. They brought in the appetizers, and the hostess announced that we were being served aphrodisiacs.

An extremely muscular and divine-looking man, who looked as if he'd been sculpted from bronze, served the wine. Stunningly handsome, he was clad in only a loin-cloth. He was poetry in motion as he moved among the guests, pouring wine.

Not wanting to give the impression that I was staring at the tremendous bulge beneath the tiny fabric that barely covered his loins, I focused my attention on the lovely floral arrangement that was set in the center of the table.

Noticing that the wine server was being admired by the women seated at the table, Madam Midnight commented, "Sergio belongs to me. I acquired Sergio during a trip to Venezuela a few weeks ago," she said, referring to the handsome wine server. "He's hung like a horse and none of the loincloths I had on hand were large enough to properly cover his assets."

There were titters of laughter, and the server named Sergio went about his duties with a straight face. I gasped when he bent to pour my wine. His bulge brushed against my arm. A tingling sensation shot through my body that was so pleasurable, it was almost painful. I was very much attracted to that bulge. I wanted to lift the cloth and admire it. Lick it and kiss it. My pussy was close to convulsing each time I gazed at Sergio. Afraid that I might very well start panting, I held my breath. Mr. Lord was sitting right next to me and I didn't want him to know how badly I was lusting for the wine server.

"Is something wrong, my dear?" Madam Midnight asked me. "You don't look well; are you feeling a little indisposed?"

Mr. Lord and the other guests examined my face intently.

I shook my head adamantly. "Nothing's wrong; I'm fine," I said, dropping my gaze. It was embarrassing to be caught ogling another man's jewels with Mr. Lord sitting right next to me.

"She's a lovely girl, Harrison," Madam Midnight said. I'd never heard Mr. Lord referred to by his first name, and it took me a moment to realize she was talking about me.

"Where are your manners, Princess?" he said.

"Thank you for the compliment, Madam," I quickly uttered.

"How long have you had her?" a rather old woman wearing heavy makeup and dressed in a red evening gown inquired.

"I've had her for ten years. Since she was a child," Mr. Lord replied.

There was an eruption of surprised murmurs at the table. "Since she was child?" said the elderly, male escort of the lady in red. "How did you manage that? Did her parents give you permission to train her for our society?"

"Her father was never involved in her life, and believe it or not, her mother belonged to me. When I acquired the mother, the daughter became part of the package."

"Two for one! That's brilliant, Harrison. Absolutely brilliant!" the old guy said.

"But the mother didn't work out. The daughter was much more pliable. Much easier to mold."

"Human property is a lot like horses," Madam Midnight said. "Sometimes the colt is much more malleable than the mare."

There was a sprinkling of laughter, and I felt self-conscious listening to people talk about my mother and me. I squirmed as I noticed inquisitive eyes latching onto me. It wasn't pleasant being under their microscope.

"Tell me, did you physically discipline both parent and child?" asked Madam Midnight.

"Not at first. When Fonia was a child, I never had to lift a hand to her. She was a joy and a delight—eager to please—a very obedient child. But her mother…" He shook his head at the memory of trying to discipline my mother. "Trying to mold the mother was a nightmare. I had to remove her from my life."

"But, obviously you kept the child," the woman in red said.

"I did. And it wasn't until Fonia became an adult that she began to require a firm hand."

My face burned with humiliation as Mr. Lord and the other guests spoke of me as if I wasn't present. I drank more wine, and felt a tiny thrill that Mr. Lord had allowed me to join the other adults and drink an alcoholic beverage. A warm feeling began to course through me and the feeling of shame drifted away. *I am the property of Mr. Lord*, I thought to myself. *And that's nothing to be ashamed of.* Reminding myself that I should be honored and not ashamed of my status, I lifted my head and offered Mr. Lord a grateful smile.

"Oysters!" a female server announced as she brought a large bowl of oysters to the table. The server's nipples peeked through a top that was made of thin, silver chains.

"I'm not fond of oysters," Colden remarked.

"The sauce is heavenly," Madam Midnight commented.

"I'll pass," Colden insisted.

"Let him try the sauce!" Madam Midnight said in a stern voice to the serving girl.

The young woman bent over, dipping a nipple into the sauce.

"You, taste it," Colden said to his date, Melanee.

Melanee swiped her finger against the server's nipple and brought her finger to her tongue. She lapped the creamy sauce and said to Colden, "The sauce is delicious, sir."

Wondering what kind of dinner party this was, I cast

a confused gaze toward Mr. Lord. "Eat your food, Fonia," he said, ignoring my inquiring stare.

Next, a bowl of mussels were brought in. Attempting to outdo Colden, Mr. Lord requested that Sergio, the wine server, allow me to taste the mussel sauce. The guests, including myself were riveted to Sergio's crotch. He lifted the fabric and revealed a normal-sized penis, which he used to stir the mussel sauce. He then turned to me and I froze with fear. Mr. Lord would never give me permission to taste another man's private part.

"Go ahead, Princess, taste the sauce."

A white, thick sauce dripped from the head of Sergio's dick. I couldn't disobey Mr. Lord, and as embarrassed as I was, I fought my shame, stretched out my neck and lapped the sauce from Sergio's dick. Instantly, his private began to flicker and pulse. Before everyone's eyes, it grew to an enormous length.

Not wanting to antagonize Mr. Lord, I pulled away from Sergio.

"What's wrong, Fonia? Don't you want to suck off Sergio?" Mr. Lord asked me.

There was a hush at the table as the guests waited for my response. And though I was dying to get that dick embedded in my throat, I shook my head, no.

"I'm very disappointed in you, Fonia. You know that I'm aware of your lustful desires, but you're not being honest with me, are you?" Mr. Lord said.

"No, I'm not."

"I brought you here this evening to show off your fine training and, already, you've embarrassed me in front of my good friends."

"I didn't mean to embarrass you, Mr. Lord. I'm feeling very lustful, and yes, I want to suck off Sergio," I admitted in a tiny, shameful voice.

"Then commence," Mr. Lord said, gesturing for me to open my mouth and receive Sergio's burgeoning erection.

The guests were completely silent as I sat in my seat, my hands in my lap like a perfect lady while my head bobbed up and down as I tried my best to deep-throat Sergio.

"Save some for Melanee," Colden spoke up.

"That's enough, Fonia," Mr. Lord said, patting my head.

I felt abandoned as I watched Sergio move on to Melanee, giving her the goods.

"Theodore is next," Madam Midnight said, stroking her boy toy on the side of his face.

After a few moments, Madam Midnight interrupted Melanee, physically extracting Sergio's length from between Melanie's suckling lips. Holding Sergio by the base of his dick, she led him over to Theodore. With a long and slender hand, she held on to Sergio's throbbing member and guided it into the open mouth of her handsome, young lover.

I was transfixed as I watched Theodore pleasure Sergio. I'd never seen a man giving another man head, and I was terribly aroused and somewhat envious of Theodore's abilities.

I gathered that Melanee, Theodore and I were all the possessions of the people we had accompanied to the dinner party. Theodore and I both seemed pleased with our status, but there was a look of sadness in Melanee's eyes and a jumpiness that reminded me of the way my mother used to look and act whenever she was in Mr. Lord's presence.

The remainder of the meal was uneventful. The food was divine, and though I was only allowed one glass of wine, I felt completely satisfied.

Madam Midnight tapped a glass with a spoon. "The dinner segment is over; shall we join the rest of the guests in the south wing?"

Everyone stood. I had no idea there were other guests on the premises. Excitedly, I linked my arm in Mr. Lord's and walked with him to the opposite side of the large house.

FONIA

W hile the other six dinner guests streamed toward a large open area that was filled with laughter and seemingly fun-filled, decadent activities, Mr. Lord steered me toward a flight of stairs. Looking over my shoulder, I caught a glimpse of two servant girls engaged in a deeply passionate kiss. I'd never had any sexual urges toward another woman, but the sight was very beautiful and extremely erotic.

The further down we traveled, the dimmer the lighting became. I longed to be upstairs, where I stood a better chance of being allowed to suck Sergio's dick again. When we reached the basement level, I noticed that the mood of the place was charged with something darker than sexual openness.

"Are any of the dinner guests coming down here?" I asked Mr. Lord, wishing for the familiarity of the people I'd dined with.

"No," he said ushering me into a small, dark room that was illuminated by candlelight.

I could barely see, but I sensed the presence of others,

lurking in the shadows. "Is anyone else down here with us?" I asked in a frightened whisper.

"Shh. You're being impudent; don't ask questions."

I swallowed fearfully and nodded.

"Tonight is your initiation. Hopefully, you'll advance to the next level."

"What do you mean?"

"There will be dire consequences if you fail."

"What do I have to do?" I asked, looking around the darkness, wondering who was in the room, watching us.

He led me to a four-poster bed. The bed and a chair were the only items of furniture in the room. "Take off your clothes, and lie on the bed, Fonia," he said firmly. Knowing that pairs of eyes were on me, I stripped out of my beautiful gown. When I attempted to fold it neatly, Mr. Lord knocked it out of my hands and kicked it across the floor. I gasped at the harshness of his actions. If he treated my exquisite dress with such of a lack of respect, then what did he have in store for me?

"Are you upset with me, Mr. Lord?"

"Very. Running away from me and throwing away your precious virginity was unforgiveable. If you pass the tests tonight, I will finally be able to forgive you. Do you think you can pass?"

"I hope so. What do you want me to do?"

"Lie down. I'm going to bind you to the bed."

My eyes darted to the bedposts and I saw the leather straps that were attached to them. Trying to swallow my fear, I sank down on the bed.

"Take off your underwear," he said gruffly and I obliged. He flung my lovely articles of lingerie as if ridding himself of pieces of trash. I closed my eyes and swallowed huge knots of fear as he strapped my wrists and then my ankles to the wooden posts. Naked and spread-eagle on the bed, I felt helpless and scared. And very vulnerable.

From the shadows, people began to emerge—two men and one woman—completely nude except for the masks that concealed their faces. I shuddered, not knowing what to expect.

"It's time to test your loyalty. These people are here to give you pleasure, but you mustn't orgasm under any circumstances. Be strong, and call on your willpower. You can't cum until I give you permission. If you lose control and succumb to an orgasm, I'm going to make you regret it," he said in a sinister tone, and then pulled the chair close to the bed and took a seat.

I watched helplessly as the two men approached me while the woman moved toward the chair where Mr. Lord sat. He stood up while the woman helped him out of his pants and briefs. She positioned herself between his legs, and took him inside her mouth.

Seeing someone else performing fellatio on the man I worshipped was unbearable. Jealousy cut through me like a hot knife, but those emotions quickly dissipated when I felt a pair of cool hands cupping my breast while a moist tongue circled my nipple.

An instant later, the other anonymous man crouched inside the space between my legs. Soft hair tickled my thighs as he leisurely made circles on my clit with his tongue. I gasped long and loud, while thrusting my pelvis upward and arching my back. I wanted to scream at my mystery lovers to stop teasing me with their tongues. I wanted to scream for them to put suction holds on my clit and nipples. To suck so hard that I cried out in sweet pain.

But Mr. Lord was watching, and I couldn't express my needs; all I could do was endure the sexual torture.

The tongue ceased lathing my nipple and I tried to rise up in protest, but I relaxed and released a blissful sigh when his velvet lips began tugging on the aching tip while his teeth nipped softly, drawing from me a sharp cry.

The man between my thighs ran his tongue along my velvety slit and then plunged into the hot juices, coercing my hips to engage in winding motions that I could not control. With my hands and ankles bound, I was unable to pull away; I was a prisoner to the passion.

Waves of sensations rolled over me, but I willed myself not to cum. After a while, I grew accustomed to the stimulation and was able to endure and actually enjoy the pleasure without the fear of toppling over the edge of ecstasy.

My anonymous lovers switched places, and this time I didn't feel soft hair between my legs, I felt hard masculine thighs brushing against mine as he climbed atop me. Realizing that I was about to get fucked, I shuddered in anticipation. Mr. Lord would only fuck me in the ass, and though I had learned to enjoy anal sex, I yearned to have a hard dick ramming my pussy.

The masked man entered me gently, and excitement prickled my skin. My legs were already spread wide, but I would have welcomed this desperately needed dick by throwing my legs open even wider had they not been tethered to the bedposts.

As he plunged deeper, I made guttural sounds of lust that were quieted when the other man who hovered over me bent down and kissed my lips. His tongue lashed into my mouth, persuading me to open it for him. And with my jaws apart, taking in his sweet kiss, he replaced his tongue with his dick.

Both men were catering to my desires, and I groaned with lust and happiness.

But the man stroking into my core hit a nerve and I jerked as an orgasm threatened to take me over. I turned my head, forcing the dick out of my mouth. "Please stop!" I pleaded to the man who was fucking me. I cut a fearful eye at Mr. Lord. He patted the shoulder of the girl who was crouched before him, and she released his dick from her mouth and scurried away.

Mr. Lord rose from the chair and stood over me. "I forbid you to climax, Fonia."

"I'm not," I panted desperately. I willed my hips to stop moving but I had no control over my body movements. With pleasure mounting, I strained and struggled against the tidal wave of pleasure that overtook me. But I couldn't stop it.

I screamed and my body shook fiercely. It was a long and intensely violent orgasm.

Gasping for breath, I panted, "I'm sorry, Mr. Lord. I tried to hold—"

"Shh. Save your breath. You don't have to explain," he said, speaking in a tone of understanding. "You're all dismissed," he told the three masked guests. They dutifully left the room at once.

Mr. Lord began undoing the leather binds and tenderly massaged my wrists and ankles. I could have cried with relief. He wasn't upset with me. He understood that my heart and soul belonged to him. It was my whoring body that had betrayed me.

"Turn over," he said in a gentle whisper. Realizing that anal penetration was next, I eagerly did as he ordered. As I lay on my tummy, I was surprised when he began binding my limbs to the bedposts again. This would be the first time that he tied me down while ass-fucking me.

With my face buried into the mattress, I heard him walk across the room. I waited for him to return to the bed and rub cool lubrication on my anus.

But the next sensation was not cool. It was fiery hot and I shrieked in pain when a harsh blow landed upon my buttocks. It was not the usual sting of the paddle that I was accustomed to. Mr. Lord was using tremendous force and imploring me to kiss the paddle each time he hit me.

JAGUAR

Today was Curt's birthday, and I took a balloon bouquet to the nursing home. I wanted so badly to brighten Curt's world, and I wished we could have really celebrated with champagne and strippers. I would have settled for bringing him cake and ice cream if he wasn't being fed through a feeding tube. The options were limited when the person you wanted to cheer up was technically brain dead.

Having recently discovered that talking to Curt helped me resolve a lot of my issues, I pulled a chair up to his bed. Even though he couldn't offer his opinion or give feedback, just having his ear was comforting. I'd been telling him about Fonia for quite a while. I told him how pretty and how special she was. How badly I wished I had a way to contact her.

"That chick, Fonia, still has my nose wide open," I said, shaking my head at the absurdity of the situation. "I know it sounds crazy, man, but deep in my heart, I believe that we are supposed to be together. I'm not going to search for her...you know what I mean? If it's meant to be, I'm sure we'll find each other," I said, speaking more to myself than to Curt.

I didn't stay with Curt as long as I usually did. I had to get some rest before making the drive out to the boondocks for the freak event that I had agreed to bartend.

The estate where the event was being held was huge. Again, I had to tend bar with a bare chest that glistened from oil. This time, I was oiled up by a voluptuous beauty named Trina. Trina had big boobs, a ridiculously tiny waist, and a super big ass that was so disproportionate to her waistline, it had to have been plumped up with injections.

While she slathered oil down my arm, I took the liberty to cop a feel. Her ass was soft and actually felt normal.

"It's real." Trina smiled proudly.

I didn't say anything; my dick shot out, speaking for me.

"I can take care of that if you'd like," she said, eyeballing my engorged phallus.

I had told myself that I would do my job and turn down any sexual favors. But…with that big ol' swollen ass right in my face, I felt weak. As far as my vow of celibacy, I'd already fallen off the wagon, so why not go all out?

"Yeah, you can take care of it," I said, feeling a little ashamed of the weakness of the flesh problem I'd been battling.

"Madam said that I could offer you a hand job or you can cum on my ass," she said in a matter-of-fact tone. "What would you like?"

I tried to match Trina's nonchalance, but my voice came out raspy and lustful when I said, "Uh, I'll cum on your ass."

She slathered up her gigantic mounds as well as the crack of her ass, and then settled on the sofa, lying on her stomach with her chin resting on the top of her hands.

Not wanting to get oil on my pants, I had to strip out of them before climbing on top of that mountainous ass and sliding up and down the crack. I'm not going to front, my dick kept slipping inside the crack, trying to work its way into her butt hole, but figuring that was a restricted area, I kept guiding it back to the permissible areas. That ass was nice and soft and cushiony. It only took about seven or eight strokes for me to bust. I held my dick and spray-painted her brown ass with white dollops.

Trina cleaned herself off with wipes and then cleaned off my dick, giving it a kiss when she finished.

Releasing cum made me feel a little lighter—physically. But on a spiritual level, I definitely felt that I'd corrupted my soul, again! As soon as I got the money I needed for an apartment, I planned to stay away from bartending in this hedonistic environment. In fact, once I actually started working in the legal profession, I was going to turn my life around and stop allowing my penis to dictate my actions.

The bar was stocked with expensive brands of liquor and aside from Madam Midnight, there seemed to be an entirely new crowd of people. This time, some of the dominants came to the bar, walking their subs on leashes. The dominants were fully clothed in evening attire while the subs were barely covered.

Everyone was in good spirits. Dominants seemed to be treating their subs with decency, and from my vantage point behind the bar, there was nothing happening that caused me to raise a brow. I surmised that the beat-freak that had attended the last party hadn't been invited back.

When it was time to take a half-hour break, Trina escorted me from the bar to another wing of the large estate where I could relax and enjoy refreshments. It was quite a hike to the other wing of the house. En route, we took numerous turns that led to winding corridors. It was like going through a maze.

I took notice of the architecture and the décor. The estate was old; there was a great deal of history inside the walls. The place reminded me of a castle with its elaborate suits of armor that was displayed and the ancient weaponry that adorned the walls.

"There's even more cool stuff downstairs," Trina said. "Old guns from…like…the Civil War era, if you're into that sort of thing."

I nodded, not wanting to admit to how very much I was into ancient weaponry. Seeing old guns, cannons, swords, and shields gave me a rush. Viewing the collection of armor and weaponry at the Philadelphia Museum of Art during my grade school years had piqued an interest in ancient weaponry.

We reached the lounge and Trina waved toward a table that was spread with an assortment of seafood and pasta dishes. "Help yourself. I'll be back to get you in a half-hour," Trina said and then sashayed away.

Good thing she planned to return; I'd probably get lost in the maze of corridors and never find my way back to the bar.

I ate a couple of shrimp and some lobster, but didn't have much of an appetite. I was more interested in checking out the gun collection downstairs than stuffing my face.

The white stone stairs curved as I descended. Every few steps, I stopped and admired the ancient swords and spears that were encased and displayed along the walls. Hoping I'd be able to actually touch the gun collection, I hurried along and as I reached the bottom of the stairs, I heard muffled cries and the sound of slapping.

Knowing what was going on, I rushed toward the sound. I didn't give a damn about consensual adults or any of that crap. I'd turned a blind eye the first time, but that wouldn't happen again. It was dark in the lower level with only a few candles lighting the way. Following the sound of the muffled cries, I walked briskly.

Finally, I reached the closed door from where the sounds emanated. "Kiss it!" I heard that horribly cruel voice demand. Without a second thought, I pushed open the door, grabbed the shadowy male figure that hovered over a poor, crying girl and tried my best to knock his head off with a punch fueled by outrage and fury.

He went down like a sack of potatoes. *Punk ass, mutha-fucka*, I thought as I attempted to lift the naked girl from the bed. She groaned and muttered something I couldn't make out. Through the hazy glow of candlelight, I realized she was tied to the bedposts, and I quickly began undoing the leather straps.

The beat-freak on the floor started to come to with a groan and I kicked him in the head, knocking him out again. I had no plan devised, but I had to get the girl away from the crazy sadist. While carrying her toward the door, I tripped on something and looking down at my feet, I realized it was a dress. I picked it up and covered her with the dress and began to make my way back to the stairs.

How would Madam Midnight and her guests respond if they found out that I'd interfered with a punishment? Would I end up tussling with a pack of subs that wanted to return the girl to the torture chamber? Maybe it wasn't a good idea to take her back upstairs.

Trying to figure out my next move, I stood in the dim hallway and looked down at her face. For a brief moment, I thought I was seeing things. It couldn't be her. Scowling in confusion, I looked closer. "Oh, my God. Fonia?"

She opened her eyes and then squeezed them shut. "What are you doing here, Jag?" she whispered in a hoarse, tearful voice.

"Don't worry about me; I have to get you out of here."

"No, I can't leave," she said in protest. "Mr. Lord is going to be upset with me."

Believing that she'd been traumatized and was unaware of what she was saying, I ignored her protests and fled down the hall, searching for an exit. At the end of the hall, there was a heavy wooden door; I pushed it open, and was deliriously happy to find myself outside. The cool night air breezed against my bare back and arms as I trotted along a path that I hoped would lead to a land-mark that I recognized.

"Take me back," she murmured, but I continued run-ning, looking left and right for the gravelly area where my truck was parked.

"You don't understand. He's going to be furious; you have to take me back," she insisted, struggling to get out of my arms. I couldn't run while she was struggling, so I set her on her feet. The dress that covered her floated down to the ground. I picked it up and helped her get into it.

"How'd you get mixed up with those people?"

"I belong to Mr. Lord."

I thought about Sharif's description of the games the people played. How the submissives often tried to run away as part of the game. "Those people are only playing games, but the man who was beating you half to death was taking the game too far."

"It's not a game. He was punishing me because I...I ran away. He told me if I ever run away again, I'm going to wish I were dead." She started crying and I reached for her hand and held it tight.

"Listen, you don't belong to that sick muthafucka or anyone else. He's got you brainwashed. Now, work with me, baby. Try to walk a little faster. I think I see the spot where I parked my truck."

Stumbling and crying, Fonia ran along with me. It didn't matter that I'd left my shirt behind the bar. And I could forget about getting paid for the hours I'd worked behind the bar. Sharif would never hook me up with another side job, but I really didn't care. All that mattered was getting Fonia out of harm's way. It hurt me to my heart that such a sweet and innocent girl had somehow gotten involved with those S&M crazies.

We made it to my truck without being chased down by a mob wearing chains and loincloths and with dog leashes trailing behind them. I helped Fonia into the passenger's seat and she'd been beaten so severely, she could barely sit down.

I had no idea where I was taking her, but I had to get her away from the psycho-sadist she referred to as Mr. Lord.

JAGUAR

"Where do you live?" I asked as we drove past gardens and horse trails that wound through a nearly five-acre property.

"In Philly. Downtown."

"Downtown…where?"

"Delancey Place…but Mr. Lord owns the house."

"Shit." I rubbed the side of my face. I'd have to take her back to my hotel.

"I sort of have an apartment off Lindbergh Boulevard."

"Sort of? What do you mean?"

"Mr. Lord took the key from me. I don't have any way to get inside."

This Mr. Lord character sounded like a piece of work. I should have broken that bully's arm or cracked a kneecap to give him a taste of his own medicine. "Can't someone in the rental office let you in?"

"It closes at five," she said softly.

"I'm staying at a hotel; you can stay with me until the rental office opens tomorrow. Okay?"

"Okay," she murmured in a broken voice that sounded like a little girl's.

We rode in silence for the duration of the ride. The events of the night were starting to seem surreal. I'd been hoping to see Fonia again since the last time I'd seen her, and never in my wildest dreams did I imagine her being a part of that S&M club. A million questions raced through my mind. Did Sharif know her? Was she a regular at those S&M events? And what was wrong with her? She had to be a somewhat cuckoo to allow a beat-freak muthafucka to whip her ass like that.

We arrived at my hotel and I helped her out of the truck. I put my arm around her as we walked toward the front door. Despite her shocking, sexually deviant lifestyle, she still seemed fragile and innocent, and I felt protective toward her.

People gawked at Fonia and me as we entered the hotel. I was bare-chested and slathered with oil. She was barefoot in a wrinkled and dusty evening gown. Her hair was tangled and messy, and her makeup was streaked. We caused a stir as we made our way through the brightly lit lobby. Beyond my line of vision, I heard teeth sucking and derisive murmurs, but I was too focused on getting Fonia to safety to care. I kept an arm around her, holding her close as I guided her toward the elevator.

Frazzled by the stares of curious onlookers, Fonia's uttered a pitiful whimper and her steps began to falter.

"Fuck those people; let 'em stare," I growled as I nudged her along.

I ushered her into the elevator and when the doors closed, she fell against me and sobbed. I'd reached the end of my reserves. Tired and emotionally drained, I didn't have any comforting words to offer. The best I could do was rub her back and caress her hair. She cried harder and my hand meandered to her shoulder, giving it a consoling squeeze. That squeeze sent a shock of pain through my hand—the results of the knockout blow I'd delivered to that sadistic freak.

On the fifth floor, we stepped out of the elevator and I led her to my room. Inside the room, I motioned for her to have a seat on the bed. She sat sort of lopsided.

I was so stressed, I immediately reached for the Scotch on the bedside table and began drinking straight from the bottle.

"Want some of this?" I offered her bottle, but she shook her head and continued sniffling. Another gulp of the mind-numbing liquid and I headed to the bathroom to tend to the scrapes on my knuckles.

Inside the privacy of the bathroom, I searched through my toiletries for something specifically for abrasions, but I couldn't find so much as a Band-Aid. What had I gotten myself into? Fending for myself had been difficult enough, but now I'd taken on the additional responsibility of caring for an emotionally damaged adult.

My initial impression of Fonia was that she was a wholesome, rich girl—someone who had led a sheltered life and didn't know how to maneuver in an urban environment. But I'd read her wrong. She was much more worldly than I could have ever imagined.

Sharif would be less than thrilled when he found out

how badly I'd bungled the job, and there was no way I'd be able to explain my actions. It didn't matter; I was through with the S&M scene, and no amount of money could lure me back.

Though I planned to drop Fonia off at her apartment tomorrow, I was concerned about her safety. Maybe it would best if she stayed with me for a few days. But on second thought, was I actually qualified to deal with someone with her problems? She had to have some really deep-seated issues to have allowed someone to treat her that way. She needed more than I could provide. She needed a shrink, or a support group at the least.

To clear my head, I took a cold shower, groaning each time the spray of water hit my raw knuckles.

After the shower, I dried off, brushed my teeth, and reentered the room with a towel cinched at my waist. Fonia was curled on the bed with her eyes closed. I put on briefs and sank down on the other side of the bed.

"Is it okay if I take a shower?" she asked timidly.

"Sure, go ahead," I muttered in an exhausted tone of voice.

She padded to the bathroom and soon the sound of running water lulled me to sleep.

The morning was bright and sunny and I felt bad for Fonia. I was comfortable in jeans and a T-shirt while she had to traipse around in an evening gown. I waited in the truck while she went to retrieve her key from the rental office.

A few minutes later, she returned to the truck dangling a key. "Do you want to come in for a minute?"

"No, I don't think so. I have a lot to do today."

"Please. I feel like I owe you an explanation—"

"You don't owe me anything. I don't want to sound judgmental, you know, regarding your sexual preferences, but you're playing a dangerous game. Dealing with that sicko could get you killed. You need to cut him loose."

"He won't let me. He's going to come here looking for me, and he'll force me to go back home."

"He can't make you do anything," I blurted in annoyance.

"Yes, he can."

The slight tremble in her shoulders told me she was terrified. The fear and hopelessness in her voice broke through my hard exterior. Though I didn't want to admit it to myself, the fact was I still had feelings for Fonia. And I'd be damned if I'd leave her in a vulnerable position. The thought of that beat-freak raising his hand to her was infuriating.

I cut the engine and got out. We walked in silence to her apartment. Inside, she sat in a chair and I sat across from her on the sofa.

"My relationship with Mr. Lord started when I was eleven."

My eyebrows shot up and a look of revulsion contorted my face. "Eleven?" I asked incredulously.

She nodded. "My mother was his personal secretary.

From the day she introduced us, Mr. Lord began to have a special interest in me. He took charge of my mother's life and mine. Moved us into a beautiful townhouse, told us what to wear and how to behave. He wanted us to present as well-bred, proper ladies."

Apparently, the beat-freak wanted Fonia and her mother to look good on the outside while he was whipping their asses behind closed doors. I couldn't hold back a sound of disgust.

"Mr. Lord never touched me during my adolescence. He only spanked my mother."

I gave a groan of exasperation. The story was more twisted than I could have imagined. "Where's your mother? Can't you move in with her?"

Fonia's eyes clouded and she shook her head. "No. She's an alcoholic and only calls me when she wants money. I changed my cell number and she has no way to contact me. And that's a good thing because it's going to take a long time before I can forgive her."

I couldn't blame Fonia for not wanting to deal with her mother. But my beef was with the sadist. I was itching to punch his lights out, and had to lace my fingers together as a way to quell the rage that was building. Fonia rose from the chair and joined me on the sofa. Sensing my discomfort, she placed a delicate hand over mine.

"I want to tell you everything. Maybe you'll understand me a little more…maybe you'll have some compassion for me after you hear the whole story."

She recounted her ten-year relationship with Harrison Lord, and by the end of the sordid tale, she was sobbing and I was so infuriated, I wanted to beat the crap out of both her mother and the sadist. Fonia had been systematically brainwashed. Her life had been stolen from her.

"I'm not going to let him hurt you," I promised. "I'll stay here with you if you'd like."

"But…he's a powerful man. He'll have his spies watching us. He'll figure out our pattern and he'll come for me after you've gone to work."

"Then I'll take you to work with me," I said, reluctantly taking on the role of Fonia's bodyguard. I wanted to suggest that she file a restraining order against her tormentor, but I knew she wouldn't go through it. She thought Harrison Lord was all-knowing and omnipotent, with the police force and other powers-that-be in his back pocket. Over time, I'd convince her that Harrison Lord was nothing more than a man—a pathetic man—who enjoyed bullying women and defenseless, little girls.

"I hate to be a burden, but can you loan me some money for some toiletries and clothes? All I have is the dress I'm wearing."

"Sure," I responded, knowing full well that my finances were in critical condition. I'd have to hustle my ass off tonight at work. I'd never been responsible for anyone other than myself before. Now I had to worry about providing food and clothing for two. I could only pray that I hadn't bitten off more than I could handle.

FONIA

I'd told Jag the horror of my life, but I'd conveniently left out that I enjoyed getting spankings. Not the extreme beat-down that he'd rescued me from, but the ordinary paddling that I'd grown accustomed to.

We were headed for the nearby strip mall, when Jaguar had a change of heart about buying me a few outfits.

"Why should I spend money on a few cheap outfits when you already own an extensive wardrobe. We need to go to your place and get your shit. You earned all the luxuries he bought you."

"But I can't get in. Mr. Lord took away my key."

"I'm from the streets, baby; I know how to get past a locked door." Eyes narrowed, he glanced at me. "What's the address?"

I gave him the address of the townhouse and he made a U-turn, and eased into the lane that led to the expressway.

We arrived at the pretty house that had been my prison for almost half of my life. Most of the neighbors were at work, and the block was peaceful with the pleasant background sounds of birds chirping. I steered Jaguar down the little cobblestone path that led to the back of the house. Standing outside the patio door, he smashed one of the small, stained glass windowpanes, stuck his hand inside, and unlocked the door.

The burglar alarm blared in protest and I raced to the control panel and punched in the alarm code. Still, the alarm company called to make sure everything was okay. I told the representative that I was fine, but she insisted that I give her the secret password.

In an uncertain voice, I gave her the password and she accepted it. I was relieved that Mr. Lord hadn't changed it.

"Okay, let's work as quickly as possible," Jaguar said when I hung up the phone. "Where's your room?"

"Top of the stairs."

"Grab some trash bags," he instructed.

"But…I have luggage."

"We're taking all your shit, so grab some trash bags," he said firmly.

I rushed to the kitchen while he ascended the stairs. By the time I joined him, he had already emptied out my closet and was stuffing clothing into Louis Vuitton luggage that included suitcases, a trunk, and a couple of duffle bags.

"Toss your shoe collection into the trash bags," Jaguar told me as he dumped jewelry boxes and the contents of my dresser drawers into a trash bag and then headed to my bathroom to get toiletries.

We were in and out of the townhouse in less than an

hour, and I was impressed with Jaguar's take-charge attitude and fearless demeanor.

Being back at the bar as Jag's guest was a lot of fun. I was enjoying a tasty Margarita as his friend, Buddha, tried to teach me to shoot pool. I was a hopeless student and so Buddha moved on to play a real game with one of his friends. Next, I shot darts with a couple of college girls that Jag introduced me to, but I was as bad at throwing darts as I was at shooting pool. My lack of skills didn't matter. For the first time in my adult life, I was laughing and having fun with people my age. I couldn't recall ever feeling so happy and free. Jag told me to have a good time and that's what I was doing. Every so often, I'd catch his eye while he was hustling behind the bar, and the big, beautiful smile that he sent my way filled me with joy and a strong sense of security.

By closing time, I was slightly tipsy. "Tonight was so fun," I told Jag. "Felt like it was my birthday. Thanks for the good time," I said and leaned over and kissed him on the cheek.

The kiss was a sincere gesture of appreciation, yet the moment my lips brushed against his smooth, handsome face, the heat of arousal began to warm my body. Strong yearning coiled in my belly and my clit throbbed with an urgent need.

Panicked, I pulled away suddenly, strapped the seatbelt across my chest, and sat erect.

"Something wrong?" Jaguar asked.

"No, I'm fine," I said brusquely.

"Hey, what's happening? You were just telling me what a good time you had and now you're suddenly acting jittery. Did you see someone?" he asked, looking over his shoulder. "Did that freak send one of his henchmen to spy on you?" Jaguar turned off the engine and opened the car door.

I reached for his arm. "It's okay; I didn't see anyone. Honestly. I just had a moment." I rubbed my forehead.

He scrutinized my face. "You had a moment? What do you mean—something like a flashback?"

I nodded. It was easier to lie than tell him that I was fighting an overwhelming craving to fuck his brains out. How could I tell the man that had so gallantly rescued me that my carnal yearnings were so intense—so primal— the desire was causing my head to ache?

During the drive back to my apartment, I stole glances at Jag and he stole glances at me. But we were looking at each other for different reasons. He was concerned about my emotional well-being and I was trying to figure out an approach to get into his pants. I had no doubt that he was a normal, red-blooded man with a healthy sexual appetite, but after what I'd endured last night, he'd been handling me with kid gloves, and probably thought I was too fragile for the hot, sweaty sex I hungered for.

He had no idea that I was a sex-craving nympho, and

that I wanted him to pull the car over right now so I could straddle him and slide up and down his dick until we both passed out from pleasure.

Thighs clenched tightly together to stave off the pressure of my throbbing pussy, I folded my hands in my lap and looked out the window.

"You sure you're okay?" he asked.

"Uh-huh." I kept my gaze trained on the city scenery that we passed by.

"I'll sleep on the couch," Jag offered when we returned to the apartment.

With my raging sexual appetite, it was probably a good idea, but it didn't seem fair for such a big, muscular guy to have to spend the night on an uncomfortable couch. I'd have to exercise some self-discipline. Perhaps a long shower would cool me down. "We can share the bed—I don't bite," I said playfully and headed for the shower.

I'd recently discovered that holding the shower nozzle over my clit could get me off quickly. After soaping my body and rinsing off, I came twice before I trusted myself enough to get in the bed with Jag lying next to me.

I stepped inside the dim bedroom and bit down on my bottom lip. Lying on his side, chest bare and wearing clingy boxer briefs, Jag was a big hunk of gorgeous masculinity. Eyes closed as he snored softly, I fought an overwhelming desire to kiss his full, succulent lips—the lips that had spread into a warm smile each time he'd laid eyes on me tonight.

I climbed into bed and snuggled close. With Jag sound asleep, I took the liberty of slipping an arm around his waist and basked in his warmth.

JAGUAR

I woke up with a massive erection. It could have been my imagination or perhaps it had been a dream, but I had the impression that Fonia had been stroking my dick all night. Shaking the cobwebs away, I eased out of bed, glanced down at her sleeping form, and then stumbled to the bathroom. A long gush of piss would rid me of the hard-on.

I returned to the bedroom and she sat up. "Good morning, Jag," she said in a sweet tone. She was a natural beauty—as pretty in the morning with her hair tousled and her face scrubbed clean as she'd been in the bar last night.

"Morning," I murmured and glanced at the clock. Seven in the morning was too early to face the day, and so I climbed back under the covers.

"Want some breakfast?" she asked.

"No, I'm good." I pulled the covers over my shoulders and slipped back into sleep. But not for long. The smell of coffee and others scents pulled me out of sleep. I threw on a pair of jeans and joined Fonia in the kitchen.

She pointed to a spread of bagels, bacon and eggs and grits. "I ordered this from the deli, but I made the coffee," she said, offering a smile.

I sat down at the table and began to chow down. "Where'd you go to high school?" I asked, curious to know more about her background.

Her face clouded. "I went to a private school. Downtown," she muttered, her tone of voice indicating that a trip down memory lane was not a joyful experience.

"I went to Bartram," I told her, deciding to reveal some of my past. "I was a bad-ass kid, raised by my grandmother. I called her Mom-Mom and it's a shame the way I caused her so much grief. Hustling on the streets and always involved in some sort of scam. I was definitely headed for jail or an early grave until I decided to turn my life around."

"What made you decide to turn your life around?"

I told her about Curt and how his tragic accident had motivated me to deviate from the destructive path I'd been on. Her eyes widened in awe when I told her that I'd recently graduated from law school.

"Law school? That's quite an accomplishment. I guess your grandmother's proud of you."

"She was proud and I'm glad that she was able to attend my graduation from undergrad school, but she's deceased now."

"Sorry to hear that."

"Yeah. It's tough being alone in this world, but I've

gotten used to it. I guess you're wondering why I'm tending bar."

"Well, yeah."

"It's only a summer job to help me survive until I start my internship in September. Additionally, I have to start paying down my student loans. Getting an education is expensive, and I have so much debt, I'll be an old man before those loans are paid in full."

"The rent on this apartment is paid up for six months, and you're welcome to stay here…you know, rent free."

Staying with Fonia had been a spur-of-the-moment idea. We'd been sort of winging it, and hadn't discussed a more permanent situation. Staying at the hotel was costly and to be able to live rent-free would be extremely helpful. The way I saw it, we'd be helping each other. My presence would protect her from the beat-freak and she could help me save money. A win-win situation if we could make it work.

Problem was, I still had feelings for her and I sensed she was feeling me, too. That erotic dream I'd had about her didn't help things. Getting into a sexual relationship with someone that had been abused and misguided by a sadistic, control freak wasn't a wise decision. But how long could we sleep in the same bed before we found our way into each other's arms?

"Hearing your story has inspired me. I got good grades in school, but Mr. Lord didn't want me to pursue higher education."

"No, I guess he didn't. He didn't want you to do anything that would encourage you to think for yourself—to be independent. He wanted to keep you as his human chattel forever," I said bitterly.

Fonia dropped her eyes.

"I'm sorry; I didn't mean to throw your past in your face. I know you're ready to move forward."

"I am," she said with a wistful look in her eyes. "It's time to start thinking about a career—to figure out what I enjoy—what I'm good at. I have to figure out how I'm going to support myself."

Nodding, I sank my fork into a pile of scrambled eggs.

I took Fonia with me to visit Curt. "What's up, man? I brought a friend with me. This is Fonia, the girl of my dreams that I've been telling you about," I said in a cheerful tone as we entered his room.

Fonia blushed and said a nervous, "Hi." I could tell that Curt's condition and his blank stare was startling and made her uncomfortable.

I pulled open the curtains, letting sunshine fill his room. "I make sure that I visit my man at least once or twice a week, but if this is too much for you, you can wait for me in the visitor's lounge down the hall," I told her.

"No, I'm all right. He's your friend, and I want to be here with you."

Noticing that a soap opera was playing on the TV, I said kiddingly, "Are you into soap operas now, Curt? Let me find out that you can't miss a day of watching *The Young and the Restless*."

Though his mouth remained in a fixed position, I thought I saw a glimmer of something in his eyes. It was as if he was trying to tell me that he didn't like soap operas.

"When the nurses are giving him care, they have a tendency to turn on their favorite shows," I explained to Fonia in a confidential whisper. "I may be laughing and busting it up with Curt right now, but inside I'm pissed off."

"Why?"

"Some of the people that provide his care don't have enough respect to change the channel to something he'd enjoy before they roll out. I'm Curt's only advocate, and whenever I come through I try to make sure that his quality of life is up-to-par."

"You're a good friend," Fonia murmured as I flipped through the channels, trying to find something that I thought would appeal to my man. He didn't have any premium channels with fairly current movies, and so I settled on a rerun of *Martin*, recalling how Curt and I both used to have a crush on the character, Gina.

Fonia glanced around the room. "At least it's nice and cheerful in here."

"Yeah," I agreed, feeling good that I'd made the effort to brighten up his room with plants, photos, and posters.

The helium balloons that I'd bought for his birthday were looking a little deflated as they bobbed around the ceiling. I grabbed the string and pulled them down. It was time to get rid of them. They'd be bobbing around the ceiling until his next birthday if I didn't trash them.

Thinking of all the years I'd left Curt here, lingering without a visit, filled me with guilt and hurt my heart. *I'm so sorry, man. I was young and dumb and didn't put up a fight when they kicked me out. But I got your back from now on.*

"Is there something I can do?" Fonia asked.

"Yeah, fill up that that pitcher on his nightstand and water the plants."

While Fonia was in the bathroom filling the pitcher, I rubbed Curt's hand. "I got your back, man. You know that, right? I'm going to stay on top of your caregivers and make sure they treat you with dignity."

After Fonia watered the plants, she looked at the pictures of Curt during happier and healthier times. "Is that you?" she asked, gazing at the photograph of Curt and me.

"Yeah, that's when I was a young knucklehead."

She glanced from the photo to my face. "You've changed."

"I have?"

"Yes, you were handsome back then, but now you're more than handsome…you're hot!"

The compliment took me off-guard, caused me to drop my gaze and bite down on my lower lip to stifle a smile.

I'd been hearing that I was hot since I was in my teens… and I heard it night after night while working behind the bar, yet the compliment had an unexpected effect when it came from the mouth of someone I cared about.

Fonia and I visited with Curt for an hour and before we left, I spoke with the charge nurse, and firmly requested that she speak to the care staff about leaving soap operas playing in Curt's room. "I didn't buy that TV for their enjoyment," I reminded her. "I have the channel set on TV One; he likes those old reruns and other African-American shows." I didn't matter to me that Curt was considered to be a vegetable by the medical profession. My man had certain likes and dislikes and it was my duty as his friend to be his mouthpiece.

"I'll speak to the care staff about changing the channel in Curtis's room," she said. "It won't happen again."

"One more thing…"

"Yes?"

"Can't the nurses open the curtains in his room? He shouldn't have to lie in a darkened, dreary room."

"You're absolutely right, and if you could start attending his quarterly care conference meetings, you could express all your concerns with the care team. That way, your requests will be documented in his chart and the staff will be obligated to follow through or face disciplinary action."

"I'll be at the next meeting," I said with conviction. It wasn't that I wanted to get any of the staff in trouble, but Curt was a human being—not a vegetable, and as long as he had breath in his body, I planned to be an advocate for his rights.

Wearing a scowl, Sharif walked into The Dive about fifteen minutes after Fonia and I arrived. "Hennessy and Coke," he said as he took a seat on a barstool. "Is that the girl?" he asked, nudging his head toward Fonia who was standing in front of the jukebox, selecting music.

I knew he'd heard about what had gone down at the dinner party, and it would be a waste of time to try to conceal Fonia's identity. "Yeah, that's her."

"That stunt you pulled the other night wasn't cool. You should realize that you're in over your head, man," Sharif advised.

"I know what I'm doing; I got this."

"I don't think so. You're messing with the property of a very powerful man."

I scoffed at the word, "property."

"I'm serious; you should return the girl to her owner before you dig yourself into a hole that's too deep to climb out of."

"Do you hear yourself? Fonia is not property and that punk-ass, beat-freak is not her owner."

Sharif shook his head in a condescending manner. "Leave the heroics for police and firemen and shit. You're just a regular dude who's playing with fire and bound to get burned."

"Are you suggesting that I need to come to work strapped? Because I'll do whatever it takes to keep that maniac away from her."

"Do what you think is best," Sharif said, tossing back his drink. "But you need to know it's only a matter of time before he comes for the girl." Sharif slid off the stool and headed for the door.

Nervous about Fonia wandering too far from my sight, I told her that I needed help behind the bar. She was able to hand out bottled beer while I mixed drinks and poured hard liquor. For the rest of the night, I kept my eyes on the door, worried that the bar would be stormed by a crew of hired gunmen that would shoot up the place and scoop up Fonia during a barrage of bullets.

At the end of the night, Ben came in to clean the place and Harvey arrived to count money and take inventory. Harvey cast a disapproving gaze at Fonia. "Your girlfriend can't be here while we're closing."

I stepped to Harvey in a confrontational manner, and I know my eyes were looking crazy. "She's not going anywhere, so do your job and don't worry about her." Harvey mumbled something under his breath, but he took heed and went about his business.

It had been a profitable night, and I had a thick knot of cash in my pocket. On the way home, I swung by the hotel. With Fonia's assistance, I packed up all of my belongings and then went to the front desk and settled my bill.

"It's official; we're roomies," I said in a playful manner

that I didn't feel. I was deeply concerned about her safety. And mine. First thing tomorrow, I planned to register for a gun.

Who was I kidding? There was an undeniable spark between Fonia, and me, and when she slipped into an innocent-looking, polka-dot, cotton nightshirt, my dick began to swell up, conducting itself as if she'd walked in the room wearing a see-through negligee. I'm not a pervert, at least I've never thought of myself as one, but I'm the first person to admit that there's no rhyme or reason for the circumstances and conditions that cause a dick to brick up.

She sat on the side of the bed slathering lotion on her legs. "Smells good," I said, referring to the fragrant scent that floated over to my side of the bed.

"Thanks. Want some?" She extended her arm, offering the container of lotion.

"No thanks. Smells good on you, but I'm not into smelling fruity."

"What kind of lotion do you use?"

Figuring she was merely making friendly conversation, I said, "Different brands. I prefer unscented. Anything that'll keep the ash off my black ass."

"Oh, do you have a problem with dry skin?"

I nodded.

"Me, too. I have something that you'll like." She got

up and went into the bathroom and returned with a circular container. "This is called Skin Silk and it doesn't have a scent."

"Cool." I reached for the container.

"Let me rub you down."

I gave her a surprised look.

"You've been on your feet all night. It's the least I can do."

Realizing that I was going deeper down a troubled path, I was helpless to resist. Turning over on my stomach, I surrendered to her soft hands.

Initially, I was able to enjoy the feeling of my muscles being kneaded and plied...and the shimmery sensation of the lotion being slathered over my skin, but when Fonia's lips brushed against the back of my neck, her warm breath tickling my flesh, I sat up and enveloped her in my arms. At first I simply held her. She felt so small and delicate, I held her tightly as if my body alone could shield her from harm. When she whispered my name, it was all over. My mouth sought her lips and I nearly devoured her with my kiss.

"I want you so badly, Jag," she said softly.

"I want you, too," I said, panting with lust. It took great effort not to rip off her nightshirt and violently plunge inside her, filling her with my substantial girth. But realizing that she'd endured enough animalistic brutality, I willed myself to take it slow...to be gentle and take my time with her.

"Been waiting for this moment for a long time," I said

hoarsely as I gently lifted the cotton fabric over her head. She shivered and I warmed her velvety skin with hot kisses. Fonia gave a sharp intake of breath as my lips captured her nipple, sucking gently as my hand wandered down to the apex between her thighs.

She squirmed and arched upward, whimpering my name. "Jag! Oh, Jag," she cried.

"I'm right here, beautiful—I'm not going anywhere," I murmured and I meant it. Fonia had a hold on me from the moment I'd set eyes on her.

Gently, my finger probed inside her silken interior. Her intimate muscles clenched around my fingers, and a moan escaped my throat as I imagined how good those tiny muscles would feel if they were gripping my dick.

But I was devoted to giving her pleasure…to taking it slowly. Moving southward, I licked open the slit of her pussy, lapping it up and down with warm, wet tongue strokes. Moaning and writhing, Fonia parted her thighs, inviting me to delve deeper. And I obliged, stretching my tongue as deeply as possible and then pulling out and alternately licking pussy and sucking her swollen clit.

She wriggled under my tongue's gentle assault. Twisting and turning, she murmured pleadingly—incoherent words as she struggled to hold an orgasm at bay. But I was relentless. My dick thickened with the need for release, yet I continued gripping her slender hips and sucking on her pussy that tasted as sweet as honeydew.

Somehow she squirmed out of my grasp and worked

her way down to my groin. The warm, moistness of her mouth as it closed around my dick, drove me to babbling quietly. Her suckling lips pulled and tugged on the sensitive head, her velvet tongue thrashed against it. Eyes squeezed shut in blissful torture, I drove myself in a little deeper, and she widened her mouth accepting even more of my length.

Pleasure spiked, tightening my nut sac. As if sensing this, Fonia lowered her hand, cupping my balls and fondling them. Quickening the rhythm, I glided in and out of her mouth at a faster pace, but was careful not to choke or cause her to gag.

"I need to feel you inside me," she said desperately. And I didn't hesitate to accommodate her, pulling her to her knees and entering her from behind. Being sheathed inside her tight sex was utter bliss. I caught a glimpse of my reflection in the bedroom mirror, and my eyes were heavy-lidded with passion and my mouth was slackened with lust. The bed rocked from the thrusts and Fonia's hair bounced around her shoulders as I made love to her.

"You're so beautiful," I said, watching her through the mirror. My breathing became ragged and rough as I increased the tempo. Clutching her hips, I urged her body to move in tandem with mine. Soon we were both panting, chests heaving, and our bodies glistening with sweat.

This was the closeness I'd been yearning for. Being inside her, exploring her most intimate parts was torture, igniting a fever in my blood. Something similar to lightning raced across my skin. Scorching and tingling, as if my body was on fire.

I turned her over; I had to see her lovely face. Lying on top of her, our eyes met, and the raw, carnal hunger in her gaze matched mine.

"Don't be gentle with me. Fuck me hard; treat me like a whore," she demanded. The incongruity of those coarse words coming from such delicately curved lips provoked something primal inside me. Adrenaline blasted through me and every muscle in my body hardened. Holding her in place, my thrusts became deep and fervent. Delivering fierce strokes, I drove into her relentlessly. I rode her until her hips circled frantically...until her body gave a sudden and violent jolt. Her pussy went into a spasm, sucking hard on my swollen dick. Crying out my name over and over, her inner muscles contracted uncontrollably as she climaxed.

I didn't give in to my own need for release until her cries died down and her legs fell apart in exhaustion. As I exploded, I shouted lewd words of praise, remarking on how good her pussy felt and how sweet it tasted.

FONIA

"Do you want to go out for dinner or maybe catch a movie? We can do whatever you'd like," Jag said.

"As long as I'm with you, it doesn't matter." I gave him a nonchalant smile, but a strong craving for sex was boiling inside me. It was his night off from the bar and I'd prefer spending our free time lying in bed with our bodies molded together, rather than going out in public.

Since the first night we'd made love, Jag and I had become inseparable, doing laundry together, cooking meals together, and even showering together. Night after night, he consistently made love to me until the sun came up. Amazingly, his stamina and sex drive matched mine, yet I still wasn't totally satisfied.

Despite our frequent and passionate lovemaking, I found myself yearning for him to take it up a notch—to get a little rough with me. When his dick was embedded inside me, pressing on my pleasure spot, I longed for him to call me filthy names. I wanted him to spank me, but I didn't know how to tell him. I didn't want to shock him or scare him away by disclosing my perverse desires.

The need to be humiliated, controlled, and disciplined was so overwhelming, on several occasions, I purposely made blunders, such as overcooking food or pouring too much bleach in the laundry, hoping he'd lash out at me with some form of belittlement or physical punishment. But he never did. He was always kind, loving, and encouraging.

"If you don't mind, let's stay in," he said after some thought. "We can order pizza and watch TV," he suggested and then quickly added, "If you want to."

"Sure. Whatever you want to do is fine with me." I gave him the practiced smile that I used to give Mr. Lord whenever I agreed with one of his demands.

"You don't have to agree with me, Fonia. This isn't a dictatorship. You get to make decisions, you know," Jag reminded with a patient expression.

"I'm happy to be with you; it doesn't matter where we are."

"I feel the same way," he said and flashed that beautiful smile of his that had the ability to light up the world.

I should have felt extremely lucky to be cherished by such a wonderful man...such a big, hunk of chocolate gorgeousness, but I felt like something was missing. Jag didn't get me. He didn't realize that I didn't want choices. I wanted...no, I *needed* to be controlled with a firm hand. I *needed* discipline. That was how I was wired. I could never be completely satisfied in a relationship that didn't include punishment for my wrongdoing.

Being on the edge and anxious—not knowing if I'd offended or pleased was sexually arousing, and it was a great relief when the mystery was resolved with an ass spanking that was followed with the reward of penetration. My mouth, my ass, or my pussy. It didn't matter which hole was invaded.

Jag had placed me on a pedestal, giving me tender love and utmost respect. The problem was, I didn't feel worthy of his respect. It was important that I earned the dick that he rammed inside me; but I was afraid that expressing my true feelings would disgust and frighten him away.

We were snuggled together, eating pizza and watching *Criminal Minds*, but I couldn't concentrate on the show; my mind was wandering and my hormones were raging as usual. I waited as patiently as I could for the program to end, but unable to hold back my lust for one second longer, I pounced on Jag during a commercial.

He responded by helping me out of my clothes and then shedding his. I climbed on top of him, and the instant he entered me, I blurted, "Slap my ass."

He indulged my wishes with a moderate smack. "Harder," I gasped.

There was an echo when the slap of his hand landed heavily against my skin. The shock of pain, sharp and searing, sent me spiraling over the edge of ecstasy. I collapsed onto his chest and panted. The suddenness and intensity of the orgasm had me shaking violently and sobbing with pleasure.

Jag's movements became still and he and gazed at me in bafflement. "Are you okay?"

"More than okay; I'm ecstatic," I cried as I wiped away tears.

He eased my body off of him, and looked down at me. "What's going on here, Fonia?"

"Nothing."

"Something's going on. You suddenly busted a big-ass nut when I slapped your ass. And now you're crying tears of joy. Does getting your ass whipped really turn you on?"

"Can I be completely honest? Will you hear me out without being judgmental?"

He nodded, and then I lowered my teary eyes, ashamedly. "I like being degraded and spanked. Jag, I can't help it. I need a man to take control of me."

"Baby, nooo!" Jag protested. "That's not healthy. I could kill that fuckin' sadist for screwing with your head and giving you such a twisted perspective on sex and love."

"I'm sorry, Jag. I can't help it. I like pain."

"But that's not me; I'm not into that lifestyle. I don't want to have to whip your ass to make you cum. I want to be tender and loving when I give you pleasure."

"For me, pain is pleasure."

"You're misguided. He manipulated you and got into your head."

"What you're saying is true, he did manipulate me. But it's too late for me to change. And believe it or not, I really don't want to change. I know you don't want to hear what I'm saying, but I'm being completely honest with you."

"But…that night when I heard your cries in the basement of that house in Chadds Ford…" His voice trailed off and he looked at me intensely. "Were you crying tears of joy when I caught that lunatic beating the hell out of you?"

"No, that beating was extreme. He'd never whipped me like that before, and I was truly afraid he was going to kill me."

"But you liked the milder whippings he gave you?"

"Yes, very much," I admitted. Not wanting to see the hurt and disappointment in Jag's eye, I shifted my gaze from his face. "When I told you how he'd molded me and trained me to be submissive, I conveniently left out the fact that I derived pleasure from everything he did to me—the fear he instilled gave me shivers of pleasure, the dominion he had over me stimulated me beyond words, and the spankings made me ravenous with sexual desire—at least up until that night."

"Fonia," he said softly. "Baby, do you realize that I'm falling for you? Hard. Fuck it, I might as well admit it… I'm in love with you and I want to take care of you."

"And I love you, too."

"But I can't be the sadistic muthafucka you want me to be."

"Can you try?" I asked weakly.

"No! I'm not a monster. I don't want to dominate and control you. And I damn sure don't want to whip your ass. That's insanity; it's not love."

"It feels like love to me."

"Baby, baby," he murmured, gazing at me with a mixture of pity and revulsion in his eyes. "Listen to me." He cupped my face between his hands. "Love isn't supposed to hurt."

"But I want it to hurt," I said in a tiny voice that cracked.

Groaning in frustration, Jag got up and went to the bathroom.

I heard him peeing and then I heard the sound of water when he turned the nozzle in the shower stall. I sat on the edge of the bed, holding my head in my hands. It was over. I'd revealed too much of my twisted nature, and now he was cleaning off the stain of my juices and washing away my scent. He was through with me. I could feel it. And who could blame him?

I knew what was next. Jag was going to get dressed, pack his bags, and leave me.

After what seemed like an eternity, he came out of the bathroom. He seemed relaxed and at peace, like he'd come to a final decision. I wasn't surprised when he crossed the room and opened a drawer. He put on a pair of briefs and then threw on his jeans and T-shirt. He quietly fiddled with his phone for a few minutes, and I assumed he was looking for a nearby hotel.

Finally, he treaded toward the closet, and took a medium-sized duffle bag from the shelf.

I gave a soft cry of pain. He was about to pack up and walk away from our relationship, and the idea of living without him, hurt me to the core.

"Jag," I murmured softly…pleadingly. "Please don't leave me. I don't want to lose you. Had I known that my confession would drive you away, I wouldn't have told you my secret desires. But I thought I could be honest. Jag…please. I'll do whatever it takes to try to change the way I am."

"You can't help the way you are, and I don't expect you to change. I asked you to be honest with me and you were. I have to respect that."

"Then why are you leaving me?"

He peered at me as if I'd lost my mind. "I'm not going anywhere. We're going out for a little while."

"Where are we going?"

"It's a surprise. Now, go freshen up. Wash those tears away and put on some clothes."

I had no idea what Jag had in mind. Was he taking me to a sex addict's support meeting or dragging me to an emergency appointment with a therapist? Actually, it didn't matter; I'd do whatever he wanted me to do, as long as he didn't give up on our love.

JAGUAR

I didn't want to risk bumping into anyone I knew in Philly, and so I steered the truck onto the Pennsylvania Turnpike. Riding shotgun, Fonia didn't have a clue where I was taking her, but I could tell by the sparkle in her eyes, she found the mysterious getaway to be very exciting.

I'd noticed a Town Car had been tailing me for the past ten minutes, and recalled that Fonia had mentioned that Harrison Lord's chauffer drove a Town Car. Was the sadist following us?

I veered off at Exit 31, which took us into Lansdale, Pennsylvania, and after another ten miles, I glided into the rear parking lot of Naturally Naughty, an adult novelty store.

"I've never been in any of these places," she said as she got out of the truck.

"First time for everything." I grabbed the duffle bag, planning to load it up with a variety of bondage gear and sex toys.

"Go check out the paddles," I told Fonia.

"Really?" Her eyes brightened in delight.

"Pick out a variety."

She smiled and went inside the store. I reached inside my glove box and picked up my new Glock. With my gun stuck inside the front of my pants and covered with my T-shirt, I stood in the parking lot and waited. A few minutes later, the Town Car cruised into the lot. The driver slid his window down and I saw the silhouette of a man in the back seat.

I strode over to the car. "This is your first and last warning, Harrison Lord. Fonia's with me now, and if you value your life—if you value your wife, Sylvia's life—you'd better leave Fonia alone. Sylvia goes to the Mainline Gym every morning at nine…am I right?"

I'd done my homework on Harrison Lord, and to let him know how very serious my threat was, I lifted my shirt, revealing my weapon.

"Oh, my God; he has a gun! Go! Go! Pull off," the sadist shouted hysterically, ducking down to the floor. The way the vehicle skidded out of the parking lot, you would have thought that I'd actually opened fire.

What a pussy! Punk-ass Harrison Lord doesn't want any trouble out of me. I had a feeling that tonight would be last time that he'd ever entertain the thought of harassing and terrorizing my girl.

I entered the store and Fonia sent me a smile as she held the handle of a carrier that she filled with an assortment of paddles that varied in size, shape, and color. I watched her for a few moments as she examined paddles and slappers. I noticed a slight smile on her face as she fondled a wooden paddle that had a series of heart-shaped rubber impressions on one side while *XOXO* was imprinted on the other. In the new world that I was exploring, I supposed nothing said "I love you" quite like the sting of a paddle.

Totally in touch with her submissiveness, Fonia picked up and examined crops and hand-held floggers.

It was time for me to explore my dominant side. I felt a rush of anticipation as I browsed aisles that featured blindfolds, restraints, leashes and collars.

I spent a whopping four hundred dollars on our starter kit of BDSM novelties, and I was sure we'd be back soon to add to our treasure chest of sex toys.

In the dimly lit parking lot, outside the truck, I put a sleek, leather blindfold over her eyes. A white Volvo entered the parking lot and I knew Fonia was excited when she heard the sound of tires crunching over gravel.

Car doors opened and closed and the occupants of the car watched in fascination as I handcuffed Fonia's hands together. "Bend over, baby," I said, and then stuck my hand up her dress and pulled down her panties, exposing her ass.

At this point, a couple that had exited the store as well as the occupants of the Volvo had moved closer, riveted by the peepshow that was unfolding before them. "Now spread your legs." Fonia was bent over with her legs widened, and from behind, I inserted Ben Wa balls into her vagina.

"You have to hold them in your pussy; you'll be in big trouble if they drop out. Do you understand?"

There was a murmur of excitement from the onlookers that were getting a private viewing of the sort of activity that would usually take place behind closed doors. Goose bumps broke out on Fonia's arms as she came to realize that the onlookers, only a few feet away could see her ass, had heard me instruct her to keep the balls inside her pussy, and could also see the object I had taken out of the duffle bag.

Fonia shivered and let out a soft moan of anticipation as she waited for what was going to happen next. "Clench up your pussy, baby," I instructed as I leveled a moderate smack across her ass. She let out a long groan. Not from pain, but from the effort she had to exert to keep the Ben Wa balls secured inside her tightened walls. I delivered a series of intense whacks, but Fonia determinedly kept the balls in place.

Finally, when I could see the impression of hearts that decorated her ass, I gently pulled the string that dangled from her pussy. With one hand, I slowly extracted the balls, and with the other, I clenched my baby around the waist, securing her—keeping her from toppling over as her body shuddered from multiple orgasms.

Our small audience applauded, and Fonia's face was flushed with a mixture of pride and embarrassment after

I removed the blindfold. I pulled up her panties and removed the cuffs and she fell into my arms. "Thank you, Jag. You're so good to me and I love you so much."

"And I love you, too."

"Awww!" our audience exclaimed before going on about their business. I opened the door for my baby and held her arm as I assisted her into the passenger's seat.

I hadn't planned on falling in love with Fonia, but I had. And being in love meant being willing to cooperate and compromise. I'd been closed-minded and judgmental, but no more. Our journey together had only begun, and I planned on being an imaginative lover who lovingly indulged all her kinky desires and needs.

Inside the truck, Fonia and I both strapped on our seatbelts and I started the engine. But I was having difficulty getting comfortable. Embracing the dominant aspect of my personality was a surprising turn-on and my dick was as hard as granite.

Sensing something was wrong, she gazed at me questioningly. I unbuckled my seatbelt, lifted up, and unzipped my pants. "I can't drive in this condition. Take your seatbelt off and get on this," I told her in a no-nonsense tone of voice.

With an expression that told me she was more than happy to oblige, Fonia buried her face in my lap, and sucked my dick until she depleted me.

ABOUT THE AUTHOR

Allison Hobbs is a national bestselling author of twenty-five novels and has been featured in such periodicals as *Romantic Times* and *The Philadelphia Inquirer*. She lives in Philadelphia, Pennsylvania. Visit the author at AllisonHobbs.com and Facebook.com/Allisonhobbs eroticaauthor.

IF YOU ENOYED "NO BOUNDARIES," WE
ENCOURAGE YOU TO CHECK OUT

THE SECRETS *of* SILK

BY ALLISON HOBBS
AVAILABLE FROM STREBOR BOOKS

CHAPTER 1

How the infant found its way into the backwoods Louisiana shack of Mattie Moreaux was as much of a mystery as the ingredients in the potions Mattie sold to white folks who lived on the right side of the tracks. Some of the residents of Devil's Swamp said the baby was the unwanted offspring of some hot-to-trot white gal with a penchant for colored boys.

More imaginative gossipers said the child was one of many discarded fetuses that old Mattie had helped desperate women purge from their wombs.

But there was one secret that the townsfolk only dared to whisper. According to legend, when the old voodoo woman put one particular fetus in the ground, as she had with all the others that fertilized her unnaturally bountiful garden, the tiny, dead baby came to life, howling and screaming in fury. And the resurrected baby girl that she named Silk on account of her straight, blue-black hair, had been raising hell ever since.

The Low Moon, a honky-tonk in Devil's Swamp, had seen better days and more illustrious entertainment than was currently available on the weekends. Old-timers enjoyed reminiscing about the time Bessie Smith had put on a bawdy show that raised the roof from eight o'clock Saturday night until it was time for Sunday morning sermon. The glory days of the Low Moon spanned the Depression Era through the early 1950s when Big Mama Thornton charged onto the stage singing her hit record, "Hound Dog," the same song that catapulted Elvis Presley into an international celebrity when he recorded it a few years later.

By 1962, The Low Moon was nothing more than a dilapidated, wood-frame structure that leaned a bit to the right side. The dimly lit, one-room establishment with its uneven, wood-plank floor, littered with cigarette butts, housed an untuned piano as a testament to the days when Fats Waller came through, tinkling the ivories, and had the joint jumping. Nowadays, a dusty, old juke box that was filled with mostly out-of-date music was the only source of entertainment, but that didn't deter the locals from filling the place to the rafters every Friday and Saturday night.

Wearing a low-cut, tight, pink dress and a pair of black, spike heels, Silk Moreaux looked gloriously scandalous as she came wiggling into the honky-tonk around ten o'clock when the place was in full swing. She brusquely pushed past dancing couples as she made her way to the bar.

Pudgy Hales, who was as drunk as a skunk on a combination of beer purchased from the bar and the homemade corn liquor he had stashed inside his seersucker jacket, took the liberty of grabbing Silk by the wrist. "Come on, gal; let's shake a tail feather," he slurred, his eyes bucking as his plump body shook comically from his shoulders down to his feet as he invited Silk to join him in a lewd, fast-moving dance.

The average woman would have rebuffed Pudgy in a more courteous manner, but not Silk. "Keep your filthy fucking hands off me or I'll cut you too short to shit."

Becoming instantly sober, Pudgy backed up, both palms held up in surrender. "I ain't mean no harm, Silk. The way you all dolled-up, I thought you was looking for a good time tonight."

"Not with your fat ass," Silk scoffed, giving Pudgy a searing look of disgust.

As she continued her tantalizing sashay across the bar room, couples that had momentarily paused to observe the fireworks now scrambled to get out of her way. Silk was known to use her switchblade for lesser offenses than being asked to dance, and if she didn't get you first, the all-seeing eyes of her blind-as-a-bat, voodoo mama would locate you no matter how cleverly you hid. If you messed with her baby girl, Mattie would put some roots on you that the most experienced voodoo priestess was hard-pressed to remove.

Only a few months ago, Darcy Nesbit developed severe facial spasms and started walking with a terrible limp after she began spreading the rumor that Silk was carrying on with the husband of one of the white women she delivered Mattie's passion potion to once a month.

At that very moment, there were at least two of Silk's victims inside The Low Moon, women who bore physical evidence of the sharp, slicing stroke of Silk's knife.

Silk sat atop the ripped, plastic seat of the barstool and smiled at the bartender. "I'd like a rum and Coke, please," she said in a honey-laced voice that was guaranteed to earn her free drinks with a generous shot of liquor added to each Dixie cup.

Drink in hand, Silk swiveled around on her stool, crossed her legs and leaned back against the bar. Slowly sipping her strong cocktail, she scanned the room, weighing her options among the men whom she felt were all at her disposal.

The mood in the place changed when the first few beats of a slow song poured from the jukebox. On cue, the space closed up between couples who moments earlier had been frenziedly dancing to a driving upbeat tempo. As if hypnotized, they reached out and clung to each other, their eyes filled with a primal longing. Their bodies were pressed together as they rhythmically dry-humped and grinded. In the midst of this public display of unbridled passion, tight skirts inched upward, while groping male hands palmed and squeezed the plump derrieres of their partners.

During these intimate moments at The Low Moon, when the room became muggy with body heat, there was bound to be an unwelcome tap on the male partner's shoulder by a fellow who found himself deprived of a female dance partner, and who desperately wanted to get in on the erotic action. The intrusion was handled in various ways. Some men bowed out gracefully, reluctantly handing over his dance partner and others flat out refused to allow another man to cut in, growling in objection. On rare occasions, a fistfight would break out.

It was unheard of for a female to do the shoulder tapping and cut in on another woman's slow dance.

Warmed by the effects of the alcohol, Silk started off innocently enough, moving sensually to the music while sitting atop the barstool, her black hair swaying back and forth like a satin curtain blowing in the night breeze.

But when she slid off the stool, and sauntered in the direction of her old beau, Duke Durnell, who was thoroughly engaged in a slow grind with Gwen Withers, a hush fell over the room. Silk didn't merely tap Gwen on the shoulder; she gave her a harsh and impatient smack on the back, and when Gwen didn't let go of Duke fast enough, Silk bunched up the fabric of Gwen's yellow blouse into her fist and roughly snatched Gwen out of Duke's tight embrace.

Several expressions crossed Gwen's face: surprise, annoyance, embarrassment, and finally acceptance as she skulked away to join Brenda and Fayette, two lonely wallflowers who sat at a table in the back, sour-faced and bordering on drunk. Gwen flopped down on a wooden chair and without asking permission, she picked up Brenda's drink and guzzled it down.

The record was coming to an end when Duke welcomed Silk into his arms with an inviting smile. Another slow song immediately followed, and Silk and Duke launched into a lustful dance that was so provocative, tongues quickly began wagging.

"Looks like they need the privacy of a rented room," Fayette groused, noticing how Duke's hands freely roamed over Silk's body as he hunched over, kissing and sucking the side of her neck.

"Duke ain't nothing but a fool when it comes to Silk," Brenda added. "She treats him any way she wants and all he does is take it with a big, ol' stupid smile plastered on his face."

"Mmm-hmm," Fayette agreed with her lips twisted to the side. "He could have at least told her to wait for the next record instead of letting her embarrass Gwen in front of everybody."

Gwen nodded in agreement as she finished off Brenda's drink and now reached for Fayette's half-filled cup of gin, hoping to numb the pain of humiliation.

While Silk and Duke were carrying on as if they had the place to themselves, the door burst open and trouble entered in the form of a well-dressed, scowling white man, whose fierce eyes scanned the semi-darkened room. A few people recognized Nathan Lee Willard as a city-slick politician, but since none of the coloreds ventured into the city much, nor did any of them have the legal right to show up at the polls and vote, most had never set eyes on the man.

Figuring an innocent colored man was about to be accused of some petty crime or perceived misconduct, male patrons attempted to make themselves scarce...or even invisible. Bunny Carter kept his face obscured by lowering his head as he studied the repertoire of music in the jukebox, Aaron Joseph made a beeline to the john, and Tad Pritchard scanned the packs of smokes inside the cigarette machine as if considering changing his regular brand. Those who were left without cover, mopped nervous perspiration from their brow and quickly downed stiff drinks.

The shift in atmosphere went unnoticed by Silk and Duke, who were enthralled in their wanton display of passion and lust. The white man stalked across the dusty floor, and yanked Silk by the wrist, pulling her out of Duke's arms. "What the hell do you think you're doing?" he shouted.

"What's it look like," Silk answered, snatching her wrist out of his grasp. She turned back to Duke, but he backed away without uttering a single word, relinquishing her to the white man.

"Come on here, gal. We're gonna talk this thing out in private." Nathan Lee took hold of Silk again. She laughed derisively, stumbling over her high-heels as he jostled her out of the honky-tonk and down the dirt path that led to the small parking area in the rear.

"Get in," he demanded, pointing to his flashy, brand-new Plymouth. Silk got in and slammed the door. Nathan Lee got into the driver's seat, and he too, slammed the door. "I waited under the bridge for two solid hours. What do you have to say for yourself?" he demanded, his face turning red with anger.

"I ain't got nothing to say." Silk examined her fingernails briefly and then turned her head and looked out the window.

"You can't treat me like I'm one of those jiggaboos you got wrapped around your finger."

"And you can't treat me like I'm nothing more than a good-time girl. I'm tired of meeting you under the bridge and by the lake. When are we gonna run away up North like you promised?" Silk had an image of her and Nathan Lee living together in a place like New York or Chicago where interracial couples could cohabitate without any-one batting an eye. In her fantasy, Nathan Lee bought her a shiny Chevrolet like the one his wife had. She day-dreamed about him keeping her jewelry box overflowing with trinkets, and providing her with plenty of help around a house that was much too large for her to even consider cleaning.

"We're gonna run away together as soon as I get some things straightened out." Nathan Lee's tone softened as he placed a gentle hand on her shoulder, his fingers mean-dering upward, caressing the soft hairs at the nape of her neck, and then moving around to the side and lightly stroking.

Silk flinched as his fingers touched bruised skin. With the glint of moonlight shining into the car, Nathan Lee detected the bluish-purple, passion mark that Duke had left on Silk's fair skin. Enraged, he grabbed her by both shoulders and shook her. "How'd you get that love bite on your neck? You been two-timing me, you dirty tramp!" he accused and then slapped her soundly.

Silk laughed tauntingly and offered him her other cheek. "Go ahead and smack me around if that's what it takes to make you feel like a big, strong man. Maybe if you'd hit me enough times in the past, you would've felt virile enough to get your wife knocked up without the help of Big Mama's potions!"

A stunned look appeared on his face. "How you'd know about Dolly's pregnancy?"

"Not much gets past Big Mama's all-seeing eyes. She has

a special way of knowing when her remedies take hold."

Nathan Lee reached inside his shirt pocket and pulled out a pack of filter-tipped menthols. He shook one out of the pack and fired it up, using a lighter that was engraved with his initials. "I'm sorry for losing my temper, honey." Looking remorseful, he extended a hand, but Silk leaned out of his reach.

"Now that the missus is carrying your baby, I suppose that puts the brakes on our plans." She waited for him to respond, but he puffed away at his cigarette without speaking. "When were you planning on telling me, Nathan Lee?"

He shrugged.

"Did you change your mind about our big plans?" she persisted.

He looked down guiltily. "No, but we'll have to postpone things for at least nine months."

Silk made a scoffing sound. "That's a mighty long time to wait when I done already been waiting for over a year. What happens after nine months have passed? Oh, let me guess…you're gonna tell me we have to wait for your little crumb-snatcher to start school. And after that, you'll try to keep me on standby, doing nothing but twiddling my thumbs until he finishes college."

"You're exaggerating the circumstances; it's not going to take that long."

"I'm not exaggerating a damn thing. Every word I spoke is the truth, and you know it. What kind of fool do you take me for?" Silk asked bitterly.

"All I'm asking for is a little more patience, sugar plum."

"Don't try to sweet-talk me 'cause I done ran clean out of patience." Silk glanced out the window to keep from having to look at his puppy-dog expression, which enraged her rather than softening her heart.

"I can't leave Dolly high and dry with a new baby on the way. I need some time to figure things out," he said softly as his hand wandered beneath her dress and then lightly caressed her firm thigh. "I miss you, Silk. Let's take a drive over to the lake, and look at the moonlight together."

Silk chortled. "I done lay on my back and watched enough moonlight to last me a lifetime. What I'd like to watch is a picture show or even a little bit of television every once in a while."

"I'd buy you a TV set if your mama had some electricity in that ramshackle hut y'all live in."

"You're a politician; why can't you get some electricity to run through our place?"

"That area's not wired for it."

"And that's one of the reasons why I want to leave this godforsaken town."

"I know, I know," he murmured in a placating tone, while his fingers took more liberties, rubbing on the crotch of her panties.

Silk jerked his hand out from under her dress. "I'm going back inside the honky-tonk and finish having me some fun."

"No, the hell you're not," he said brusquely, roughing

her up as she reached for the door handle. "I didn't buy that dress and those snazzy shoes on your feet for you to prance around, enticing a bunch of black bucks." He put a vise-like grip around her forearm and spoke through clenched teeth. "You try to step foot out of this here car and I swear for God, I'll break your neck. Now get your ass in the backseat and take those drawers off. I'm not gonna waste any more time fooling around with your uppity nigger-ass tonight."

"Fuck you, cracker!" Silk looked him dead in the eyes, staring so defiantly, she didn't see the hand coming that flew up and backhanded her hard across the face, splitting her bottom lip. The metallic taste of blood that filled her mouth sent her into a blind rage. But she didn't kick, bite, or scratch as was common among most women who found themselves in the sudden position of having to defend themselves.

Silk stuck her hand down in her bosom and pulled out her switchblade, and quick as lightning, Nathan Lee's throat was slashed from ear to ear, presenting a deep, crescent-shaped gash that flowed dark red. Staring at Silk in horror and disbelief, he clutched his neck, attempting to staunch the gush of blood that squirted through his fingers, splashing the insides of the car. The interior of the new Plymouth suddenly looked as if it had been spray-painted carmine red.

There were also blood splotches on Silk's arms, her face, her dress, and her shoes. She sat paralyzed for a moment or two. But when Nathan Lee's body fell heavily against hers, she let out a little shriek and scrambled out of the car.

She looked right and left, searching for prying eyes, but there was no one to be seen in the desolate back lot. The only other car was an old beat-up Ford that belonged to Mr. Roland, the elderly owner of the honky-tonk. And by the time Mr. Roland or anyone else discovered Nathan Lee's dead body, Silk would be long gone.

CHAPTER 2

Silk took her heels off and ran barefoot through a dark field of damp, muddy grass and wild flowers with thorns and bristles. Running for her life, she darted past low-hanging trees with moss-covered branches that seemed to reach down and grab her, trying to slow her down so the law could catch up with her and dispense justice.

Night creatures made sounds that she should have been accustomed to, but the sudden noisy squawks and whistling sounds of large-winged birds were as startling as a police siren. Adrenaline kept her legs pumping and prevented her from reacting to the scrape of sharp-edged stones and the prick of knotty twigs that lacerated her bare feet.

Silk had drawn blood from plenty of people who had provoked her, but it was only the second time she'd killed a man. It was an unnerving sensation, yet thrilling at the same time. But there was no time to bask in her excitement. In about three hours, The Low Moon would shut down for the night, and when old man Roland came outside to get in his car, he'd discover the bloody murder scene she'd left behind. She ran faster, rushing to get home and pack her things. A pretty gal like her wouldn't have any trouble hitching a ride to Baton Rouge, and from there, she'd hop on the first thing smoking, and get the hell out of the state of Louisiana.

Silk was counting on the fact that witnesses to the spat she'd had with Nathan Lee would be too afraid of Big Mama's wrath to accuse her of harming the white politician. They'd have no choice but to suggest that her old beau, Duke Durnell, had gone into a jealous rage and murdered Nathan Lee. Duke would be lucky if Sheriff Thompson got to him and locked him behind bars before an angry mob of Klansmen came calling to string him up, vigilante style.

If and when somebody put two and two together, and figured out that Silk had committed the crime, she'd be somewhere up North, living the good life.

She glanced up at the sky and squinted at the bright half-moon. She was in luck. Big Mama always went out on the nights of the half-moon to do a little night hunting and to dig around in the ground until dawn. Although blinded by cataracts, Big Mama could see amazingly well in the moonlight, when she went out to hunt down the mysterious assortment of small critters, worms, insects, and vegetation required to prepare her occult remedies.

At last Silk reached the shack in the woods she shared with the peculiar old woman who had loved her as mightily as any natural mother would…in her own way.

She crept into the darkened place, feeling her way around as she searched for Big Mama's battered old suitcase. The scrapes and cuts on her feet left a trail of smeared blood as she roamed the wood cabin. She pulled the suitcase out of a closet and dumped the contents: yellowed documents, old invoices, and faded black-and-white photographs of Big Mama's relatives—people Silk had never known. After stuffing her fanciest clothes into the suitcase, Silk stripped out of the bloodied pink dress and stuffed it under the mattress. She would have burned it if she had more time.

She hastily washed her face, neck, and arms with water from a bowl on a table near the sturdy bed with its iron headboard and footboard, the same bed Silk had shared with Big Mama since the day she was born.

Wearing only underwear, she tiptoed to the area of the shack where Big Mama cooked up her remedies in a pot-bellied stove. She hated stealing from Big Mama, but had no choice. Silk fumbled in the dark, looking for the tin breadbox that was Big Mama's money vault. To hasten her mission, she was tempted to, but dared not light the kerosene lamp or a candle. A mere flicker of light would draw Big Mama back to the house with her shotgun cocked, ready to mow down an intruder.

Feeling her way around in the dark, she touched items near at hand. Her fingers skimmed across pots and pans, straw baskets, and other objects. Finally, she tapped against the smooth surface of the breadbox. With a sigh of relief, she opened the lid, reached inside and grabbed handfuls of paper money, but her heart dropped in disappointment. Though she was holding what seemed to be a lot of cash, it wasn't anywhere close to the piles of money Big Mama had been squirreling away over the years. Where could that money be? Big Mama loved to brag about the ten thousand dollars she'd been saving up and planned to share with Silk on her twenty-first birthday.

Silk figured that since it was technically her own money, Big Mama wouldn't have too much to complain about when she discovered her savings were gone. But where was the bulk of the money? With no time to search any further, Silk smoothed out the crumpled bills from the breadbox, and concluded that she'd have to make do with whatever amount she'd scrounged from the tin money vault.

She dressed hurriedly in a navy-and-white, polka dot swing dress with a sailor collar. It was a decent-looking garment with a full skirt and a tight bodice that showed off her trim waistline. It was pretty enough to travel in, but not so provocative that it would draw unwanted attention to Silk. She didn't feel the pain of her cut feet until she slipped her feet halfway into a pair of navy patent leather shoes that were tucked beneath the bed. No time to give in to discomfort, she pushed her right foot and then the left into the glossy, flat shoes.

Next, she doused her hands in the bowl of water and applied her wet hands to her hair, slicking it back and twisting it into a hastily styled bun. Unable to see her reflection in the dark, she imagined she looked as innocent as a schoolteacher.

Ready to go, she picked up the suitcase. But before she made it out of the cabin, the door burst open and the shimmering moonlight lit up the place. With her shotgun pointed at Silk, Big Mama's wide body filled the doorframe. The snow-white, coarse, little beads of hair that covered her dark-brown head seemed to glow ethereally in the darkness.

Silk gasped in alarm. "Big Mama!"

Big Mama sniffed at the air. "I can smell your blood on the floor and someone else's is on that dress you hid under the mattress. What have you done, chile?"

"I ain't done nothing," Silk protested in a quavering voice.

Big Mama lowered the shotgun and came inside, slowly closing the door behind her. Wearing a man's shirt, a long, wide skirt, and a pair of black brogan boots, she lifted the skirt and sat down heavily on a wooden chair.

"Don't lie to me, Silk. You know Big Mama's got eyes in the back of her head. I had a vision about you," Big Mama said in an ominous tone and then nudged her head toward the bedroom area. "These blind eyes saw the vision right there in that basin of water that's now red with blood." She shook her head. "Stealing my money and running up North ain't gonna solve your problems. From what I seen, it ain't likely that you'll ever find the easy living you're hoping for. If you could be faithful to one man, you could live like a queen. But you ain't nothing but a tramp. You'll spread your legs for any man who got hisself a shiny car and some folding money in his pocket. I tried to keep your nature down with my potions and the womanly attention I gave you. But you're jest like that white-trash woman who borned you—headed for disaster."

Despite her blindness, Big Mama was always several steps ahead of Silk. No matter how hard she tried, Silk had never been able to outslick Big Mama, and it was frustrating.

"I'm sorry, Big Mama, but I ain't got time to go back and forth with you. I gots to get out of town before the sheriff and his men come looking for me."

"The sheriff ain't looking for you, not yet. He ain't coming for you until morning. Now, tell me, something…" Big Mama looked at Silk intently as if she could actually see her.

"What do you want to know, Big Mama?"

...